What is Abram?
Here are some one-liners.

The story of Abraham
without supernatural references

The story of Abraham
for a post 9/11 world

The story of Abraham
believable to atheists
yet not atheistic

The monotheistic operating system
upgraded for the nuclear age

Catcher in the Rye
for truth seekers

ABRAM

by Cary Cook

Sanity Quest Publishing
Tustin, California

www.SanityQuestPublishing.com

This book is a work of fiction. Except for parts taken from Genesis, the characters, incidents, and dialogue either are the products of the author's imagination or are used fictitiously. Any resemblance to actual events, or persons, living or dead, is coincidental.

ABRAM

Published by Sanity Quest Publishing
Tustin, CA 92780
www.SanityQuestPublishing.com

First published 2007
Printed in the United States of America

ISBN 978-1-934584-00-2
Library of Congress Catalog Number: 2007906114

Book design/cover illustration by Cary E. Cook

DEDICATION

This book is dedicated to:
truth seekers
religious terrorists
Steven Spielberg

ACKNOWLEDGMENTS

First I want to thank all of the conservative Biblical schollars and critical thinkers who have helped me, and now probably don't want their names associated with what I've become. They provided a foundation from which to judge all the liberal schollars, whom I want to thank next - but who probably think I am not sufficiently weaned. Besides Dr. Price, I want to thank Walter Reinhold Warttig Mattfeld y de la Torre for his excellent website:
www.homestead.com/bibleorigins*net/index.html.

Thanks to Dave Cunningham and his Pure Fiction League, whose free literary criticism proved more valuable than the criticism I paid for.
http://groups.msn.com/PureFictionLeague

Thanks also to Candace Sinclair of The Writers' Mentor for cost-effective self-publishing consultation.
www.writersmentoru.com/mentoring.html

FOREWORD

Abraham has always loomed large over the history of Mid-Eastern and Western religion. He is the sole link between Judaism, Christianity, and Islam. And that is quite appropriate, given the ancient function of the Genesis patriarchs as fictive/mythic links between hitherto (or otherwise-) feuding tribes and clans. If any of them forged political bonds, military alliances, or trade covenants, they would henceforth consider themselves blood brothers and seal the deal by positing a previously unknown ancestor from the remote past, someone from whom they could claim common ancestry. The most famous example would be Jacob (aka Israel), ostensibly the father of twelve sons, each of whose descendants forms a whole tribe. They remained united (in some measure) as "children of Israel." What actually must have happened is that twelve originally disparate Canaanite groups decided, for mutual benefit, to form an "amphictyony," or twelve-tribe league (a common arrangement all over the ancient Mediterranean) centered on rotating custodianship of a central shrine dedicated to a "federal god" whom all tribes would worship in addition to their own ancestral totems. In fact, the names of several of the Israelite tribes reflect either their religious allegiances or geographical locations: Gad was the god of good fortune all over the region, while Asher is named for the goddess Asherah, Yahve's queen. Zebulun is named for the god Zebul. Issachar means "migrant laborer," while "Ephraim," not at first a personal name at all, denotes "those who live on Mount Ephrath." "Benjamin" signals "sons of the right hand," i.e., the south. And so on. Once they decided to federate, they chose as a common ancestor the mythic figure Israel/Jacob (probably already a fusion of two heroes, joined for similar ecumenical purposes, uniting Jacobites and Israelites!).

Somewhere along the line, before or after, the tribe named for Isaac and venerating his god ("the Fear of Isaac") had similarly joined with the Jacob group (worshipping "the Strong One of Jacob") as well as the Abrahamic group (worshipping "the God of Abraham"), with the result that, according no doubt to tribal seniority, the three patriarchs became, purely on the political-geological drawing board, father, son, and grandson. Nor was this the end. When the Ammonites and Moabites allied with Israel, they all agreed that Abraham and Lot (already the symbolic progenitor of the other two) were uncle and nephew. When relations (rocky though they often were) with the Edomites were achieved, the national ancestor/stereotype Esau was added to the family tree. When covenants were forged with the Arab amphictyony, Ishmael became the first son of Abraham. And so on and so on. And this is what I mean about Abraham's central symbolic role today. He is a helpful though tenuous link between Arabs, Jews, and Christians in an unstable region. If not for the ancient fiction that they are all related Peoples of the Book with an Abrahamic heritage in common, who knows how much worse the violence might be?

Had Abraham been an historical figure? There is no particular reason to think so. Conservative scholars, striving to secure an historical basis for every bit of the Bible they could, used to point out features of the Abraham stories that reflected social conditions of the second millennium BCE when Abraham was supposed to have lived. Such arguments are equivocal and unconvincing. And, as Hermann Gunkel observed, who can believe the Israelite nation preserved not one shard of memory of their whole 430 year sojourn in Egypt but did manage to preserve specific verbal exchanges between Abraham, his wives, slaves, and foes from centuries before that? No, it has to be fiction. And they were fictions of a particular kind. Many of them, on one level, are ceremonial etiologies, official stories circulated to legitimatize certain Israelite religious or dietary practices, especially new ones requiring the clout of Abraham. One of these is the story of Abraham nearly sacrificing Isaac at Yahve's behest, then being told to forget it and to sacrifice a sheep instead (Genesis 22). It must reflect the transition from the early law of firstborn sacrifice (Exodus 22:29-30) to the substitution of an animal for one's son (Exodus 13:12-13). Well, if it was good enough for Abraham…

But the Abraham stories had an earlier meaning still. At first Abraham was the moon personified. He was the "father of a multitude" not of Israelites, but of the stars, smiling protectors of the shepherding nomads who blessed the moon but execrated the blistering sun. Isaac was the sun. "Isaac" means "he laughs" and reflects the image of the smiling or laughing ("beaming") of the sun: "he who sits in the heavens laughs" (Psalm 2::4). When Abraham sought to destroy his son, but was prevented, the first meaning was to depict the cycle by which the moon seeks to supplant the sun, ruling the night sky, only to be cast down daily as the sun rises. (Isaiah refers to the identical myth, this time told of Venus, the upstart morning star, brightest object in the sky until the obliterating return of the sun, in Isaiah 14.) Many other Patriarchal characters and stories preserve ancient astronomy, as Ignaz Goldziher (*Mythology among the Hebrews*) showed, under the influence of Max Müller's once dominant solar mythology paradigm. He is still correct, as far as I am concerned.

Now what of this freshest treatment of Father Abraham? This new telling and transformation of his tale by Cary Cook? It, too, is naturally a fiction. But this one is a very different kind of fiction. Cook has decided to depict the human reality that might have laid behind the chief Abraham stories had they actually been historical in character. The Genesis text provided him with only disparate, scattered dots. Its narrative is just one thing after another, with little in the way of either historical or psychological connection. Partly this is because it is an ancient narrative of the kind discussed by Tzvetan Todorov, in which the didactic point is thrown at the reader again and again in catechetical fashion and with catechetical intent. Abraham's descendents will inherit the land, ad nauseam. Also, the Bible writers rarely share their characters' thoughts with the readers, much less their motivations. So this leaves a huge amount for Cook to fill in. The scope of his achievement may be measured by the distance between the events of the story and any plausible modern parallel.

Can he depict such alien events in such a way that modern readers can empathize? You can decide for yourself, but I render a big Yes for a verdict.

Melchizedek, fascinating in Genesis precisely because of how little is said of him, becomes all the more fascinating as a priest of the archaic religion Cook must imagine for his world of Abram. Using Melchizedek, Abram, and various others as indices, Cook depicts the winds of the Axial Age beginning to blow. Will religion become more nearly humanized? Will such breezes one day gather strength and form a cyclone of pure Humanism? Cook uses Sodom and Gomorrah as a test case for whether tolerance was an idea that had come before its time. And the story of the *Akedah Isaac*, Isaac's near- sacrifice, Cook turns on its head: rather than using it as a sacred paradigm to dictate ritual reform, he employs it as a window through which to catch a glimpse of the budding human conscience that might first have recognized the barbarism of infant sacrifice and risked the social ostracism it must have taken to buck tradition. In all these ways, Cary Cook does not so much defend Genesis as a record of real people; rather, he imagines what might have happened if these myths did involve real individuals. Only by such a brilliant *tour de force*, I suppose, can the ancient tales be made, against their own tendency, to shed light on the possibilities of human nature.

Robert M. Price Ph.D.
teacher of philosophy & religion
Johnston Community College, Smithfield, NC.

Scripture doesn't lobotomize people.

People lobotomize people.

PREFACE

Genesis 22:2 *-paraphrased*

> And God said, "Take your son and offer him for a burnt offering."

Verse 10

> And Abraham stretched forth his hand to slay his son.

Verses 11 & 12

> And the Lord said, "Don't slay him."

Verses 16 & 17

> "Because you have not withheld your only son, therefore I will bless you."

In both Torah and Koran God told Abraham to sacrifice his son. Of course, the Moslems say it was Ishmael, not Isaac, but that's beside the theological point. The point is, he heard a voice from God… *knows where*, telling him to kill his son. Did he check it out with the local priesthood? No. He just assumed it was the god to whom he was accountable, though *God* as we use the term today wasn't even imagined in the Bronze Age. And then he did it – almost. But just as he raised the dagger, God stopped him, congratulated him for passing the test of faith, and promised him reward for obedience.

> Message: Obey God, and you will be rewarded.
>
> In fact: Obey what you *believe* to be the voice of God, and you will be rewarded.
>
> In fact: Obey what you believe to be the voice of God, no matter how insane or immoral those directions may appear, and you will be rewarded.

But now that we have the Word of God written down, such voices in the sky (or head) are generally regarded as unreliable. Now it's:

> Obey what you believe your Holy Scriptures are telling you, no matter how insane or immoral those directions may appear, and you will be rewarded.

Abraham was rewarded just as God promised. And Abraham's progeny took over Canaan and survived through the millennia just as God promised. And that proves Abraham obeyed God, and God pays off on his promises. Therefore, go thou and do as Abraham did. On this foundation was built Mosaic Law, then all of Judaism, then Christianity, then Islam. Regardless of which branch is chosen, and whether believers actually obeyed it or not, the maxim itself has remained the Prime Directive of monotheism for four thousand years. Even when one group of monotheists, in obedience to the Prime Directive, murders other monotheists, the maxim itself is never challenged. Should it be challenged?

What if a God *does* exist, and He acted the same four thousand years ago as He appears to act today? What if Abram (as he was originally called) were not a special person selected by an arbitrary cosmic Tyrant for supernatural communication? What if he were simply a sincere truth-seeker whose efforts to find a God worthy of the capital G met with about the same success as those of any truth-seeker today? What if he simply *chose* to bet his life on a righteous God, as opposed to the evil gods of his society? *Now* what's the moral of the story? Insist on a righteous God, no matter what your society tells you, and you will be rewarded. Does not that message make better sense to everyone from the most sincere and ardent believer to the blatant hypocrite?

Would such a scenario fit with the Torah? Certainly not with a literal interpretation of it. Would this scenario fit with a *realistic* interpretation of Torah? Judge for yourself. Whether you're as liberal as Dr. Price or as conservative as any Bible thumper, which is more realistic – your present interpretation of Genesis, or this fiction?

HISTORICAL BACKGROUND

If data dumps bore you, skip this part. Just remember it's here if you run into questions.

Starting with Genesis, we are told that Abraham came from Ur of the Chaldees. So right away we have a disagreement between the Torah and historians who date Abraham anywhere from 2200 to 1500 BCE, but date the Chaldeans at no earlier than 900 BCE. Likewise, it says Abraham sojourned with Philistines at Gerar, but the Philistines didn't arrive in Canaan until c.1200 BCE.

> The E might be interpreted as a statement of religious neutrality. Don't let it fool you.

Of course, the Fundamentalists would insist that the Bible is totally correct, and the historians are hopelessly confused, and their disagreement proves it. On the other end, liberal scholars deny Abraham's existence altogether. The not-quite-so-liberal would happily grant a late date for Abe, but then deny the Exodus. A middle-ground interpretation, favored here, would assume that Abraham existed, but either his story was not written until long after the alleged events, or it was embellished by copyists with contemporary references to make better sense to the readers of their time. But even then, after you add in the absurdly long life spans in Genesis (among other strange anomalies), you need some seriously faith colored glasses to avoid the conclusion that the writers were not highly concerned with factual accuracy.

Other parts require no faith at all. Terah had three sons, Abram, Nahor, and Haran, listed in that order, but this does not necessarily imply that Abram was the eldest. Remember that the story was recorded by Abram's descendants. It is more likely that Haran was the eldest. Haran's daughter would eventually marry Nahor, who was named after Terah's father. If Haran were older the age gap between his daughter and Nahor would be diminished. Also note that Haran is named after the town where Terah would die. Coincidence? Possibly. But more likely Terah was born in Haran, migrated out, and named his son after his home town. If Terah had been born in Ur, why would he name his son after a small town very far away?

Ur was the greatest city in Mesopotamia for about a hundred years just prior to the time of Abraham (assuming a date of c.2000 BCE. for Abraham). Built on the coast of a vast and fertile flood plain, the city and everything in it was made of mud or what grew in mud. It was first settled around 4000 BCE as a trading and fishing village where the Euphrates emptied into the Persian Gulf. The original town, like all of eastern Mesopotamia, was covered over with a deep layer of silt deposited by a great flood around 3500 BCE. Though Mesopotamian civilization was interrupted by many floods, this one was unlike any before or since. Still, Ur was not completely buried.

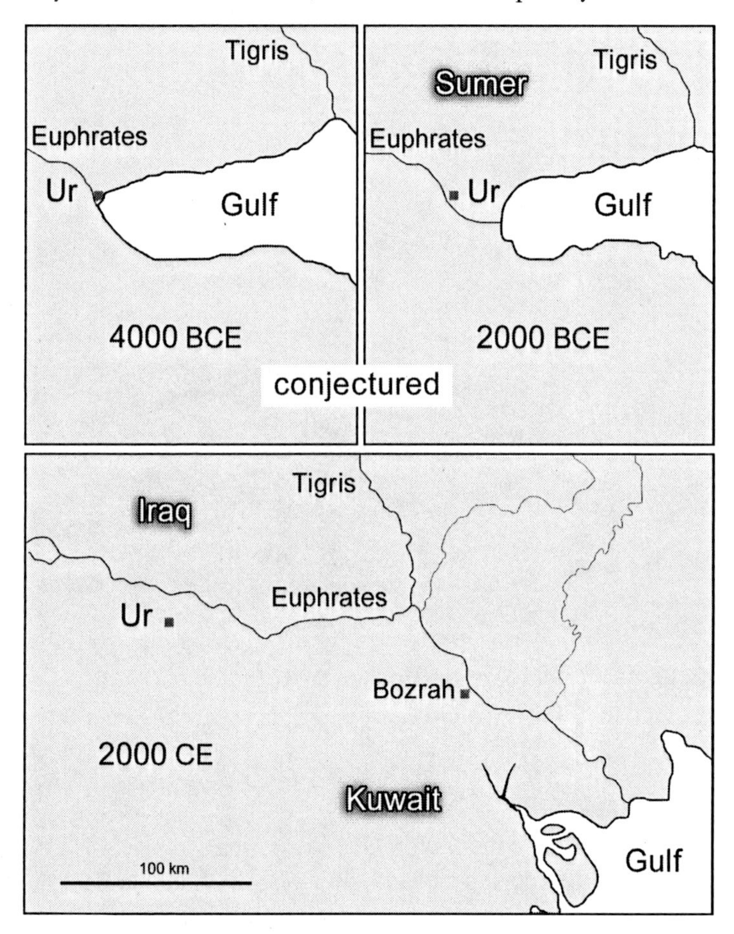

The new city, built on the ruins of the original town, was inhabited first by Sumerians, then by others until the meandering Euphrates would eventually abandon it in the fourth century BCE.

Still standing at Ur is the remnant of a ziggurat, a man made mountain of mud brick sixty-three by forty-three meters at its base. When completed, it was over seventeen meters tall.

> Why use metric measurements in an American book? Because metric is simply a better system. And this book is a shameless advertisement for better systems over traditional systems.

But meters are even more boring than dates, and fiction can ill afford such condescension to reality. Therefore all efforts to separate such dull facts from juicier speculation will henceforth be abandoned.

Unlike most post-diluvian dwellers on the plain, the Sumerians of Ur had the foresight to take precautions against the possibility of such a disaster happening again. They built a mound of bricks to which they might flee in case of another deluge. Each succeeding generation, whether heirs or conquerors, took civic pride in adding more bricks to the mound and crowning it with a temple to whatever god or gods were in fashion. Around 2500 BCE Ur became the Sumerian capital.

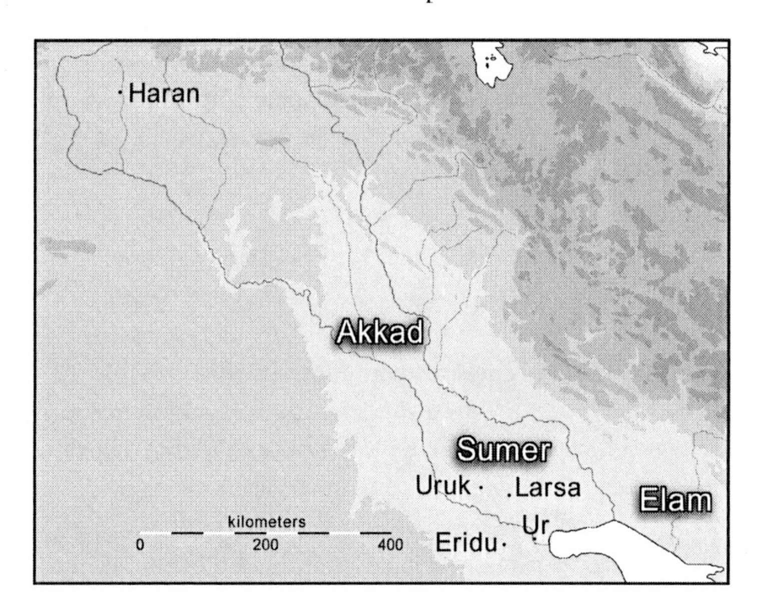

At the same time the first Semites began migrating down the Tigris and Euphrates into Mesopotamia. These soon founded the kingdom of Akkad northwest of Sumeria. Two centuries later the Akkadian king Sargon dominated all Sumeria. Around 2100 BCE a dynastic change moved the Akkadian capital to Ur, where the new king, Ur-Nammu, founded Mesopotamia's most majestic kingdom to that time – the Third Dynasty of Ur. He also built the now holy mound to unprecedented grandeur, a rectangular three tiered step-pyramid, the Great Ziggurat.

The temple at its top he dedicated to a deity common to both peoples, a moon god known to the Sumerians as Nanna and to the Akkadians as Suen.

> The moon was the chief heavenly body to early Mesopotamians because their planting seasons had always been coordinated to lunar cycles. Unlike the Egyptian solar year of about 365 days, which made the moon out of step, the Mesopotamian year consisted of twelve months of thirty days – an extra month being added as needed. The moon was seen as the leader, which the inferior sun followed behind.

But alas, the reign of the Third Dynasty was short lived. The next expansion of western Semites began around 2100 BCE, just as the Akkadians had done three centuries before. These new immigrants were desert dwellers, called Amorites. Innocently encroaching like a camel with its nose in the tent, they would within a century reduce the Sumero-Akkadian empire to little more than the capital itself.

Near the turn of the millennium the Amorites allied themselves with the kingdom of Elam in what would later be Persia on the northeast. Caught between these two ascending powers, Ur was surrounded and besieged in 2004 BCE.

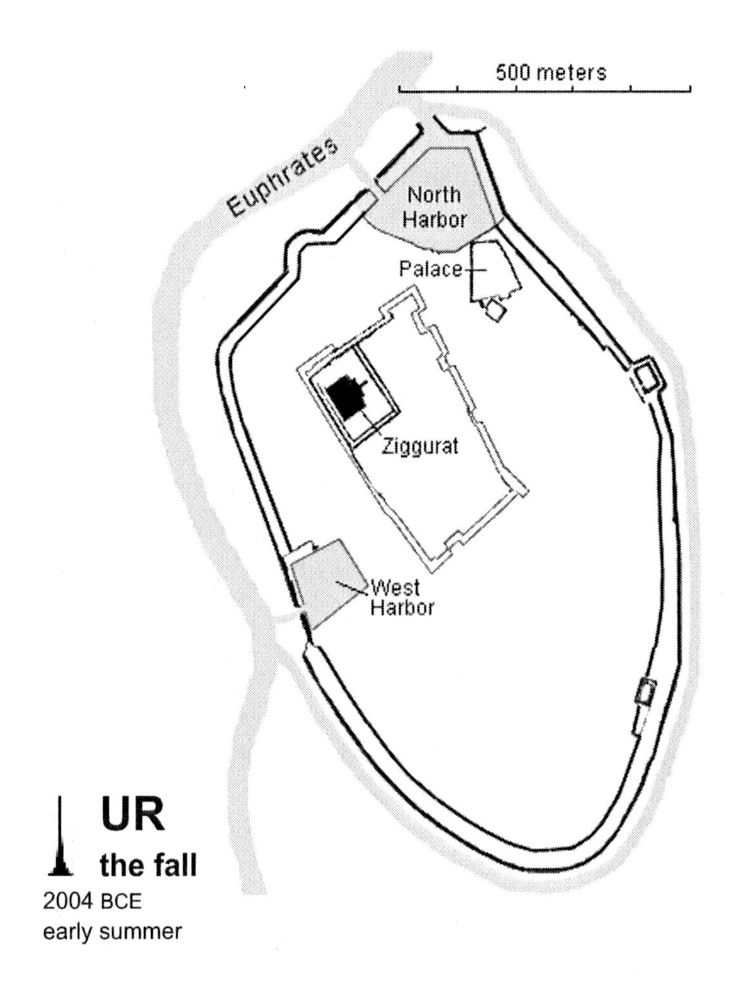

UR

the fall

2004 BCE
early summer

Abram kissed his crescent amulet. “Holy and blessed Suen, protect your city from the evil ones. Protect your people. Protect us.”

Ur was ablaze. Flaming arrows arcing in waves over the east wall ignited reed huts and palm thatch roofs in a wide swath down that side of the city. Fires were quenched at first by the defenders, well prepared with water pots and wet fleeces. But the waves kept coming, and the only water sources were on the north and west.

Besieged within by Amorites on the east and Elamites attacking the south wall, the Akkadian Third Dynasty of Ur clung desperately to life. The defensive canal outside the east wall had been dammed up at the north end by Amorites. Now all that stood between Ur and two hostile armies was a muddy trench.

Haran patted Abram on his leather helmet. "Fret not, little brother. If Ur were to fall, the star gazers would have seen it."

"And if they saw it," said Terah, "who would they tell?"

Terah with his three sons, Haran, Nahor, and Abram were in a detachment of three hundred soldiers defending the royal palace against a potential boat attack through the north harbor.

All of these men were lean and fit as Bronze Age life required of all but the rich. Terah, in his forties, was barely less agile than his sons. A hard-faced man with clearly furrowed lines, he wore the no-nonsense scowl of a determined survivor.

Terah, squinted intently up at the partly clouded sky.

Also praying? thought Abram. *How unlike father.*

"Saru!" shouted Terah to the captain. "Skyward!"

Looking up with reddened eyes, the soldiers saw the next wave of smoke-tailed arrows heading for them.

"Raise shields!" commanded the saru.

Abram dropped the ceramic crescent amulet back down the front of his tunic. The company raised shields. Burning darts pelted the area like hail. Soldiers now dropped their weapons and grabbed water-soaked fleeces to beat out the flames.

> Shields were leather stretched over a wicker frame. Arrows would stick, but not penetrate far.

"Why must we stay back here like women?" complained Lot to his uncle. "The fighting is at the wall."

"His Majesty cannot close the harbor," answered Abram. "And the Amuru have all the boats of the river."

"Amuru are desert rats," said Lot. "They know naught of boats."

"The king commands it," returned Abram. "Be content. If he feared not a boat invasion he would not have fled to the Ziggurat."

From the south an envoy hurried toward them on a fiercely beaten donkey. Terah paused to watch as the envoy took his saru aside and spoke urgently to him in private.

"Seize your weapons," shouted the saru. "To the south wall!"

"We have been breached," said Terah quietly.

The company grabbed weapons and marched southward, then broke into a trot as the saru ordered double-time. It was a crooked and smoky route through the poor district of the east city. They detoured west to take advantage of the better streets near the center. Soon the noise of battle increased. Ghostly silhouettes of running men appeared through the haze. *Enemy?* thought they all, but no, these were battered comrades fleeing toward them.

"Turn, you cowards!" commanded the saru. "We are here to help you."

Some stopped; some ignored him. A bloodied Sumerian staggered past Abram and Lot.

Haran grabbed his arm. "Turn and fight with us, friend."

The Sumerian whirled, clumsily slashing with his bronze two-edge, then continued on his way. Haran was dazed by a tingling at his throat. His next breath flooded his lungs with liquid. He coughed up a stream of blood and fell to his knees.

"Father!" shouted Lot.

The saru barked another hoarse command through the smoke, but few understood it and fewer cared.

Chaos.

Yet high atop the Great Ziggurat, in the temple of Suen, was neither panic nor disorder. The King and his priestly entourage went about ritual sacrifices calmly – or at least with that appearance – in willful disregard of the enemy at the walls. With the populace down to starvation rations, the gods would receive meals on time without interruption. The king saw to it, for this was his duty. And duty, specifically cultic duty, was all – all to the king, all to the priests, to the nobles, to every foot-soldier, down to every mother with child. As each new report brought diminishing hopes of victory, theocratic resolve intensified. Their final breath would be in service to their god.

A noble act of martyrdom? Possibly. A mindless act of stupidity for nothing nobler than group loyalty and dread of dishonor? Also possible. But should these questions even be asked? Is the self sacrifice of a hive for its queen noble or stupid? Neither, it's instinctual. And whether by instinct or honor or peer pressure, Bronze Age men lived by the mentality of the herd. They did what was expected of them – some to be hacked apart at altars, while others, for the same reason, did the hacking.

Amid the tumult in the smoke-filled streets, four sweating and exhausted soldiers jogged panting to the gate of their home near the north harbor.

"Open it!" shouted Terah to the women inside.

"Quickly!"

His wife, Havah, untied the reed binders, and the men rushed in.

"Hitch up the cart," ordered Terah. "The time has come."

"Make ready the children," Nahor ordered his breast-feeding wife.

"Where is Haran?" asked Zilha, the man's widow.

Terah ignored her. "Gather up all your shoes."

"Where is Haran?" she insisted.

"Seize what you can find to eat," commanded Terah.

"Where is my husband?" she cried.

"Father is dead," snapped Lot to his mother.

"Be silent, Beardless," returned Terah. "Fetch his bow."

"Grieve afterward, Zilha," whispered Abram to his sister-in-law. "We must hurry."

Abram was the youngest of Terah's three sons, all by his first wife. Now at the age of twenty, he wasn't quite sure of it, the counting of winters being the job of mothers, and Abram's being long since deceased. Average of height and build, Abram was nevertheless a man you would notice in a crowd, not because he was particularly handsome – the long hair and beard of the time made masculine beauty irrelevant. And why even care about appearance when marriages were arranged by status minded parents? No, you would notice Abram because of his clear and innocent eyes – not piercing, because he was careful to avoid that sort of thing. People didn't like it, so he didn't do it. Abram seemed to know instinctively the right thing to do, and generally did it. But he never could figure out exactly *why* it was right. This question – "why?"

troubled his heart, yet somehow didn't seem to bother others. As a child, Abram had found adults strange, but figured that he would understand them once he became one. Now as an adult, he still found them strange, and now this too troubled him. Abram couldn't possibly know that his mind was evolving a strange new appendage. Whereas *their* identities were effectively crimped by culture into little more than the sum of their roles, Abram was developing an incorrigible sense of self. Like a sane man born into a lunatic asylum, he would require more than the usual period of adjustment, whether to embrace his society or reject it.

> The heart was believed to be the seat of all mental activity until at least the Renaissance.

The wicker cart, now full of most needed possessions, was hitched to a donkey and pulled out into a street fast becoming choked with more of the same. Traffic, congested as lava, flowed toward the east gate of the city wall – the only exit from which they might escape by land.

To their right stood the Ziggurat where victorious Elamites panted their way up the long steps, while comrades loaded with sacred spoils descended. Soon the most holy of all treasures was ripped from its temple and dragged outside. This statue of imported limestone now appeared at the top terrace for all Ur to gaze upon. The image was of an old man with floor-length beard and a crescent moon behind his head, its upward curving ends being easily mistaken for a pair of horns. This was the god Suen. Though just his image to the more enlightened, this white rock was the god himself to the majority, for the commoners perceived no distinction.

Traffic slowed as fleeing citizens turned to gawk at this spectacle through streaks in the haze. Some, including Abram, stopped dead in their tracks to take it fully in. All else faded from his consciousness. Here was his god, the Blessed One, the Holy One, the center of all things worldly and divine, now nothing more than a prize captured by laughing demons. The scene eclipsed all thought.

"Abram, hurry," interrupted Sarai, his wife. "Father waits not."

By "Father" she meant literally that Terah was her father, not just Abram's father. The daughter of Havah, Sarai had been espoused to her half-brother Abram when they were children. There had been no courtship and never a doubt as to whom each would marry. Had Terah suspected how attractive Sarai would grow up to be, he would surely have held back her hand as bargaining goods for social advancement.

Squeezing through the east gate, Terah strained to see above the throng. Which way were they going? Which way was the enemy? It didn't really matter. They would have to stay with the crowd regardless.

Abram turned for a final glance at the Ziggurat. His god, now supine on skids made of palm trunks torn from its own garden, slid slowly down the steps from its heavenly perch. The image burnt into Abram's memory to be preserved for the rest of his life. Then he too was pushed through the gate as through a birth-canal.

Northward along the wall seemed to be the decision of whoever led this herd. Bodies of citizens dead and dying cluttered their path. These were pierced with arrows from the Amorites massed on the far side of the muddy trench. But now the Amorites had lowered their bows and just stood there laughing and jeering.

"They could slay us all." Said Sarai. "Why do they spare us?"

"So as not to block the gate with bodies," said Abram. "The sooner we leave, the sooner they can enter."

At the north end of the trench the refugee column hurried across on the dam built by their enemies. Now they were fair game and the Amorites resumed the arrow barrage. The right side took several hits. On the left many were pushed westward into the reed swamps of the river edge – those in first trampled by those that followed. Still the column stumbled relentlessly over once beautiful farmland up the river toward the afternoon sun. As shadows lengthened, the glare forced all eyes downward, as if heaven itself demanded further humiliation.

Dusk. Their oppressors had by now lost interest, preferring the greater spoils inside the city. The battered fugitives rested at the river bank, tending wounds, gathering food, cooking, and preparing for night. Widows and orphans wandered among family units hoping to see a friendly face. A girl not yet pubescent approached Havah's stewing fire.

"I can spin and sew and weave beautiful baskets. I am exceeding strong."

Havah glanced at Terah. The answer was no. The girl moved on.

Abram's attention drifted to a blind old woman sitting in a cart and ignored by her despondent kindred. She now offered the only thing she had left to justify her keep – her knowledge of cult stories.

> "And Anu said to Tiamat, 'Wherefore shall these our children make this noise? They disturb our sleep. Let us destroy them all.' And the gods trembled in fear of Anu, their father. And they said, 'Who can save us from the wrath of Anu and Tiamat?' And Enlil, mightiest of the gods, opened his mouth and spake, 'I will go up and smite the ancient ones.'"

Abram listened passively, his mind numb. The story, often repeated by his deceased mother, had been etched into his mind as sacred truth. Now it sounded hollow and remote, like one of many solicitous harangues in a market place.

A boy gave the old woman a bowl full of something hot. The woman ate. Abram, however, was not hungry. The day's events required all the digesting he could manage. As the four Terahite men sat circled around supper dishes, Abram alone did not dip bread. The women and children sat in another circle huddled around the newly widowed Zilha, whose wailing and rocking and breast-beating had passed their pitiful crest and were now becoming tiresome.

Terah broke silence, "Lot, fetch more reeds for the fire."

Lot complied without hesitation, though clearly no more fuel was needed.

Terah then turned to Nahor, his eldest son now that Haran was gone. "Would that Zilha be not over grieved. The Blessed One forbid she should set her heart to follow her husband."

"All gods forbid it!" agreed Nahor, then taking a large bite of dipped bread.

Apparently little affected by the day's tragedies, Nahor's face was calm and blank – his usual look. Detached emotionally, he was the perfect Bronze-Ager, in fact the most common creature of all ages, a natural born conformist dedicated to nothing in particular. Nahor remained firmly grounded in the needs of the present, whatever they might be.

Terah, hoping for greater acknowledgement of those needs, pressed forward. "Skillful on the spindle, is she not?"

"None finer."

"Earns her mutton, that one."

Feeling the drift of the conversation, Nahor declined to respond.

Terah continued, "I would greatly miss her date-nut cakes."

Nahor nodded in agreement. "Would that I were older, I would clutch her to my own bosom."

"It is your right."

"Ahh, would that I were older."

After pausing to be sure that Nahor would not change his mind, Terah spoke again, "Zilha. Be comforted. You shall be my concubine."

The statement was neither rude nor shocking. It was what all the women expected and some hoped for, though Zilha would have rather heard it come from Abram. With timidly raised brows, the new concubine made eye-contact with the wife. Havah opened wide her arms, and the tension was broken. The two collided into their assigned roles with a fresh round of tears.

Abram breathed a sigh of relief.

Nahor now turned to Terah with a counter offer, "I would happily unburden you of her daughter."

"In due season," returned Terah.

"Surely," agreed Nahor.

Two days of monotonous marching lengthened the column as the stronger moved forward and the weak lagged behind. Custom now separated each family into two groups, the men ten paces ahead of their women and children. The evening of the third day brought the first sliver of new moon to the sky. All gazed toward it, some in tears, some in whispers, most in silence.

Lot prodded Abram. "Abi, the moon returns as before. How can this be?"

Of all the men in Terah's family, Abram and Lot were closest – Abram being the only one with a rudimentary sense of humor, and Lot being the only one to laugh in the right places. Lot was three years younger, unattractive, and socially withdrawn. Having little identity of his own, he allowed Abram to do most of his thinking for him. But a moon rising without its god was beyond even Abram's understanding of cosmology.

"Father," said Abram. "What does this mean?"

"Surely, it means the Blessed One lives. Rejoice in it." But there was no joy in Terah's tone.

"Does it mean he escaped from the Elamu?" asked Lot.

"Perhaps."

"Do you think he now hates us Akkadu and loves Elamu?" asked Abram."

"Perhaps that too."

"Will he be angry at us?" asked Lot.

"Am I a priest?" snapped Terah. "Make of it what you will."

Terah and Nahor exchanged a peevish glance indicating their mutual disdain for such "childish" questions. Abram caught it.

Why do you roll the eyes? he thought. *These are needful and heavy things to know.*

On the following day many families split off from the main column and headed eastward.

"They go to Larsa, father," said Nahor. "Shall we join them?"

"No. Follow the river."

"The children are weary," said Havah.

"No," repeated Terah. "If mighty Ur fell, can Larsa be far behind?"

"Then where shall we go, father?" asked Abram.

"The one place I have kindred – Haran."

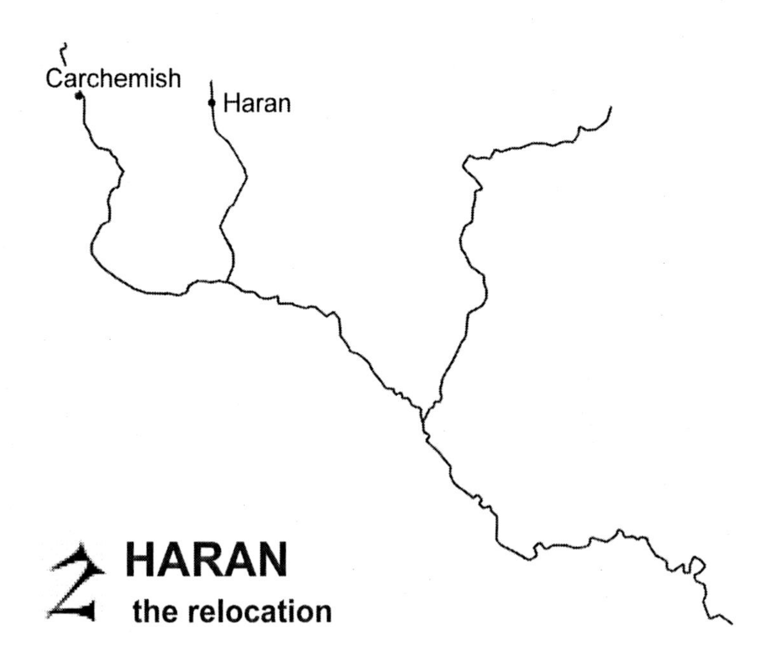

HARAN
the relocation

> The name Haran meant caravan, much like a highway restaurant might be named Truckers.

The names were not identical by coincidence. Terah was born and raised in Haran. Having been drafted into the Akkadian army to fight anything non-Akkadian, he still clung to his home town by naming his first-born after it. Haran was located in the hills of western Mesopotamia on the trade route from Carchemish on the west to the old Akkadian capital where the road was severed by a southbound Euphrates tributary. Here an ancient rest stop grew into a village, now an unwalled town of some four thousand.

Still at the Euphrates on an autumn night drizzling with rain Sarai huddled close to Abram. "Three moons have come and gone, Abi," she said. "How much farther?"

"Father says it is near."

"He said it was near when we came to the oak trees. He always says it is near."

"Then it is near. Be content with it." Abram turned away from her. *Be content. Be content. Always the chide of the higher to the lower. And now I pass it on like a right bestowed by the gods. Yet I have never been content.*

The next day Terah and his sons waded into the Euphrates to drag a stolen fishnet. In the tall grass he noticed an old and rotted pine cone. Picking it up, he smiled and tossed it to Nahor.

"What be this?" asked Nahor.

"Fruit of the tall trees of my youth," said Terah.

Nahor sniffed the cone. "Not the best, I hope."

"Far from it. Truly our home is near."

A week's trek brought the column into gently rolling hill country forested in part with oak, ash, and pine, soon after that to a fork in the river.

"The river of Haran!" came a shout from the front. This was echoed down the line to the end. By now, all animals, carts, and elderly were gone. The ragged remnant numbered less than a hundred. In a week they arrived in the wooded and fertile valley south of Haran.

Terah, impatient to get back to the land of his birth, hurried his family to the front of the column. The first familiar rock formations brought moisture to his eyes. Climbing to the top of a hill, he searched for the homes of former neighbors. The first sign of habitation was a black goat-hair tent, clustered among livestock pens.

"Food!" he shouted down to the column.

Several young men trotted ahead to beg for the sake of their families but stopped at the edge of a ravine. Terah ran down the hill to join them. He thought he heard the sound of bees, but no; they were flies. This once-pristine river bed was now used as a dump. A gathering place of hyenas and vultures, the stinking crevasse revealed more than the men wanted to see. Scattered throughout the unburned refuse were human skeletons.

Terah peered between the trees at the black tent and noticed camels among the livestock. "Amuru." He turned and shouted the warning to the rest. "Amuru!"

> The Amorites, who would later found the Babylonian Empire, were barbaric nomads at this time. They ate their meat raw and buried neither their dung nor their dead.
>
> Historians disagree on when camels were first domesticated (4000-1400 BCE). Arbitrarily assuming that the Amorites used them as pack animals, they would still not figure out how to ride them for another millennium. Apart from references in Genesis (possibly added after even Moses' time), there is no record of camels being ridden until the eighth century BCE.

Trudging the last leg of their journey on bandaged feet, the vanquished parade again entertained an Amorite audience. This time both were careful to appear non-threatening, equally careful to appear ready for defense. Stepping over abandoned irrigation ditches, the Akkadians' contempt welled up for these agriculturally apathetic nomads turned squatter. Shallow furrows once green with wheat and barley now bore only straggly stalks among the weeds. Neglected citrus trees and melon patches showed a few small fruits, barely tempting. Terah seethed as they passed by the ruined dwellings of his childhood friends, houses left unoccupied by the Amorites for fear of ghosts.

Terah stopped. There before him were the broken walls of his former home. The tiled roof was collapsed over the charred remains of its rafters. By now his grief was spent, leaving only a smoldering anger. The family gathered silently behind him, and waited as the column trudged past them.

A young Amorite girl ran down to the procession offering a block of cheese. Hungry children would have eagerly accepted the gift, but were restrained by their parents. Nahor's boy bolted forth, grabbed it, and took a large bite. Terah ran to him and seized his arm. Wrenching the cheese from his hand, he threw it down. Then holding the boy by the back of the neck and bending him over, Terah commanded, "Spit it!" The boy obeyed.

After accepting a man's food, it was considered impolite to kill him.

On the highest hill next to Haran stood a much reduced imitation of the ziggurat temple. Here, in a location having an ample supply of stone, they still chose the traditional baked brick, but compromised with pillars of pine sculpted to resemble the reed and palm ornamentation at Ur. At its front a rectangular altar of uncut stones proclaimed to the observer that the image inside was a god, the god Suen, with the characteristic crescent behind its head. Once again, no coincidence – Haran had been conquered by Akkadian worshippers of the moon god three centuries previously.

Clad only in loin cloth and skullcap, two shaven-headed priests scrubbed soot and blood from the altar and surrounding trough – not at all menial labor in view of its proximity to holiness. Glancing southward, they noticed a curious sight and paused in their work.

"Be that an army?"

"Perhaps a caravan?"

"Not much of either, but it comes this way. We must tell the king."

Reaching the outskirts of Haran, men shouted out their family names in hopes of being reunited with relatives. The residents, surprised but sympathetic, dropped everything and helped in whatever way they could. Terah's family gratefully accepted food and drink.

"I am Terah, son of Nahor, son of Serug. Does my father live?"

The question was politely ignored.

"Be any here of clan Serug?" shouted Terah. The appeal was absorbed into a clamor of other kinship queries.

The king, having taken the time to don his royal regalia, arrived on donkey with a small entourage of priests and guards. The bewilderment on their faces was addressed by a subject rushing past.

"Your Piety, Ur is fallen!"

Finding themselves irrelevant in a situation needing no supervision, the administrators nevertheless barked a few cosmetic orders.

A tent-camp developed along the riverbanks for those not quickly adopted by relatives. Here the family rested in hopes of being rescued by Terah's father, or at least by a rich and generous uncle. As the sun sank in the west any kinsman would have been welcome.

"Be you of clan Serug?" asked a voice.

They looked up to see a man in his forties, too pale and pudgy for physical labor, he appeared to be some kind of cleric. Terah stood, clasped hands in front of his chest, and bowed. "Terah, son of Nahor."

"I am Odum," said the man, "son of Almodad, who was brother to the wife of Nahor."

"The peace of the Blessed, my cousin." He reached for Odum's right hand to kiss it as a servant.

Odum courteously refused the gesture, and with that same hand clutched Terah's beard, and drew him up that they might kiss cheeks as equals. Formalities fulfilled, Terah asked, "Does Nahor live?"

"Alas," said Odum. "About ten harvests has it been."

Terah lowered his eyes and pressed his lips together just long enough to register the proper remorse before asking, "And what of my uncles?"

"They lived in the valley," Odum said gesturing. "Many years ago the Amuru began to move in."

"Where are my uncles now?" Terah asked.

Odum struggled for the right words.

"Dead?" asked Terah.

"Slain in battle against the Amuru," Odum replied.

"Avenged?"

"Their sons also perished."

Terah stared at Odum until the man fidgeted.

"And the men of Haran did naught?"

Odum squirmed. "We fought them as lions, truly. There were battles and truces and more battles, bargains and betrayals. In time it… settled."

Terah's lips tightened to control his temper until he regained composure. "Amuru were they who sacked Ur. Now you tell me that my father and his kindred are all slain by Amuru?" He turned to Havah. "Woman! Fetch my teraph."

Havah hurried to comply. She picked up what appeared to be a bundle of filthy rags and handed it to Terah. He unwrapped the package impatiently. It was about the size of a shoe – a clay figurine clumsily resembling a dwarfish man. Terah held it up before Odum's face.

"My father made this thirty years ago. It has a lock of his beard baked inside. He told me he would always be with me, and he has been. On the journey here I saw other teraphim thrown in the dirt because they were too heavy to carry. *My father was not too heavy.*" Terah began to tremble. "Forgive me." He turned and walked away.

Nahor rose to fill the vacuum. "Father has lost much. We had an elder brother at Ur. He died in glory at the wall as the Amuru horde broke through."

Actually they were Elamites who breached the wall, and Haran was killed accidentally by a fleeing Sumerian, but such details were not expedient to the desired goal.

Nahor continued. "Lot here is the son of our dear brother."

Odum saluted Lot. "May the peace of the Blessed Suen fill your heart."

"And yours, uncle. I am Nahor the younger." Then with a hand gesture, "My brother, Abram."

Abram rose and bowed.

Nahor's wife pinched the child in her arms until it cried.

Odum capitulated. "You must stay at my house."

Nahor politely declined. "We would not think to impose. The tent is more than enough."

Odum insisted; Nahor demurred. This humble haggling was all part of a time-honored hospitality formula, and therefore indispensable. None of the women were introduced, nor did they expect to be.

Odum's house in western Haran was not lavish, but showed him to be a man of comfortable means. Once inside the gate, he called for water jugs. These were brought by his teenage children, revealing to his guests that he had no slaves. Terah and his family removed their worn out sandals but forbade Odum's children to wash their feet, insisting rather on doing it themselves. Both gestures were also part of the hospitality dance, but the guests were equally concerned for their abrasions. These were washed and treated with onion juice and poultices. By lamp and torch light the family sat down to enjoy their first full meal since the fateful day.

"Olives!" exclaimed Terah, popping one into his mouth. "These above all have I missed."

That night, he and his two sons slept on comfortable grain sacks in a storage room. Not the ideal arrangement, but the men's right to the best accommodations was considered more important than conjugal relations for now. Some geese and goats in the backyard were displaced to accommodate tents for the rest of the family, where Lot was not yet old enough to outrank the wives for the choice spots farthest from the pig pen.

Pig bones found in Bronze Age archaeological sites indicate that pigs were eaten by Akkadians and Sumerians.

The next day at the town center market place a meeting was held – free adult men only. The king, who doubled as high priest, did his best to appear king-priestly, rending his garment in grief and directing public lamentation for kinsmen lost, notably his own cousin, the king of Ur, whose fate was unknown to any of those present. After prayers and eulogies he got down to business.

"Alas, it would appear that the Son of Suen is no more, and the Blessed is without a son upon the earth."

"You, O king, are now that son," came the expected response from the robed choir of shaven headed priests.

"Aahh," wailed the king, "would that I were worthy to kiss the shoe of such a one."

It went on until the king, lacking the popular landslide necessary for deification, decided to postpone his rejection of the title until a more favorable time. Next order of business.

"We know not why the gods allowed this grievous thing." He glanced toward his clergy. "Perhaps for priestly offenses." His eyes roamed the audience, "unatoned sins, holding back at the altar." He shrugged. "We know not, so we care not. It is a time to welcome our brothers and make room. For those who have no kindred among us, let us take up alms to help them find new homes in other lands as the gods will."

"Perhaps in the south valley, your Piety?" came an unexpected question from the back of the crowd. Heads turned around to see its source. Terah stood, somber and chin held high.

The king responded, "Any man is welcome to live in the valley, but the neighbors may be…"

A chuckle from the audience saved him from having to complete the sentence.

Terah inquired, "Does not the south valley belong to Haran?"

"It did," came an anonymous voice.

"It does still," came another. "The Amuru are tenants – so it was said."

"Truly!" shouted another. "When do they pay their rent?"

Terah was emboldened. "I and my sons have fought Amuru all our life. Give me fifty men; I will drive the sand lizards back into the desert."

"It has been done," came an objection. "They return."

Another: "The Amuru now serve the Blessed One."

Another: "They have sacrificed at the temple."

Terah pushed through to the front and faced the crowd. "When the Amuru covet your land, they first kiss the feet of your gods. They sung hymns to Suen as they crept into Akkad. They made great offerings to Enlil and Ishtar all the while they ravaged Sumer."

A priest spoke up. "But *these* Amuru are honorable. They have taken the sacraments of the Blessed Suen."

Terah looked him straight in the eye. "The Amuru will worship a dog but to steal its bone. Then they will slay it upon the altar of Baal."

The crowd murmured. "Many of us have broken bread with them." "Some have made oaths." "They are not evil folk."

Terah shouted above it. "Be any oath greater than the bond of blood? Be any law greater than to avenge blood?" He looked around at sullen faces. "My grandfather was Serug, son of Reu. My blood is yours. My first-born son I named Haran. He was murdered by Amuru. Would any man here forbid me to slay every one of them?"

After a respectful silence, a noble responded, "So be it. But ask not for us to help you."

"I will help him," offered a scar-faced veteran.

"And I," echoed a sun-browned young field worker. "Tares among wheat remain tares."

Murmuring erupted again. Sensing the crowd's division, the king raised his staff and hushed them. "This matter shall be judged by the Blessed One." He thumped the staff on the ground, turned, and walked away.

No discussion followed – no bantering of pros and cons. Like field workers at sunset, the meeting quietly dispersed.

That evening after supper Terah asked Odum if he might borrow a pinch of incense and two lamps with oil.

"I would speak with my father," explained Terah.

"Surely," said Odum. "You may use our family shrine. My fathers were friends of your fathers."

Odum's shrine was in a corner of his bedroom so that the spirits of his ancestors might protect him as he slept. It consisted of a wooden bench on which five teraphim were arranged in a straight line spaced at equal intervals. These were between two brass lamps half-full of olive-oil. Cantered in front of this line was a ceramic dish blackened in the center from countless burnt offerings. The symmetry was compromised by an incense burner on one side of the dish, not quite balanced on the other by a flint dagger and a cup containing four lamb vertebrae.

Terah entered the room carrying a lighted lamp and his father's teraph. After passing on the flame to the shrine-lamps, he knelt before the bench, unwrapped his teraph, and stood it in front of the other five. He then picked up the dagger, cut off a lock of his hair, and placed it in the dish. Feeling under the bench, he found a box of incense and sprinkled some over the hair. This he ignited while muttering a pious invocation to all gods of his ancestors ending, with a request to speak with the ghost of his father.

Nahor and Abram watched silently from the doorway where they had been instructed to remain. The ceremony differed slightly from previous ones they had witnessed back at Ur. Terah had substituted a lock of hair for the customary offering of fine wheat flour. Not having any food of his own, he chose to offer part of himself rather than to borrow from another.

They could not hear what their father was saying, but when Terah picked up the cup and rattled its contents they knew he had asked a question and anticipated an answer. He dumped the bones onto the bench. As he studied them, his sons, with equal intensity, studied him. Apparently finding the results unsatisfactory, Terah scooped them back into the cup and rattled them again. Nahor and Abram watched him repeat this procedure twice more. Then he wrapped his teraph back up, snuffed out the lamps, and stood.

Nahor and Abram backed away from the doorway. Terah exited the dark room still deep in thought, then felt his sons' eyes on him.

"He wishes to be avenged," Terah said, and walked off.

On the next day the town meeting reconvened in the temple courtyard. Terah stood in the front row, Nahor, Abram, and Lot, with the other refugees, in the back. Two priests, again stripped down to loincloth, hoisted a black Billy-goat onto the altar. Despite the ropes tied to its legs, it put up a good fight until the king deftly slit its throat with a double edged flint dagger.

Though Abram had witnessed similar rituals many times feeling nothing but reverence, he now thought it strange that priests should prefer the old-fashioned flint when bronze was obviously superior. *When did the gods say that only flint-cut offerings were acceptable?* he thought. *What kind of god would be offended by a better tool?* In the past Abram would have rejected such thoughts as impious, but now they seemed perfectly reasonable.

With professional detachment the priests opened the goat as if it were a packing crate and pulled out entrails, separating them into pre-designated ceramic basins. The king, now in a white linen sleeveless mantle and cylindrical miter, stood behind reciting incantations from a cuneiform tablet. The language was formal and archaic, which made it sound all the more holy.

Lot whispered to Abram, "Think you that the gods be real?"

Abram stiffened. *The forbidden question – right out in the air where the gods can hear it!* Indeed the very thought had been suppressed until the preceding four-month trek. Now Abram realized that he was not the only one who harbored it in the shadows.

"Truly they must be," he whispered to Lot. "How can anyone be a god yet not be real?" Abram was surprised at the flippancy of his own response, but it felt justified.

Lot pondered the reasoning. He had to glance back at Abram's smirking profile before getting the joke.

King and priests now clustered in a surgeons' conference over the gore, poking and interpreting softly in jargon obscure to the onlookers.

> Vocabularies of this time swelled with names of entrail parts, yet had only love and hate to distinguish preference. Human thought and language had barely risen above Neolithic infancy. Anything pleasant was called sweet, and if sweet and edible, it was usually called honey. Bronze Age grammar could not even handle a participial phrase.

"Ah!" exclaimed the king, finding an interesting spleen-blemish and showing it to his subordinates. A definite piece of evidence, but needing confirmation. Flip it over and check the other side. What's this over here? Compare that part to this part. At length, they were in agreement. The king now raised his bloody arms and announced the divine verdict.

"I see camels flee in terror."

The crowd cheered. But most understood priestcraft well enough to know that this was no promise of a successful campaign. If it went well, Suen must get the credit. If it failed, Suen must not be blamed – nor his priests. This was permission and nothing more.

Another loin-clothed priest arrived on stage with a basin full of wet fleeces intended for clean up. But Terah interrupted.

"And who would the Blessed One have to go with us, your Piety?"

The priests looked to the king for direction. *Back to work?* No. The king had seen enough.

"Those bound by oath may not take up arms. But any other may offer his sword, to his own honor and the glory of the Blessed."

Heads looked around. Only the veteran and the field worker stepped forward to stand next to Terah. Not impressive.

Terah raised another question for the king. "If we take back the valley, who owns it?"

"Surely the temple, as always," he replied, "but its tenants receive abundant benefit."

"Would it not appear that the Amuru now own it?" asked Terah, "and offer the Blessed but a crumb of due tribute?"

All froze. Only a desperate man would dare ask such a provocative question of a king. Terah continued.

"Would not the Blessed love more to give it to his own?" then remembering his place, "your Piety?"

The king scratched his beard. "*Give* it?"

"Not free of tribute surely," replied Terah, "but perhaps as enfiefed lords and not as tenants. Your Piety might ask him."

The priests again looked toward the king. He hesitated.

Abram couldn't resist. "Be that another goat?"

Lot restrained a snicker. The rest were not amused.

The king gave a reluctant nod to the priests, who now reexamined the basins, this time silently.

Nahor leaned toward Abram. "I know not about you, Abram. You can be wise as a serpent and foolish as a goose all in one breath."

Abram reflected on his disturbing new attitude. He had never in his life been insolent or impious. Now such thoughts were escaping from his mouth before he thought to censor them. It gave him pause.

The priests showed their findings to the king. He studied the evidence until he was satisfied, then smiled, and addressed the crowd.

"The land shall belong to those who conquer it."

Their expectant silence compelled him to finish. "as enfiefed lords."

A faint, "Hmmmm," arose from the crowd.

Men made their way to the front and stood with Terah. Their number reached seven, then stopped. Terah's lips tightened around grinding teeth. It was not enough.

Then… "Ah," exclaimed the senior priest, Bildad, closely examining a slippery liver. All turned to Bildad.

"The crescent moon may favor its servants," he announced, showing the liver to the king.

"Hmmmm," growled the king, squinting closely at the liver. Wary of a subordinate's opinion, he picked through the carcass to get a good look at the kidneys. Then convinced, he nodded in prophetic certainty toward Terah's small band. "The Blessed One smiles upon a night attack at the time of crescent."

So impressive was this assurance that one more young lion dared step to Terah's side.

The king now strode to Terah and stood regally before him. "Declare your prayer."

Terah clasped hands in front of his chest. "Victory. Perfect victory. Vengeance. And a curse upon the Amuru."

"Kneel," said the king.

Terah knelt. The king put forth his bloody left fist. Terah kissed his ring.

"The magic of Baal is powerless under a crescent moon," said the king. "Take care that no clouds stop its light."

The meeting was over. People dispersed as before, except for Terah's twelve soldiers – his sons and grandson, plus nine recruits. All gathered around him for orders.

"First, I would visit the graves of my kindred," he said.

Under normal circumstances these bodies would have been interred under the floor-plaster of their homes, but those being in foreign hands, they had been buried in the public graveyard, along with others who had fallen defending the valley. Several of their surviving relatives were among the twelve. It was a politically astute move, and Terah made good use of it. At the grave of his father he sobbed audibly and beat his breast.

Abram and Lot exchanged an embarrassed glance. Having never before seen a single tear fall from those narrow slits of eyes, they could not help but wonder for whose benefit these were.

Terah had his men introduce themselves by declaring their names and relationship to any of the graves present. It was then decided that they should reconvene secretly and get to know each other over some good food and drink.

"But for now, rest well, men," Terah commanded. "We shall sleep by day and train by night. Five nights to mid crescent." Though reserved by nature, Terah could put on soldierly swagger when necessary.

That evening in a pine forest in the hills north of town they met around a crackling fire. Feasting on roast boar and strong wine, the Twelve compressed a week's worth of male bonding into a single meal. Terah learned that the south valley Amorites were one clan. If you killed one man, you would have to kill them all, or you would never see the end of it.

"Do they post guards at night?" asked Terah.

"No longer," said the veteran.

"Not even to protect their flocks?"

"They pen them at night close to the tents."

"How many families in all?" asked Terah.

"At least ten," said one man.

"Perhaps fourteen," another.

> Would they have had sheepdogs? Probably not. The earliest mention of a sheepdog is the Tibetan mastiff c.1100 BCE. In 2000 BCE sheep themselves were barely domesticated.

"How far apart be they?" asked Terah.

"Far enough to keep flocks and herds from mingling."

"Far enough that one nest will not hear what happens in the next?" asked Terah.

"Yes… unless someone screams."

"How many men in the biggest?" asked Terah.

"Five tents," said the veteran. "No more than five men."

Terah stroked his beard. "We hit the nests one at a time. But in each nest, we hit all tents at once."

The veteran cautioned, "We shall be weak in the bigger nests."

"We shall hit them last," concluded Terah, knowing that he could not afford to lose men until late in the operation.

Walking home by the light before dawn, Abram timidly offered a suggestion. "The Amuru owe much tribute to their lords, father. Perhaps they would agree to divide the land."

"Amuru will agree to anything," countered Nahor. "Their words are naught."

Lot, too, was uneasy. "You mean we shall go from tent to tent and slay them as they sleep?"

"If all goes well," said Terah, "for they slew my uncles and cousins… your clan. Be you man enough? Or will you stay at home with the women?"

"No!" exclaimed Lot. Then, *"Yes!* I am man enough."

"Good," replied Terah, "for we need every man we can get."

Lot unconsciously grabbed Abram's hand, then quickly released it. A night slaughter was no small adjustment. Both felt a need to get their bearings.

At sunrise it was Shapatu, seventh day of the week, holy to the Akkadians because after Elil caused the rains of the Great Flood for six days and nights, he rested on the seventh.

Before that, it had been holy to the Sumerians because the rain lasted seven days and nights without reference to anyone resting.

After sleeping – or trying to – through the day, the Terahite men awakened to find Odum's dining floor set out to formally welcome them. The women, after eating separately with the children, poured water over the men's hands, then sat behind them to facilitate in matters of etiquette, such as filling goblets and disposing of bones. Dinner concluded, they removed the dishes and regathered to hear Odum's aged mother officiate as mistress of the story. She continued from where she had left off on the previous Shapatu.

> "And the gods complained to Elil, their master, saying, 'Wherefore must we do all the work? Make for us servants, that we may rest.'"

Abram and Lot winced. The use of the Akkadian Elil for the familiar Enlil sounded provincial to them – indeed to all the Terahites. *Strange,* thought Abram, *how such a small change of words could sound so foreign.* Every little deviation in detail from the more "reliable" version at Ur, was like a poke in the ribs.

> "And Elil took the blood of Geshtu, the slain god, and gave it to Ninlil, his wife. For he said, 'Here. Make you a servant to the gods.' And from clay mixed with the blood of

> Geshtu, Ninlil made Adapa, the first man. And Elil put Adapa to work in the edin. And it came to pass that Elil took Adapa up to heaven and invited him to eat of the tree of life, for he said, 'Eat, that you may live forever.' But Adapa had been deceived by Ea, and he ate not. And Elil was wroth with Adapa for that he disobeyed."

edin: a Sumerian word for plain, steppe, or desert believed to be between the Tigris & Euphrates.

"What?" exclaimed Abram before he thought better of it.

Everyone froze, then turned stiff-necked toward the disruptor.

"Forgive me, I pray you," said Abram, "I learned the story differently from my youth."

"Save it for question time," said Terah.

Abram's interruption had not been totally out of place. Shapatu dinner was a time of religious instruction. Even women and children were allowed to speak up and be heard – the wooden formality being trusted to quell anything but the most respectful of expression. This ritual was to the family as temple ritual was to the community – the glue that held it together.

The story recital was resumed and took about ten minutes. After this, Odum offered a prayer to Suen. Terah followed up with one of his own – longer and more pious than was his usual custom. Odum then called for prayer requests, and this was followed by question time. None dared pre-empt Abram.

"We of Ur have been taught that Enlil wished for Adapa to serve the gods forever, and therefore offered to him the tree of life. But Ea warned Adapa not to eat of it."

Odum smiled congenially. "The Sumerian tale has a few small differences."

"But I thought Adapa was relieved of toil because he obeyed Ea," said Abram's fugitive mouth. "If he was punished with death because he disobeyed Enlil, then it is all upside down."

Odum shrugged. "But a trifle. Either way it tells us why man is not immortal."

"I pray you all forgive my son," said Terah. "He thinks much but learns little. Now that we are back home I will see to it that all my family is taught the true stories of our fathers, as well as the *manners* of our fathers."

No one else ventured a question that evening.

There could be no war training on Shapatu night, but nothing forbade the Terahite men from working out their strategy and tactics by the light of an oil lamp. Abram and Lot soon excused themselves and moved to the back yard to mull over the ethics of the situation. This quickly slid into religion and the primitive beginnings of a philosophical discussion. While finding no answers, they at least clarified some questions.

Seeing Terah step outside, Lot prodded Abram.

"Ask him."

"Not I," declined Abram. "You ask him if you dare."

Terah headed for the latrine, shooting them both a cold glance in passing. They froze, and the moment was lost.

Lot, for the first time in his life, took the lead. "I will ask him, but swear you will stand by me."

"If you must," said Abram, "but be humble about it."

The two waited silently in the darkness until Terah returned.

"Grandfather," said Lot, "a question if you will. Be Suen still our god?"

"Surely," replied Terah. "Who other?"

"How be it that men can conquer a god?" asked Lot.

"They cannot," replied Terah. "None but gods conquer gods. Men but do the dirty work."

Lot then asked, "If Suen be conquered, should we not choose another god?"

"Men choose not gods," replied Terah. "Gods choose men."

Lot risked a suggestion. "Back at Ur, many served Enlil and Ea and Ishtar. Enlil is father of Suen. Why shall we not serve Enlil?"

"Or rather *Elil* of the Akkadu," Abram added, "Would not Elil choose us if we ask him?"

Terah shook his head impatiently. "That is not the way of men and gods. A man serves the god of his fathers."

"But Enlil created the first man," dared Lot. "And we are all from the loins of the first man."

Abram offered another addition. "If one god created all men, why cannot all men serve one god?"

Terah was irritated. "No, no, the gods' ways are their own. Moreover, in the far past, Enlil was pushed aside by Ea, and then Ea by Ishtar. Then Ningizzidah got in there somehow, and everything was mixed up until it was all overthrown by Suen."

Lot shrugged. "And now Suen by Baal. Why then shall we not serve Baal?"

In a flash, Terah throttled Lot, pushed him to the ground, and threatened him with a raised fist.

Abram jumped. "It is but a question, father. He but

desired to learn. Thought happens."

Terah took a few deep breaths to regain composure, then got up and looked around to see if anyone saw it. "Suen is the god of our fathers. He is the one god who cares for us. He holds our fate. Your fathers, your king, your god – it is all one. All others are enemy. You live in my house – you serve my god."

Terah walked back inside.

The following night at camp Terah inspected weapons and began training. "I would hear no death cries. Slay quickly. If they lie on their back, slice the throat – hard and deep. If on the side, then stab through the neck and slice outward. Stab nowhere other – not even the heart. When your blade dulls, then hack open the head." He chopped through a stick with a bronze gladius, then held it up and ran his thumb over the impact-dent. "This will happen when you strike bone. Your swords will then be useless for cutting. Take a dagger with you as well – also two edge."

He then had his men beat bushes with sticks to exercise their arms. "Hack on a slant, men – forehand and back. If you hack straight down, your sword may catch on a tent."

Lot, now resolved to make the necessary adjustment, hacked harder than any of them.

Next morning in Odum's back yard, the Terahite women sewed black goat hair tunics, thin, and with sleeves short and loose so as not to impede movement.

Under a nearby oak tree, Terah sat sharpening swords on a flattened grinding stone.

Abram approached. "Father."

"What?"

"You know I run not from a fight."

Terah lay down the sword and leaned back against the tree trunk. He had been expecting this visit. "Ah, but this is different, you would say."

"This is no fight. It is murder."

"Call it what you will. It has the blessing of the Most Blessed."

"It sets ill on my heart."

Terah smirked. "And noble Abram never does what feels not right in his heart. The law is naught. Family is naught. The word of our god is naught next to Abram's dear heart."

"I meant but–"

"What would you have me do?" Terah leaned forward. "Send word, and meet them in the field, their forty or fifty to my twelve?"

"We could move on."

"This is the home of my fathers... *your* fathers. Now be my son or begone from my family."

"But to slaughter people in their sleep!"

"Amuru!" shouted Terah. "*Swine!* Enemies of the Blessed One. But if you be greater than your god, then follow your whining heart."

It was the universal kill-shot to the conscientious theist. Abram did not dare reply to it. He lowered his head and submitted.

> The Bronze Age held three values: piety toward your god, loyalty toward your kindred, and courage toward your enemy. Master these, and you could be a murdering raping thief and still be honored. Serving one's gods was not a matter of personal belief, but of civic duty.

> Faith – or the appearance of it – was expected to the degree of being a social imperative. Integrity was a concept unheard of, and not considered virtuous until Greek drama.

As the moon reached crescent, Terah waited for a cloudless evening, then sent his sons to muster the men. South of Haran in a location kept secret from curious town folk, Terah and the Twelve assembled, dressed in black, all with short swords and daggers, two with bows. Terah set down a pot of soot.

"This is from the altar of the Blessed. Rub it on all naked skin," he commanded. To the archers, "Where stand you?"

"East side."

"West side."

Terah: "What shoot you?"

"Whatsoever runs away. Whatsoever approaches from without."

Terah noticed some sashes and cords hanging from Abram's belt. He looked at Lot and saw more of the same.

"For what be those?"

Abram responded, "To tie up women and children."

Terah scowled.

"For slaves," Abram explained.

Nahor huffed, "A slave is not worth his thievery."

"So say many," returned Abram, "but we can sell them. Part of the spoils. All the men get an equal portion."

"Remove the cords," ordered Terah.

"What harm, Saru?" came a surprising objection from the field worker. "Must we slay children?"

Others murmured on both sides of the issue. Tension escalated until the whole operation was in danger of falling apart. Terah drew his sword and pointed it straight at Abram's face.

"Spare none but those you can gag. No noise. None but females, and none but young. Whatsoever speaks above a whisper is struck down."

Abram clasped hands in front of his chest and bowed in compliance.

"Prepare your gods," said Terah.

All men lifted amulets from under their tunics, kissed them, and prayed silently to their ancestors.

"The Blessed Suen, god of our fathers, wills it," said Terah.

The northernmost Amorite family lived in three tents. The angular tops of these now cast black silhouettes against a barely lighter background. Silently, the shadow-men positioned themselves at the front flaps of each. All looked toward Terah, poised in front of the largest tent. He nodded. Quickly and simultaneously the flaps were pulled wide apart to let in what little light was available. They rushed in. Blades through flesh were the only sounds. An infant's cry was silenced by a thud. Terah exited the tent and looked toward the others. The second tent was pacified by Nahor's team. A scuffle was heard in the third. Nahor rushed to it.

Inside the tent, Abram and Lot wrestled a thrashing teenage girl, stopping her mouth with a sash, and kneeling on her arms. Her legs kicked wildly until Nahor entered and jumped on them. They subdued her just as Terah arrived. A man lay dead beside her.

She was gagged and bound securely enough to pass inspection, but it was a dangerous and time-wasting move. Terah glared at Abram. All secure, they proceeded to the next complex – four tents.

All men positioned, Abram and Lot burst into a side tent. It contained an old woman, a young woman, and two children. Lot looked to Abram for a suggestion. Abram shrugged. *Now what?*

A child woke up with a questioning sound.

Lot silenced it with a sword slice.

Others began waking up.

Abram clenched his teeth and sliced the throat of the old woman.

Lot jumped on the young woman, trying to keep her from screaming.

Abram jumped on the other child.

The woman bit Lot's hand and got out a scream.

Lot clutched her throat to keep her quiet.

She clawed at Lot's eyes.

Abram hacked her head open, then turned to the child under him.

"Silence! Or you die."

A dog barked in the distance.

Nahor appeared suddenly. Looking to Abram he asked, "What be it?"

Abram reached between the child's legs. "Girl."

She too was bound and gagged, as the pack waited impatiently outside.

Walking to the next tent complex, Terah reassigned personnel.

"Here on out, Abram, you come with me. Lot, you go with Nahor."

Lot discarded the fetters from his belt. There would be no more prisoners. All breathed easier. Even Abram felt relieved now that the moral decision had been taken from him.

Six hours passed. The eastern sky showed the first violet hint of dawn.

Outside of a five-tent complex the family dog barked incessantly.

An Amorite man came out, freshly awakened, but sword in hand. He looked around, saw nothing unusual.

"Hush!" he commanded the dog.

It ran around behind him and whined.

The Amorite peered in the direction the dog was looking.

Out of the darkness appeared the figures of men walking resolutely toward him, no attempt at stealth or concealment. Head coverings were gone. Much of their clothing was gone. They were splattered with blood, expressionless, focused, beyond all need of strategy or orders, a pack of marching zombies, human only on a technicality.

The Amorite turned and hurried back toward his tent. He was hit in the shoulder by an arrow.

"Demons! Demons!" he cried.

Another arrow hit him; a third whizzed past.

First Terah, then the rest, broke into a trot. They rushed the complex, cutting tent ropes and pushing over support poles. Women and children screamed. Armed Amorite men struggled to crawl out, and were struck down. The pack, now berserk, hacked at anything rippling the tent cloth.

Abram felt as if he were watching himself from outside his body as in a dream. In a quiescent world beyond thought or emotion, he gracefully chopped and stabbed with the rest until nothing moved. The cry of a baby lingered in the air. Lot, crazed and wild-eyed, hacked at the area until it too was silenced.

Stillness. Only the distant wail of the dog remained.

As if on command, the pack sat down on the ground. No man looked at another. Nothing disturbed the song of the dog.

Terah turned his gaze toward the east horizon where a pair of kneeling camels cast dark silhouettes against the sky. They ruminated peacefully, undisturbed by the previous commotion.

At length Terah went to the camels, cut them loose, and scared them up with a shout. Then slapping one with his sword, he chased them into the sunrise. They trotted a short distance away and lost interest. It was enough to fulfill the king's prophesy.

The sound of the river now beckoned Terah. He walked down and immersed himself in the cool cleansing water. The pack got up and followed him in – all but Abram. There was unfinished business. Abram turned back north.

The sky was lighter now. Abram entered the tent where he and Lot had killed two women and a child. The remaining child, tied and gagged, stared blankly into space. Abram knelt beside her. Seeing his sword to be chinked and bent, he forced open his cramped fist and dropped it. Then taking out his dagger, he cut loose her gag. She took no notice of it.

"You can be a slave, or you can be dead," he said softly. "Which do you choose?"

The girl remained silent and expressionless.

Choice, mused Abram. *Strange little word.* The meaning of it had somehow vanished, but the child's preference was obvious. He gently lifted her head and placed the dagger blade under her chin, then suddenly slashed it through to her vertebrae.

Still operating in dream zone, Abram approached the tent where it all began. Not quite hoping to find the young widow gone, he approached the entrance and saw her struggling unsuccessfully against the cords. She froze, staring wide-eyed into Abram's blood-spattered face. His right arm was dripping red from shoulder to dagger tip.

"Fear not," he said. Clutching her firmly by the back of the neck, he brought the knife to her chin. She closed her eyes, then heard the bronze blade slice through cloth. The gag fell away. Abram then released her neck gently and sat down on the most convenient object, which was her husband.

"It is not a grievous thing to be a slave," he began. "We are all slaves. Truly kings also are slaves. Gods too, I wager. Everyone must serve someone. All, save the highest god, must serve someone. You can live as a slave, can you not?... Say yes."

She trembled uncontrollably.

"Say yes!" he demanded.

"Yes," she whimpered.

"I thank you," Abram sighed. "One may think that if life binds you to become what you hate, then why should one live at all? But when pressed to it, you do what you must. And there you are." He stared at his bloody arms. "Strange. The other side holds no hate or sorrow. It is truly peaceful." He mused on the hazy numbness. "I know not your name, and wish not to know it, but... you are the first person I have ever truly talked to."

Abram got up and turned to exit, then remembered

his manners.

"It has been a joy."

He walked to the river for baptism.

Lying on his back in the shallows he felt the water rippling around him. *It should feel cold,* he thought, *but feels not cold.* He gazed up at the crescent moon fading against blue sky and wondered if Suen were looking back down at him. *Now I am truly a part of it,* he thought. But soon, feeling the chill of reviving normalcy, he waded back to the bank and threw up.

News of their total and perfect victory brought no celebration to Haran, but rather a stunned silence. Days passed. Terah, having lost not a single man, was strangely unresponsive to congratulations. Much more concerned was he to insure that the women and children of his now-disbanded company did a good job of cleaning up the valley.

Next Shapatu was cold and cloudy. In the temple courtyard, Terah and the Twelve stood in a row, freshly bathed and dressed in white linen, hands clasped at their chests, before a blazing altar.

Naked and sweating priests slaughtered one after another of the formerly Amorite sheep and goats, as fast as the fire could consume them.

> Sumerian and Akkadian men are often portrayed naked, bald, and beardless when offering food to deities. Possibly clothing and hair would be a fire hazard.

The king, holding a hyssop branch, walked down the white linen row. He was followed by a priest carrying a basin of sacrificial sheep blood. Pausing before each man, the king sprinkled him, and dispassionately repeated an over-memorized prayer in early Akkadian.

> "Holy and Blessed Suen, king of the gods, at whose command they tremble, and whose word is not spoken twice, in prayer and humility of face we beseech thee, forgive thou the sin of this thy servant..."

It went on for a full two minutes on each man to be sure he was thoroughly purged.

Custom encouraged tears at this time, but this was not obligatory. Nahor managed to squeeze out a few for appearance sake. Lot and a few others seemed somewhat sincere about it. Abram, clinging to the last vestiges of moral apathy, remained dry eyed. He glanced at Terah and saw the same. Terah's face showed only the warm glow of vengeance fulfilled.

The atonement ceremony concluded, the band silently descended the hill, scarcely looking at one another. Lot, however, again turned to Abram with a question. "If Suen permitted us to do it, why must we make a sin offering?"

"I know not," confessed Abram. "But it feels right."

Neither would ever again bother Terah with a religious question.

The blaze at the hill top was not abated, as the priests were nowhere near finished. A hundred or so animals were sacrificed that day, about a fifth of the total take.

The final Shapatu dinner at Odum's house was more subdued than the first. At its conclusion all listened somberly to the mistress of the story.

> "And Elil said to Adapa, 'You have sinned against me. Therefore you must die.' But Ninlil, his wife, stole Adapa and put in his stead a wild ox. And Elil slew the ox. And when Elil saw what Ninlil had done, his wrath burned hot against Adapa to slay him. But Ninlil opened her mouth and spake, 'Blood is required, and blood is paid.' And so Elil skinned the ox and wrapped it round Adapa. For he said, 'This blood be upon you and your children forever.'"

None of Terah's family had heard any of this strange story before. Still, not one of them was tempted to open his mouth at question time.

Terah saw to it that the land and property were divided into thirteen equal portions, but then, as head of his household, claimed title to all four of his own family's shares. Abram and Lot, still shamed for having jeopardized the whole mission, acquiesced. Nahor, now more than ever his father's favorite, offered no objection, looking to his future inheritance as likely to be even sweeter.

Trash was burned, houses rebuilt, irrigation restored. Terah dug up his father's bones and ceremoniously reburied them in their rightful place in his patio. Now a wealthy and respected landlord, he hired workers to tend his fields and livestock. In his new found leisure he built a shrine in a corner of his bed chamber and placed in it the teraph of his father. Not satisfied, he took scoops of dirt from the graves of his grandfather and great-grandfather. These he pressed into lumps of clay and made two more teraphim for his shrine.

HARAN
the question

Four peaceful and prosperous years passed in Haran's south valley. Nahor begat another son, and took Lot's sister concubine – to help with the children, of course. Lot, finally bearded, married a neighbor's daughter – the neighbor who offered the most attractive dowry. Abram and Sarai did little more than wait for signs of pregnancy – that never arrived.

Lot's wife, however, had no such problem. Scarcely a year after marriage, she was about to deliver. On a spring afternoon, gathered around the birthing tent, the Terahites were poised for celebration. Inside, their senior women fussed about the young mother to be, jabbering advice and pleasantries. A newborn cried.

The men outside hushed for the news.

"It is a girl," came an apologetic voice.

"Aw dung," muttered Lot.

But the group was prepared for either, and celebration

would not be restrained. A pressed wineskin squirted forth a purple stream into impatient goblets. Lyres plunked, pipes piped, and tambourines tamped, but no ram's horn bleated the arrival of a man-child. Among consoling back slaps, Nahor scored the first jibe, "This is what you get for marrying outside the family."

"Fret not, boy," Terah reassured. "Many more where that came from."

"Of a truth," said Nahor, "you outdid your uncle Abram, hey?"

Party party party.

Abram would have gladly offered Lot his congratulations, but its squeaky formality could never compete with the *har har har*, so why bother? Unfortunately, his presence was obligatory for the duration of the festivities.

Inside the tent, Sarai also faded back to the periphery, as the rest cooed and fluttered over the newborn. Her effort to avoid notice had the reverse effect on her mother, Havah, who gave her a much-appreciated hug.

> Failure to produce children was grounds for divorce – always disgraceful to a woman. She would have to move back into her father's house – if he would take her. Most likely, no other man would have her. In this case, however, Terah being her father, she was fairly safe.

That night in bed, after routine sex, Sarai dared ask Abram a question that had been on her mind for years.

"Abi, Do you truly desire a child?"

Abram paused. For a second he actually let himself consider the question, but then snapped out of it. "Surely I desire a child! All men desire children."

It was the expected response, but now spoken outright, it permitted Sarai a follow up. "Zilha says my barrenness might be a curse. She says, when you live on land taken from others–"

"We made offerings for that," Abram interrupted. "It is covered." He rolled onto his side facing away from her. "Moreover, this land belonged to our fathers."

They said no more that night.

The next day Abram went to the home of Bildad, the senior priest. He took with him two sheep leashed with ropes. Upon arrival he clinked the ceramic gate-bells. When Bildad opened, Abram offered him the ropes.

"A free will offering, my rabu."

Bildad was perplexed. "This should be presented at temple."

"One is an offering," Abram clarified. "The other is for your counsel." He knelt and kissed a fold of the priest's gown.

"I pray you enter," said Bildad. "Desire you some wine?"

Abram arose and followed him. "Beer, I pray you."

> Most water being contaminated, weak beer was the most common beverage, even for children. It was generally sipped through a reed to filter out the barley husks.

Bildad's atrium was tastefully decorated. White fleeces covered stone benches, amidst flowers all scattered around an ornamental juniper tree. Less wealthy homes would have reserved those places for fruit-bearing plants.

Seated comfortably with a cup of warm beer in his hand, Abram explained his wife's condition.

Bildad reassured him, “No. You made the offering commanded by law and decreed by custom.”

“Perhaps one of my animals was blemished.”

“We examined them with care,” said Bildad defensively. “But if your heart be troubled, we can slay another.”

“I would be grateful.”

“As you wish,” conceded Bildad. “I shall choose the finer sheep, and make of it a sacrifice of appeasement. Have you tried a bit of mandrake root in her food?”

“It makes her strange.”

“Perhaps in a poultice rubbed on the belly.” He stood and walked to a wall cabinet. “Also, here is a little token for your bed chamber.” Bildad took one of many clay teraphim from a shelf.

“This is made of the holy earth of Urartu. It has piss-soaked wood from Sargon’s privy baked inside. The writing on the back is a great and terrible curse on all enemies of Akkad. No Amuru birth-demon would dare stand against it. If your wife be not with child in a few moons, we have amulets, bull stones, lion shmaku – any fate bender in Sumer and Akkad we have right here.”

“You are most gracious.”

“And how be *you?*” asked the doctor.

“Good! No troubles. No troubles, truly.”

Three more years passed. Lot's wife, again pregnant, sat under a mulberry tree teaching her daughter to braid flowers into garland. Sarai peeped out at them through a gap in her tent.

How perfectly lovely, she thought. *Perhaps some masterful artist will come and carve this motherly bliss into stone for all the ages... Perhaps she will miscarry.* Sarai released the tent flap. "No! No! I repent. Blessed Suen, keep my heart from evil thoughts." She turned her gaze to a row of teraphim and other magical fetishes above her bed. Kneeling, and clasping hands, she recited one of several prayers Bildad had advised.

On a winter's day with snow dripping from the oaks and pines, Terah took sick. In a week he was very sick, then sick enough to get his legacy in order. Havah was temporarily relieved of nurse duty and sent outside to join Zilha leading a chorus of sobbing and praying women. Nahor, Abram, and Lot entered the bedroom and stood attentively.

"Get you here," ordered Terah in a faint voice.

They knelt beside him.

Terah looked around. "The witness. Where?"

Nahor called, "Odum."

Odum entered the now crowded room. "I am here, cousin. May the Blessed One grant Terah a thousand years."

"My death is near," insisted Terah. "Let none cheat me of it."

But Odum would not be restrained. "Heaven rings with the prayers of all Haran."

Terah retched. "Can I not but die without I must hear this dung? I called Odum for what?… Oh yes, a witness. Can you witness a man's will and not see god-feathers?"

"Yes, most truly." Odum knelt to join the rest.

"You boys hear me good," said Terah. "Divide you the livestock three ways equal – the hirelings too. But the land goes to Nahor – all of it. Hear you?… Nahor, come here." Putting his right hand on Nahor's head, "You are a gushing shmaku, and you know how to get your desire.

Your branch shall flower." Terah dropped his hand.

"If I may, father," said Nahor softly, "a snippet of your hair for a teraph?" Nahor took a knife out and held it to Terah's beard making his permission superfluous.

"Yes," whispered Terah. "Do it."

Nahor sliced off a lock. "And of your other teraphim, father?"

"Huh?"

"Who is to have them?"

"Oh," Terah understood. "Yes. You get them too. Go away."

Nahor backed away.

"Lot," said Terah, "You, I think, will not amount to much. But try to have some sons, eh, for your father. Hear you?"

"Yes, grandfather."

"Abram, come here," said Terah. "You others, go. I wish not for you to hear this… Begone! Now!"

All exited but Abram.

Terah began softly, "Abi, you are a good man. That is bad. For good is dust in the wind. Bad is no greater. Us and them are true substance, and we are us, and that is all, and you must learn it. Do you take my word?"

"I try."

"You cannot be what you wish, and live. It works not. Two ways a man can go – madness or naught. That is all. One or the other. You must choose. Care not which. They are both the same. But still you must choose. Every day, every breath, madness or naught."

"Father, this–"

"–is madness? Yes, but what of it? Madness is naught. Hear my wisdom. If you try to stay in the middle, they will slay you." He grabbed Abram's beard and pulled his face close. *"They will slay you!"* He released it, exhausted. "But this too is naught." Terah laughed. It quickly turned to weeping. "Forgive me that I begat you."

Though this would have been the perfect time for death, Terah was denied the grace of a dramatic exit. The men left him as they found him in the care of Havah and Zilha.

The next day at Nahor's invitation, Abram and Lot convened at his tent. Nahor was genial. "Naught will change. You both keep what you have and get a third part more."

Abram asked, "In the same pasturage?"

"If you need more, I shall rent you more," assured Nahor, "at a good price. You are family. Either of you need a tent?"

"Grandfather has five cows and two bulls," said Lot. "How shall we divide them three ways?"

"Trade some sheep and goats for another bull."

"What of the cows?"

"Same. Buy another."

"Or sell two."

Sarai came running to the tent. "A miracle! A miracle!" she cried.

She led them back to Terah's house, now a site of subdued jubilation. Children danced outside, having been expelled from the patio for their noise. Nahor, Abram, and Lot entered the gate.

A bedraggled Terah was sitting up in a shroud of wool blankets. Havah fed him hot soup as Zilha massaged his neck.

"Our prayers are answered," declared Havah to the men.

"Behold! The power of love," added Zilha.

Terah glanced up at his heirs, then lowered his head down into the palm of his hand. A bloodshot eye stared blankly between the fingers.

Sarai hugged Abram. "He is recovered. Praise be to Suen!"

Normalcy resumed. But normalcy for Abram now included a nagging spiritual discomfort. In time he found himself again at Bildad's gate, this time with three goats. Bildad opened.

"I have questions," said Abram.

Again seated comfortably in Bildad's atrium with a beer, Abram unloaded.

"Something I fail to see."

"What?"

"I know not," replied Abram. "Something in my heart is not as it should be, and I cannot find what it is. I think it is of the gods."

"You think a god touches your heart?"

"No, no, naught so… pious. My thoughts go the other way."

"The way of doubt?" asked Bildad.

"Yes."

Bildad stroked his beard. "Doubt is of itself no sin. But it is a gate to sin. What be your thoughts?"

"Be the gods true substance, or of men's hearts and naught more?"

"They are the truest of all substance."

"How know you?"

"The fathers have told us. It is passed down."

Abram glanced at the top of Bildad's teraph cabinet where a row of plastered skulls silently observed everything in the courtyard. He leaned forward to Bildad and spoke softly.

"How know you that the fathers spoke the truth?"

"Why would they lie?"

"I know not," said Abram. "I have no children. Have you children?"

"Yes."

"Do you lie to them?"

"I do not call it *lying*."

Abram bit a lip. He clasped his hands in front of his chest so as to soften his next question. "Do you see how that answer might make a man wish to tear off your head and dash it against a wall?"

Bildad paused. "A bit of wine, perhaps?"

"Yes, you are most gracious."

Bildad commanded into the air, "Woman! Bring wine – strong." Then back to Abram, "Be your troubles caused by the fall of Ur?"

"From the fall of *Suen*," said Abram.

"Suen is not fallen," Bildad reassured him. "Caravans have brought news from the east. He was handled honorably by the Elamites. They bore him on a mason's wagon with great ceremony to their capital. They are now his servants."

Abram tightened, but could not prevent the moisture in his eyes from betraying him. "Even if I believed that, so what? If gods fight gods, and that be all, why should I care who wins?"

"Truly," cautioned Bildad, "losers become slaves."

"Or dead."

"Care you not for life?"

"Less upon less. Some days I marvel that all life be not happier dead."

"Care you for *anything*?"

Abram thought. "Truth. I care to know truth."

Bildad combed his fingers through his beard. "To know truth is for the gods. Do you wish to be a god?"

An anonymous woman silently set wine cups beside them and then hurried away so as not to hear any more than necessary. Abram waited awkwardly for her to leave before asking, "What of good and evil? Be good and evil true substance?"

"True – yes, but not substance."

"What be they?"

Bildad spoke as though the answer were common knowledge. "Good is what the Blessed One loves; evil is what he hates."

"Be that all?"

"What more need you?"

"I know not."

"Nor I." Bildad rose with his wine cup and paced thoughtfully. "These Canaanite questions are not good. Gods are for to serve, not to question. They are to bind folk together around a fire, and to comfort us when someone dies."

"*What* kind of questions?"

"Canaanite," repeated Bildad. "The Canaanites love to trick people with questions. If they care not for a man's answer, they say their god is greater than his. I charge you not, but your questions are similar."

"Be their answers any better?"

"Far from it! Their highest god is both one and many – and also a great bull. Make truth of that if you can. El they call him, but they know not from where he came. Hah! Any Akkadian can see that El is shortened from Elil. The same is Enlil of the Sumerians."

"Enlil," mused Abram. "So *their* god is the father of *our* god?"

"No. Our god is the son of Elil, who is the son of Anu, who came from the first of all things. *Their* god is a runaway child who forgot his family and imagined himself the first of all."

Abram, seeing that he had drained his mentor's storehouse, rose to leave.

"One more question, rabu. How know you what the Blessed One says?"

"Augury is a difficult art."

"Yes, but when Enlil… Forgive me – *Elil* told Ziusudra to build the Great Boat–"

"Ach!" Bildad threw up his hands. "The Sumerians have you all mixed up. It was *Ea* who told *Utnapishtim* to build the boat."

"What?"

"Ea is the brother of Elil, as you know. The Sumerian Enlil had a brother named Enki. Ea and Enki are both gods of the waters, so the foolish Sumerians mushed them together. They are the cause of much false knowledge. I have heard Akkadian priests from Sumer say that *Ea* created Adapa and put him in the forest of Eridu. Imagine that! Not the edin, but *Eridu!*"

"Forgive me again, rabu. I wish no more god problems. But tell me this. When Elil or Ea or whoever told our forefather to build the boat, how did he say it?"

"Through a wall."

"Through a wall?"

"So goes the story," said Bildad, "but between you and me, I suspect that Utnapishtim was skilled in augury or divination."

"My question is a bit different, rabu. Did Ea choose

Utnapishtim, or did Utnapishtim choose Ea?"

Bildad shrugged. "Why does it matter?"

Abram spoke slowly and carefully. "If the god of men chooses a man to speak to, how does he choose which man? Or, if a man chooses a god, how does he choose the most high god?"

"Hmm." Bildad thought. "Truly I have never heard those questions before."

Abram departed, leaving Bildad's gate never to return. *Three goats for that,* he huffed. A short distance from the house he heard Bildad's voice behind him.

"Abram."

Abram stopped.

"If you wish to hear the Most High, ask for it, but it will cost you."

Abram turned. "Yes but, how–"

No one was there.

Hmh. He went back inside. Abram turned, walked a few paces, and stopped. "Truly, he must have gone back inside." He shook his head and went home.

Evening. "He must have gone inside."

"Who?" asked Sarai.

"Naught." Abram went to bed.

Midnight. Through a slit in the tent a crescent moon shone onto Abram's face. He awakened, fully alert. Careful not to wake Sarai, he stepped outside into a clear and quiet night. Every star in the sky seemed to be looking at him. The feeling of being watched by angels or demons from some other place was not new to Abram, but this night it was more intense than ever. He moved away from the tents so as not to disturb anyone. *Naught to lose by trying,* he thought. Facing the crescent moon, he clasped hands at his chest.

"God of my fathers, if you be true substance, I pray you give me a sign."

Abram gazed into a broad expanse of starry sky.

A cow farted.

Abram lowered his head. Not quite what he had in mind. He tried again.

"Most holy Enlil, if you be true–"

Another cow fart.

Abram threw his hands apart in exasperation. "So be it! God Most High, whatsoever your name, I ask to hear you."

Nothing. No shooting star. No chirping bird. Nothing.

Abram shrugged and went back to bed.

Life's routine remained undisturbed until the next winter after Terah's illness. Then on an overcast day as Abram lunched with field workers, Lot approached. His somber face made his message almost unnecessary.

"This time, no miracle."

Terah was dead. The determined survivor had left his family in good condition and passed on in his sleep, sparing them and the gods another swan song.

Nahor took it upon himself to have a grave dug in the patio next in line to the graves of his ancestors. Bildad offered a deal on full liturgical funeral services, but Nahor and Abram agreed that Terah would probably prefer a family job with a brief interment benediction. Odum and most of the old Twelve stopped by to promise exuberant weeping at the funeral, which was nice of them. It meant there would be no need to hire professionals.

Havah and Zilha were assigned spicing and wrapping duty; the men took charge of afterlife supplies – the most important part of burial. Abram handed down jars of liquor and grains; Lot arranged them in corners of the pit.

> An unprepared ghost could have a tough time of it, and possibly seek vengeance on the living. Bulky items went in the grave first, lest while putting them in, one accidentally step on the body.

Havah came out of the bed chamber. "Which shoes do you think?"

"The field wear," answered Nahor. "Always safer in a strange land."

Zilha appeared at the doorway. "This was his most favored cup. Should it go in now?"

"Fill it with silver and seal it," said Nahor. "He may need money more."

Abram objected. "Silver in a grave is forbidden. Thieves would rob all graves."

"I would not have father's ghost disturb my sleep," countered Nahor. "No one need learn of it."

"I am so happy you are here," said Havah. "I would know not what to do."

"It is not difficult," said Nahor. "Give him whatsoever he might need… or desire. The difficult part is how much to give."

"I would give him my heart if I could," said Havah.

"You have already," said Zilha.

Nahor made an unexpected move, "Thought of it, have you?"

"What?" said Havah.

"You know," said Nahor. "The love of a truly devoted wife knows no bounds. Far be it from me to suggest such a thing, but many of the most honored widows we know have followed their husbands the full distance… It is but a word to think on."

Havah understood his meaning and lowered her eyes.

Abram tapped Nahor on the shoulder. "If I may add a thing?"

Nahor turned. Abram decked him.

The day of burial was chilly but not unpleasant. All families of the south valley were present in full, each with a gift to toss into the pit at the final procession. A solitary musician sat near the grave playing a reed pipe. The women of the family wept appropriately, Odum and others far more than appropriately, as they had promised. Abram and Nahor (with swollen cheek) remained sullen. Bildad clasped his hands in the customary prayer posture to do the honors.

> "Holy and Blessed Suen, remember this thy faithful servant, Terah, for his piety and service. Let not his ghost be troubled and wander among the dry places, but grant thou rest to him in the land of the dead. Boatman Ursanapi, take thou the ghost of Terah across the Hubur to Arallu. Nergal, god of Arallu, receive thou Terah, servant of the Blessed Suen…"

It was intended as a spiritual opiate. For Abram, however, it was now just a placebo that had lost its deception. He allowed his mind to drift for the duration of the drone.

> "…and let this watered wine numb the hearts of those who seek for that which is not."

Abram snapped out of it. *Did he truly say that?*
"Amen," said Bildad.
"Amen," agreed the crowd.

4 EXODUS
changing of the gods

On the following day Abram entered Terah's bedchamber and knelt before the bench of his shrine. He and the three teraphim stared silently at each other. Abram picked up two lamb vertebrae, put them into the wicker cup, and rattled them. "Alike, and I stay. Unlike, and I go." He dumped it over. One bone fell out, while the other stuck in the cup. *I forgot the incense. Dung! I forgot the offering also.* He put down the cup. *Who am I even talking to?*

Abram continued to kneel there, staring past the walls into the void. Not so much as a coherent thought floated up to the conscious part of his writhing mind. He got up and left.

That evening he spoke privately with Lot.

"I plan to leave."

Lot was shocked. "What, forever?"

"Yes."

"Why? Surely you can atone with Nahor."

"I wish no atonement. I hate him. I have always hated him. Naught but fear of father held my tongue on it."

"Have you asked a priest about this?"

"Why? To get a magic potion for hatred?"

"I mean about moving."

"No."

"Then how know you the will of the gods?"

Abram pursed his lips together and looked down.

Lot pressed on. "You would move from your homeland without first asking the gods?"

"Which one would you have me ask?"

"Did you at least cast bones on it?"

"None of that," said Abram. "I but know it is the right thing to do. I should have done it before we ever took this bloody valley."

"Where will you go?"

"Canaan."

"What be in Canaan?"

"Canaanites! And none of them are Nahor."

Lot glanced around, then leaned forward and spoke softly. "Take me with you?"

It was not a difficult decision. Everything was set up for Abram and Lot to move to Canaan. The question of by whom it was set up troubled none but Abram. Did he repeatedly sabotage himself? Or were circumstances being manipulated by external forces? *But,* he thought, *if one cannot know, why should one care?*

Upon announcing it to the family, Nahor alone did not express grief. Not surprisingly, Sarai's mother, Havah, would go with them. Zilha was conflicted, but feeling closer to her daughter than to her son she would remain behind. The hirelings were faced with either insecurity under a popular leader, or the reverse. Herdsmen generally chose Abram, farmers Nahor.

Hearty nomads or lazy sluggards, Abram figured he got the better of the deal.

One man in particular showed promise – a Hurian named Zimran.

Voluntary enslavement for payment of debt typically lasted three years.

Formerly a slave, he had earned his freedom and became chief herdsman of Terah's livestock.

A few years older than Abram, family man, good organizer, and most importantly, Zimran knew the territory. Abram, as usual, sought the advice of those most likely to know the subject.

"What be the best time to leave?"

"Right after spring barley harvest would be my choice," said Zimran.

"The beginning of lambing season?"

"It will not matter," said Zimran. "You must trade off all your swollen ewes and goats for yearlings. Do it soon so they can bond with their shepherds. Keep a good ram for every forty or so ewes; the rest can be castrated – or save some for offerings."

"What about milkers?" asked Abram.

"Hold back a few for that, but trade off their young right after birth. Unfortunate that your father sold the camels."

"Why?" asked Abram. "Be desert between here and Canaan?"

"No. Amuru. First we enter Ebla – what is left of it. Best to bypass the cities until we reach Dimashki. Most are in ruin anyway."

"Cursed Amuru."

"Oh, they were not destroyed by Amuru," corrected Zimran. "It was Akkadu under king Naram – the same who conquered the Huri and built Haran. Amuru but filled the hole. Best to look like them if we wish to pass through them."

Zimran was not only knowledgeable, he talked straight without fear of offending. Abram promoted him to foreman.

He also bought camels and encouraged his men to trade their artistic Akkadian fashions for the drab natural textiles of the Amorite. Sadly they abandoned their fitted skull caps for primitive kaffias banded with camel-hair ropes. Even more sadly, they began selling their pigs.

"What, no swine flesh?" exclaimed Lot.

"Until we pass through Amuru land," said Abram. "We must not offend Baal."

"Filthy Amuru will eat anything save swine. How foolish!"

"Raw swine flesh has demons. We all know that."

"But is Baal not wise enough to tell them to burn the demons out? Why forbid this most delicious meat altogether?"

Abram shrugged. "The ways of the gods."

Both men raised their eyebrows and glanced at each other. It was the same cynical glance once shared by Terah and Nahor.

After the barley harvest as the hills and plains broke into flower they left Haran forever.

Their arrival at the Euphrates was well timed, the rushing river of melted snow having receded. The water was cool and the surface smooth, but the day being a Shapatu, they refrained from crossing. That evening after a supper of fresh caught fish the group sat around the remains of a large camp fire – men on the inner circle, women and children behind. Havah was recognized as the rightful mistress of story.

> "And Elil said to the gods, 'Now has the man tasted of the forbidden thing and lived. No longer will he harken to our wisdom. He will think he knows good and evil better than we. And he will bring grief upon us. Let us then cast him forth from the edin, lest he grow strong and become as a thorn in our side.'"

It was the Akkadian version and by now familiar to all, but this time Abram heard, another story underneath it – words speaking directly to him.

> "…And so Adapa wandered beyond the river Euphrates, and he built Uruk, and became a great king. And his children were as many as the stars."

Havah sat down.

Silence.

"Abram," whispered Sarai, "it is Shapatu."

"Oh… Yes," he responded. "Lot, would you–"

"No," declined Lot, "but your grace abounds."

"So be it," Abram stood. "Who has cares to speak of?"

Silence again.

"Pray first," whispered Sarai.

Abram clasped his palms.

"God of our fathers… or… whatsoever god we answer to. Truly I know not how to do this, but uhh… I would ask that you help us to find a good place to live, with uhh… good pastures, and water, and… truly all that we need. I could say all that by list, but you know it already, yes? And we ask it humbly, if it be your will. And… of a truth, whether it be your will or not, for you know, we need it. So if it be not your will, then, uhh… well, I pray you change your will… Amen." Abram sat. "Now… who has prayer requests and all that?"

Silence.

A severely repressed laugh squeezed through Lot's nose. Then the entire group broke into laughter – its first communal event. What had been a collection of loosely acquainted families now became the Abramite tribe.

That night in bed Abram lay on his back trying to identify a new feeling.

"Sarai," he whispered to the back of his wife's head.

"Mh?"

"A strange thing I see."

"What?"

"Since we left Haran, the gods feel different."

"The gods?"

Abram whispered, "Suen still sees us, but he is not as strong out here. Truly it feels different."

"What kind of different?"

"It feels good."

"I am happy that my husband feels good."

"That too is good," said Abram. "I am happy that you are happy, but at this time I would truly like to know what you think."

Sarai paused, then rolled over onto her back.

"I may think?"

"I see no harm in it… within limits."

The next day, after crossing the Euphrates, Abram quietly buried his crescent amulet.

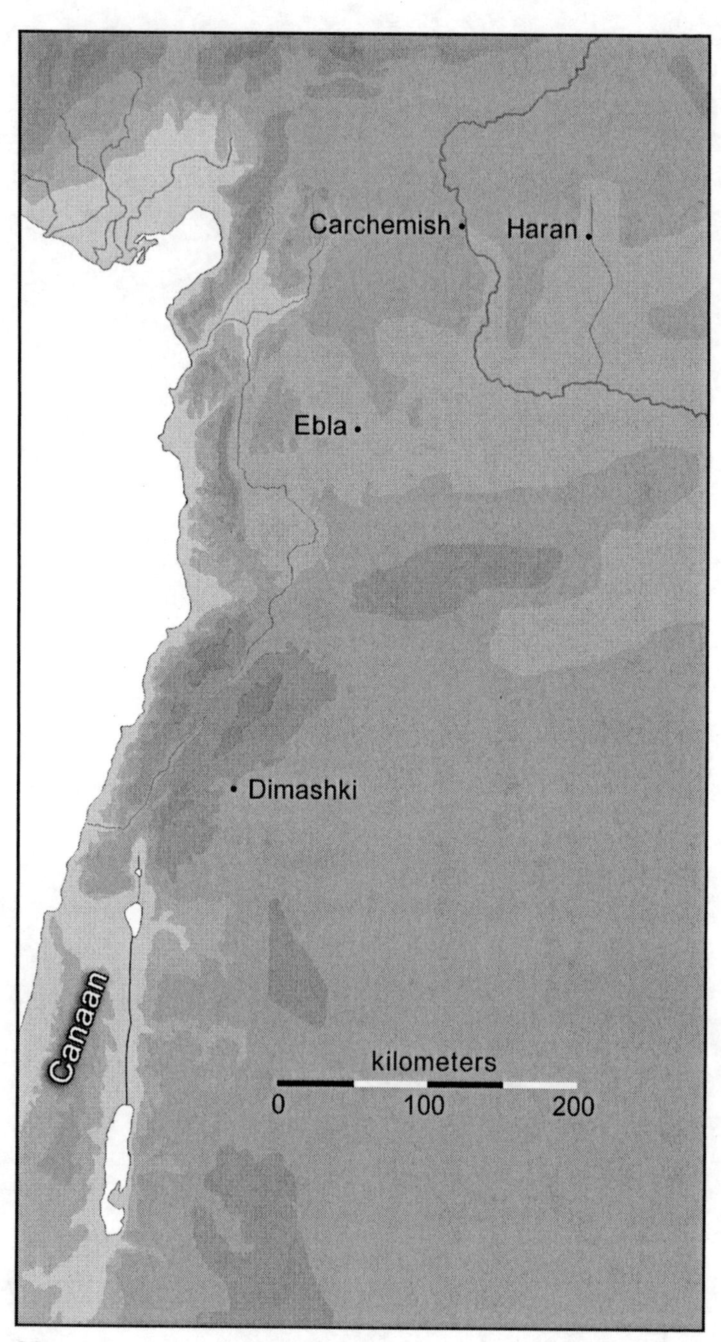

Carchemish
Haran
Ebla
Dimashki
Canaan
kilometers
0
100
200

5 DIMASHKI
the guide

Traveling south from the Euphrates through spring flowered valleys between forested hills, the tribe stayed as far as possible from refuse pits, and politely declined invitations to raw meat banquets. In a month they reached Dimashki. An ancient city built on a river flowing into the Mediterranean, Dimashki was far enough west to be on the shortest route from Mesopotamia to Egypt without crossing over sand dunes. Not yet walled, and a home to some twenty-thousand Canaanites of mixed ancestry, the indigenous population was fast losing ground to the Amorite influx.

"It is safe to be Akkadu here," said Zimran. "They have no bad memories."

"No temple?" mused Abram, seeing no predominant hill within the city.

"Hundreds of shrines," said Zimran. "Name your god."

"Be all Canaan like this?"

"I know not. I have never been farther south."

"Pitch tents here," shouted Abram to the crowd. Then to Zimran, "Load up a cart. We shall trade."

Leaving Lot in charge of camp, Abram and Zimran, with three other armed men led a donkey-cart full of trade goods into Dimashki. The herdsmen, unaccustomed to the mercantile mania of a big city market place, had to be reminded of their purpose.

"Watch the cart," chided Abram. "That is why you are here."

Stopping a pedestrian, Abram asked directions to the produce sellers and led the way through the crowd. Soon even he found himself gawking at the sites. Two beardless men in strange clothing spoke in a foreign language to a vendor. Abram could not help noticing that their eyes were painted black. He raised his brows to Zimran.

"Egyptians," responded Zimran. "They live in a great heap of sand at the south corner of the Earth."

"Hm. I have heard of them."

Deeper into the city the street was clogged with vendors of food and clothing, tools and trinkets. Amid the bargaining noises, one voice caught their attention.

"Alms for a homeless son of Akkad."

They stopped and turned to see a teen-age boy dressed in rags and leaning on a crutch. Just another handicapped beggar? Not quite. This one was Akkadian.

Zimran walked to the boy and handed him a small lump of copper.

The boy bowed gratefully, "May the Blessed Sin be gracious unto you, rabu."

Zimran forgave his odor, but not his liberal mispronunciation of the deity.

"Suen. We too are Akkadu." He returned to the group.

Abram glanced at the side of his cart where the figure of a crescent moon had been burnt into the wood. The beggar no doubt saw it.

"Ho! Boy!" called Abram, "A shiqlu of copper if you can name the sons of Sargon of Akkad."

The beggar thought, "Uh… Naram Sin."

> A shiqlu (later shekel) was a unit of weight. Coins were unknown until the seventh century BCE.

"Close," said Abram. "Naram was his grandson."

After a good laugh on the boy, and on Zimran for being fooled by him, they went on their way. Then startled by a bleat from a goat in the cart, they turned and saw the same boy running away with a roll of their woolen cloth.

"Seize him!" ordered Zimran.

Abram's three other men chased the thief as he ducked into a narrow and crooked alley. Soon they returned carrying nothing but his crutch.

"Good work," said Abram. "He will not get far without that."

In the fruit and vegetable market they received less than the expected value for their nomadic wares – Amorite competition.

"It should be better farther south," encouraged Zimran.

Abram looked at him. "I thought you said you have never been farther south."

"Uh, true, but so say many who have been there."

Abram heard the sounds of a slave auction and detoured in that direction. To the surprise of the rest, he walked over to it and inspected the slaves. An auction worker intercepted him.

"All of great health are they, rabbani. My joy to please you."

"Be any of these from the south?"

"Yes. Young and strong."

The man showed him some children, barely pubescent. Abram thanked him, but proceeded to a cage full of adults.

"Be any of you from south of here?"

They ignored him.

"Yes," assured the auction worker, "most surely, rabbani. These from Zuzim. Say Zuzimite words, dog." He prodded them without success. "Talk, swine!"

Abram walked away.

Guarding a cart now full of produce and beer, the men retraced their steps through the city. Zimran, on his own initiative, took the lead. Abram guessed why. Suddenly Zimran stopped and motioned for Abram to approach cautiously. Up ahead was the same beggar jabbering fluently in a foreign language to some wealthy Egyptians. Abram and Zimran plotted revenge.

Ten minutes later one of Abram's men approached the beggar. He turned to flee, but saw another coming from the opposite direction. Ducking into the nearest alley, the boy deftly picked his way around the trash, laundry, drunks, and children toward safety – he thought. Then, tripped by his own crutch, he fell on his face. Abram and Zimran jumped on top of him.

Zimran shook his shoulders, "The wool – where?"

"I ate it."

Abram dragged him to a wall and slammed his back up against it, "How did you know we were Akkadu?"

"I was down wind."

Zimran slapped him across the cheek. "Stinking dog!"

Abram continued, "Where did you learn the tongue of Egypt?"

"Anatolia."

Zimran raised his hand again, but Abram blocked it. "From where be you?"

The boy spat some bloody saliva. "From everywhere."

Abram pulled him up and dragged him out to the street. Noticing a man in a red mantle, he pointed to him.

"That man there – from where is he?"

"From my street, and he is my friend, and he is an assassin."

A merchant pulled a cart full of dried fish into view.

"From where is that one?" asked Abram.

"Canaan."

"What part?"

"Perhaps Chinnereth, perhaps Hazor."

"Hold him," said Abram to his men.

He approached the merchant. "Ho! Omar!"

The merchant gaped.

"You seed of a swine! Where is my money, Omar?"

"I am not Omar!" declared the wide-eyed merchant.

Abram throttled him. "You are Omar from Ebla, you dirty thief!"

"No! No! I am Ashakazi bar Kenazar from Hazor!"

"Oh." Abram released him. "Forgive me." He returned to the cart.

The beggar laughed. "You are truly up river. He is a Geshurite and a seller of goat-fish. From where would he be but Lake Chinnereth?"

Abram went to his cart and pulled out a small bunch of grapes.

"These if you can name the gods of Canaan."

The beggar looked askance. "El," then held his hand

out for the grapes.

Abram then looked askance.

"A trick question, no?" asked the beggar. "All are named El."

Abram looked to Zimran for explanation. Zimran shrugged.

"Ahh," surmised the beggar. "You truly know not. Of a truth, in Canaan are all the Semite gods and all the Egyptian gods. So many gods they try not to count them. They but call them all el."

Abram gave him the grapes. The boy popped a few into his mouth and studied his captors with new interest.

"What seek you, a guide?"

"What be your name?" asked Abram.

"Eber."

"Yes, I need a guide. Take us to the nearest bathing place."

That afternoon Abram and his men returned to camp with the cart and the newly washed beggar.

"My friends, this is Eber from Dimashki. He will be our guide… for now. He knows the land and the people."

The beggar made eye-contact with some of the local maidens. Zimran suddenly noticed that once cleaned up he was not a bad-looking fellow.

"And he is a skillful thief and liar," said Zimran, escorting his wife and daughters away from the area.

"But not beyond shame," added the beggar. "Of a truth, my name is not Eber; it is Eliezer."

eli = my god,
ezer = help

"Of a truth?" said Abram, then heaved a sigh. "Would some of you maidens care to make this man some clothing?"

The girls trotted away giggling.

At dinner time, Eliezer joined the inner circle around the fire. While voraciously attacking a leg of mutton, he briefed Abram and his men.

"Canaan has much open pasture but be watchful. There are fewer bears and wolves, but more lions. It is safer close to cities but take care that your goats get not in the farm land."

"We know that," said Zimran. "Can you show us pasture land that is not already taken?"

"I can guide you around the great tribes, but there are many small herdsmen, more so now with the 'Amo's."

"The what?" asked Abram.

"Amuru," corrected Zimran.

"Amorites," insisted Eliezer, "if you must say it rightly."

Lot spat. "Stinking dogs I call them."

Eliezer gave Lot a once over. "Not bad folk once they learn city ways. And they learn quickly when money is in it. You will bump heads at first, but–"

"We know all of that," interrupted Zimran. "What we need to know is where to find things, like clean water."

"Not truly," said Eliezer. "Springs and wells are everywhere. Look for palms or willows and you will find water. In winter the coastal plain is best. As it warms, the herdsmen move higher into the hills. But unless you wish to fight them, strive not for the best land."

"Markets?" said Zimran.

Eliezer became irritated. "Tell me not what you wish to learn. *I will tell you* what you must know. Canaan is not Dimashki. You cannot happily walk into a city with your Akkadian tongues and trade like equals. They wish to know you – from where you come; who be your gods;

who protects you? If you have not protection, you must move often. Canaan is not a kingdom. It is but a road full of merchants weary of travel. New faces come and go daily. If you wish to live there, reputation is everything. So smile, look strong, and hold not back at the altar. Religion and money are all that keeps Canaan together."

Abram was surprised. "Religion keeps them together?"

"The religion of many in one," replied Eliezer. "You can drag any god you wish into Canaan, but be sure to add El to its name. Your moon god can be El-Sin or Sin-El."

"*Suen*-El," insisted Zimran.

"As you will." Eliezer shrugged. "But be ready with a name when you get to the altar."

"I thought El was a bull," said Abram.

"Is Suen a moon?" Eliezer asked rhetorically. "Every god needs an image."

Abram's interest was aroused. "But how can so many images be mushed into one?"

"In the far past," began Eliezer, "El had many sons. These were all gods of tribes and cities, but they were all of El. So El was all that kept the gods together. In time, *el* came to mean god – *any* god. Therefore all gods were called els. So each man can worship his own el, and the priests can sacrifice to the one El. And El keeps the rains on time, and everyone is happy. See?"

They pondered it. Abram was first to comment. "Do they not find this confusing?"

Eliezer smiled. "That is the very purpose of it."

"Slippery," said Lot.

"As goose fat," agreed Eliezer.

"What happens," inquired Abram, "when two els agree not?"

"Then they take it before the judge – El Most High at Salem."

"El Most High," mused Abram with heightened interest. "Then his temple is at Salem?"

"Yes. Moreover, his son is at Salem. The king of Salem is the judge of Canaan, and the son of El."

Son of the Most High God, thought Abram. "What be his name?"

"Melchizedek."

melchi = my king,
zedek = righteous

Lot tired of the subject. "I but wonder. Be you of Canaanite blood?"

"My mother sold me when I was too young to know. I am nothing. And I love it. Now I can be anything."

Abram was still on theology. "Much like El, hey?"

They all laughed, but Eliezer seemed uneasy about the comparison. "Such jesting at the wrong time could be costly."

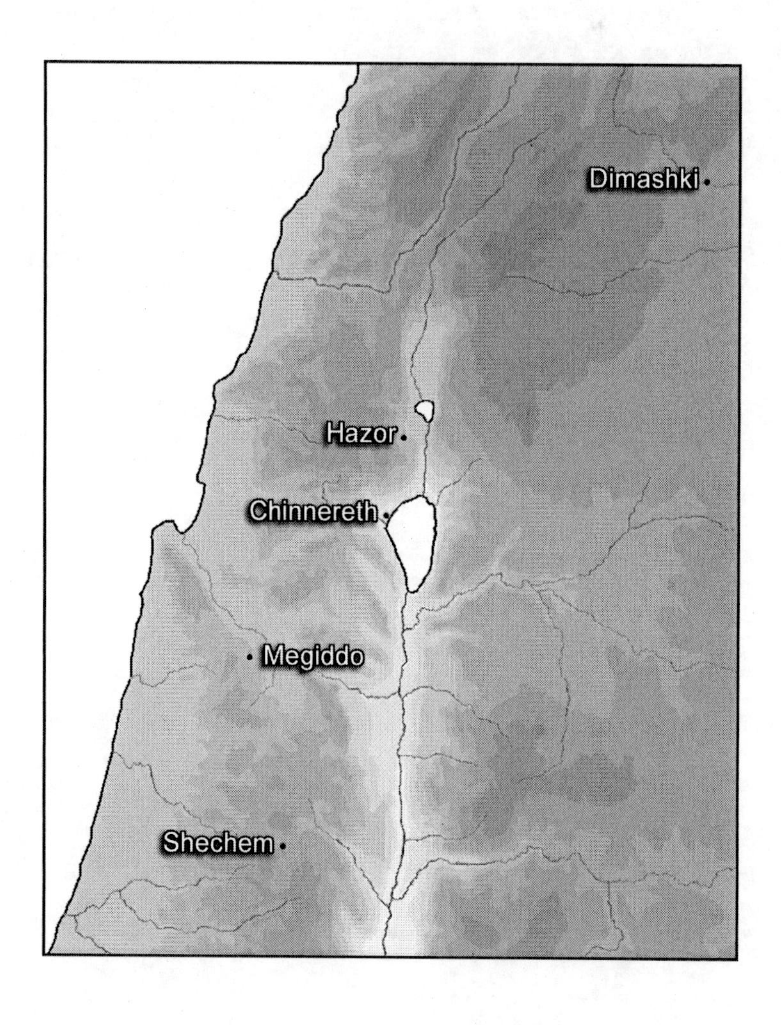
Dimashki
Hazor
Chinnereth
Megiddo
Shechem

6 SHECHEM
the debut

The road southwest from Dimashki was pleasantly shaded by forests of tall cedars. The pasture land, however, was often fowled by the summertime stink of Amorite dumps and graveyards. But the farther they went, the fewer the camels and the cleaner the air. By the time they got to Hazor the smoke of burning refuse was a welcome sight. By Lake Chinnereth the Amorites could scarcely be distinguished from other locals. Proceeding onward, through a wide valley between mountain ranges, the tribe approached a great walled city, now in ruins, and garrisoned with troops in Egyptian dress.

"Megiddo," said Eliezer. "Once the mightiest city in Canaan. It could stop an army going north or south. Pharaoh loved it not."

"Be Canaan under Pharaoh?" asked Abram.

"No, but not far from it. And that could change if Pharaoh gains strength."

"Let us stay here," suggested Lot. "The land is good, and the villagers are friendly."

"They smile and tell you their names," explained Eliezer, "so you will tell them yours. Think not that they love you. They but desire to know what can be known of you and to tell their friends. Canaan protects its own. And we have not yet paid our dues."

After three days journey that would change. Shechem was a walled city nestled between and east of two wooded hills. Second to Salem in holiness, it was first in commerce because of its location in the center of Canaan. Not only was it on the trade route north and south, but here the people of the coastal plain met those of the Jordan valley to exchange goods and information – and to pose and hustle.

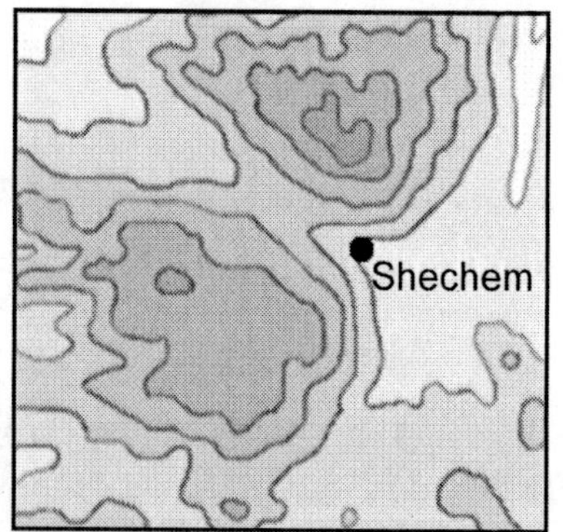

As the party prepared to enter from the west between the two hills, Eliezer explained his reasoning.

"Shechem is where you let Canaan sniff your cheese. From those hilltops one can see from the Jordan River on the east to the Great Sea on the west. The priests see everything you have at this very moment, and judge how much of it should go to them. If you give them less, they love you not. Give them more, and all Canaan marks you a fool."

"And what be the right number?" asked Abram.

"Near one in twelve of your market stock."

"That buys us what?"

"Permission to trade in Canaan for a year, and in

Shechem for as long as they smile on you. Throw in many young males. If they ask you if it is all your first-borns, say yes. All first-born males in Canaan are haram to El."

"They are what?" asked Abram.

"Haram," explained Eliezer. "Dedicated to a god for destruction. It is a very ancient law called the law of the first fruits."

"Many are the rules in this place," complained Lot.

"For the greater good of those who know them," countered Eliezer.

Nearing the base of the hills the tribe passed through tent camps of herdsmen and merchants, some from foreign lands. At his first sight of Shechem, Abram was unimpressed. "Not much of a wall," he said.

"It is all they dare," said Eliezer. "A higher wall could draw the evil eye from Pharaoh."

Around the wall was a bustling market place of shops and stalls and traveling vendors, all of it policed by armed clergy.

Eliezer cautioned, "Think not to bring a cart to market until the priests give you the nod. Otherwise you are food for thieves, and no one will help you."

Zimran muttered, "I doubt not your knowledge of that."

The atmosphere in the visitors' camp was relaxed and cordial. The sound of children playing cheerfully enhanced that of livestock and tradesmen. Nevertheless, Abram directed his men to remain armed and to pitch tents in a protective circle around their carts and animals. But the women would not be so restrained. Finally on equal footing with their neighbors, they felt safe enough to enjoy the exchange of pleasantries. The major part of the journey was over.

That night in a deep sleep, Abram dreamed vividly. As a child of about twelve, he found himself following his father through dark and nebulous surroundings. A sense of foreboding caused him to stop – or try to. But he could not. His father was pulling him on a rope. Up the Ziggurat of Ur they climbed until they came to rest at the first terrace. Suddenly hostile priests attacked them with flint daggers. Fighting them off, Terah and Abram ran up the steps to the next terrace. Again they were attacked. Tiring of the fight, Terah negotiated with the priests until they came to agreement. He then delivered Abram to them, receiving in return a square lump of silver.

Abram was confused. "Shall we not go to the top, father?"

Terah did not look at him. "All is one," he said. Then he walked away.

Paralyzed with fear, Abram pretended to be dead in hope of fooling the attackers. The priests now turned into Amorites. They closed in around him, picked him up, and carried him to an altar. But the altar changed into a well, and they dropped him in. Falling into darkness, he jerked awake in a cold sweat. It was morning.

After breakfast Abram left Zimran in charge of camp. With Lot and Eliezer he led three sheep and three goats on ropes up the south mountain of Shechem. It was not straight sided, but in rounded masses of hills. Rough hewn stone steps graciously but inconsistently aid the climbers over the steeper passages. Abram was still groggy from his dream. "Whose temple is at the top?" he asked.

"No temple," responded Eliezer, "but a tree."

"A tree?"

"The Holy Oak of Moreh."

"We sacrifice to a tree?"

"It is an exceeding ancient tree," assured Eliezer. Then grinning, "We sacrifice to whatsoever el you choose. The tree is but a token."

Biblical Hebrew contains at least five words for oak, all of which are derived from "el."

"Of what?" asked Abram.

"Of many gods in one – one trunk, many branches."

Abram felt a chill. Looking around he saw other men walking, some upward with animals, others downward holding squares of papyrus, apparently receipts. On one of the flatter areas several priests inspected sheep and goats for a line of patrons. Other priests slaughtered and butchered animals, slinging their parts on top of blazing altars.

"How far up shall we go?" asked Abram.

"Your choice again," responded Eliezer. "We can wait in a long line, or climb for a short line. Be you weary?"

"No."

"It is the same either way," said Eliezer.

"No! I would see the top."

Abram's heart raced as they pulled their animals up to another offering station. He faltered and stumbled.

"Be you well?" asked Lot.

"Yes," Abram panted.

"We will stop here," asserted Lot.

Standing pale and frozen in a waiting line, Abram could think of little but his dream. *Surely these priests will not turn into Amuru.* He glanced around at the methodical and dispassionate processing of sacrificial meat and remembered that terrible night when he had participated in a similar slaughter. Beads of sweat formed on his brow. He whispered to Eliezer, "I feel not right about this. Can we come back another time?"

Eliezer grabbed his upper arm and whispered firmly. "Of a truth! Back away from the Holy Oak of Moreh? Be you mad?"

The man in front of Abram stepped away, leaving him next in line at a table full of papyri attended by a clerk.

"El be with you," said the clerk.

Abram hesitated. Eliezer leaned around him to reply, "El be with you."

"Name?" asked the clerk.

"Abram... son of Terah."

"Have you first-borns to declare?"

"These males," said Abram, pointing.

Priests examined the sheep and goats, as the clerk applied a reed pen to papyrus in cuneiform dashes.

"From where come you?" asked the clerk.

"Haran."

"Do you sacrifice to El-Sin?"

Abram blanked for a few seconds, then somehow pulled it together. "Truly… no. Uh, we have learned that El Most High rules in Canaan. We would choose to sacrifice to him."

The clerk raised his eyebrows. "So be it. To El Most High."

All priests in earshot took a wide-eyed glance at Abram. The men in line behind them craned their necks around to get a look at this man – this obvious foreigner who came in with no god of his own, but hoped to buy the protection of the Most High. Some snickered, while others tried not to.

"Your business in Canaan?" continued the clerk.

Again Abram blanked. Then a word fell out of his mouth. "Pilgrim." He could not believe he said it.

Lot and Eliezer stiffened.

Abram took a deep breath. "We have come to pay homage to the most honored el in all the Earth – the holy and Most High El of Salem, for we have heard of him – our king has heard of his greatness." Then louder, "Truly, we are also ambassadors from the king of Haran to the king of Salem." Then even louder, "It is my mission, my sad mission, to inform the judge, and you men of Canaan, that the son of El Most High… is dead."

Total silence. Lot and Eliezer froze breathless.

The senior priest at the altar dared speak. "Uh… Which son? He has seventy."

Abram walked to the altar and turned to address the crowd.

"I speak of his son who dwelt in the great city of Ur. As you may know, Ur is burnt to the ground by evil doers. The holy and blessed El-Sin has been hauled away in a mason's wagon."

Another silence. Then Lot's rigid chest collapsed in a laugh. He immediately masked it as weeping. Eliezer picked up the cue, sobbed, and embraced Lot.

Abram continued, "I wish to add that we are not here to ask for troops or money. Our mission is but to inform an honored father and his faithful servants of this most grievous misfortune, and to console them."

A man in line felt moved to confirm it. "That is true of Ur and El-Sin. I heard it from spice traders."

Priests and merchants gathered around Lot and Eliezer to offer their own consolation.

The chief priest scratched his head. "The fall of Ur was ten years past."

Abram shrugged. "Government."

The clerk finished Abram's receipt. A slave then rolled an inked cylinder seal across the bottom, picked it up with his unblackened hand, and gave it to Abram. As Abram walked past Lot, Eliezer dropped to one knee and bowed.

"Master," he whispered.

Abram touched his shoulder. "Be brave."

The three strode down the hill like victorious generals, escorted by a priest to inform all concerned that these were very important pilgrims.

Several days of rest and relaxation followed. Abram, Lot, and Eliezer pulled a donkey cart through the market place, giving and receiving polite salutations and nodding to the smiling police-clergy.

"Buy some of those," said Eliezer, pointing to a stall selling amulets and teraphim, among other religious trinkets.

"I no longer believe in those things," said Abram.

"And you think I do?" said Eliezer. "You need not to believe in it; just buy it and wear it and let them see it."

Abram sighed. Eliezer continued. "That hill with the oak-tree on top – every morning and evening they offer prayers to it – prayers to keep the sky from falling."

"To keep the sky from falling?" repeated Abram. He walked to the stall and bought amulets for all his men.

The next Shapatu was more festive in spirit than most of them could recall. After dinner, Havah departed from the usual order of stories to tell one she considered more upbeat. It was of their ancestor, Shem – how he finally overcame the adversity of his brothers and settled down in a new land to live happily ever after. She concluded.

> "And Elil said to Shem, 'For that you have called upon my name, I will bless your name

> in all the earth.' And Shem sat beneath his vines and fig trees on the hills of Urartu, and he was happy all his days."

Abram offered no prayers that night, but only thanks giving to his still nameless God for the end of a journey and an auspicious new beginning.

One minor thing, however, continued to haunt his mind. Of Shechem's two hills, all of the sacrificial activity centered around the southwest hill, actually the smaller of the two. The other hill, except for the smoke of a fire at its top, seemed to have no activity at all, no economic or religious use. He asked Eliezer about it.

"That hill is for children," replied his guide. "You need not be troubled by it."

"How sweet!" commented Sarai.

Eliezer bit a lip. "Firstborns are passed through the fire."

Abram and Sarai both nodded as though understanding, but Eliezer was not convinced that his meaning was fully communicated. "In Canaan, Shapatu is called Shabbat. Your wife's mother is a fine mistress of story, but she knows the stories as told by Akkadians. You would be wise to have the women learn how the Canaanites tell it." This advice, if taken, would reveal to the foreigners that "passing through the fire" was a euphemism for a much harsher reality.

Over Lot's objection, Abram chose to leave Shechem before the smiles turned. The die was cast, and now all Canaan would expect them to go straight for Salem. So they did.

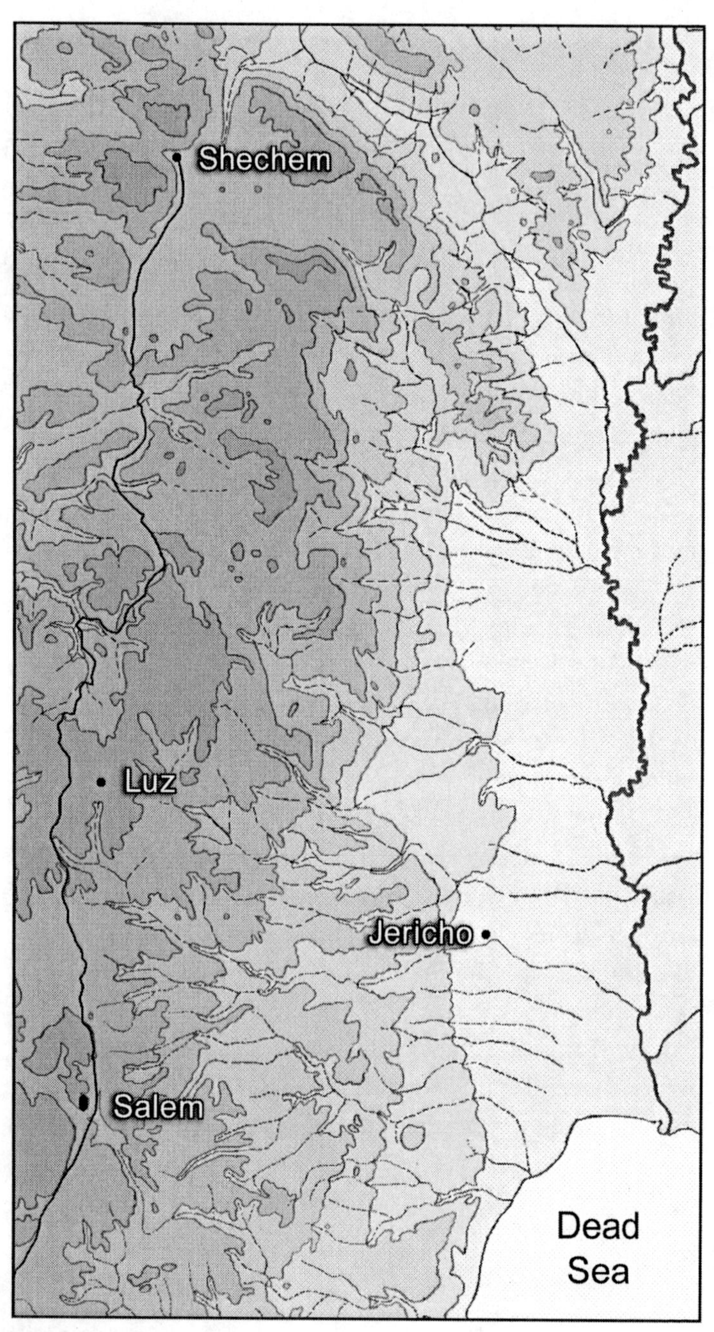
Shechem
Luz
Jericho
Salem
Dead
Sea

7 SALEM

the answer

The road south from Shechem was mostly along a ridge and was called the Ridge Road. Often it wound through hill country – a wide crest sloping gradually on the west toward the Mediterranean and on the east, toward the Jordan River. During the dry Canaanite summers these hills offered the coolest weather and the most shade trees, and were therefore now crowded with competing herdsmen.

The Abramites flashed their oak tree amulets, and settled for less favorable grazing land while smiling and bowing to make it clear that they were just passing through.

"Question, my lord ambassador," said Lot. "How will you sell this holy mission to the king of Salem?"

Abram turned to Eliezer. "Any thoughts?"

"Streets I know. Kings…" Eliezer shrugged.

"Tell me what you know of this Melchizedek."

"Wisest of all men," replied Eliezer.

"Truly?" exclaimed Lot.

Eliezer smirked. "So say the Canaanites. But surely not as wise as the king of Ur – *former* king of Ur."

"How old is he?" asked Abram.

"Two hundred and fifty years easily. I have heard as much as three hundred."

Hmm! thought Abram. *Older even than the king of Ur.*

In an age when time was seen as an endless series of cycles, and verbs had not even evolved the sophistication of past, present, and future tenses, a man's age was measured more by his stature in the community multiplied by the gray in his beard, than any counting of winters. The older you got, the older you got, especially if you happened to be a king. Even after death an honored ruler was likely to age. And when the branches of history developed independently and then came back together in conflict, the more respectful version was considered safer. By Abram's time, arithmetic was gaining ascendancy, but not soon enough to prevent Shem, the son of Noah, from outliving Abram by thirty-five years.

After trudging for a week over hill country through white thistle puffs blowing in the dry breeze, they entered a land full of almond trees, ready for harvest, their leaves now beginning to fall. Here the road ran through the peaceful town of Luz, the almond capital of Canaan. Down slope to their east lay the ruins of a much larger community under a canopy of tall palms.

"See that city?," said Eliezer, pointing to it.

"What city?" asked Abram.

"Jericho," said Eliezer. "Oldest city in Canaan. Full of beautiful springs. That is what happens to cities that displease Pharaoh. They will rebuild it. They always do."

South of Luz Abram asked an almond picker, "How far to Salem?"

"El be with you. A day's journey."

Abram turned to Lot. "Set up camp here. If I return not by Shapatu, you never heard of me."

"Surely, I go with you," said Eliezer.

"You will be needed here if I fail."

"Then take me," requested Zimran.

"No." Tired of trying to explain motivation that even he didn't understand, Abram simply knew what he had to do. He chose three of his best ewes and four goats, leashed them up, mounted a donkey and set out alone.

In his mind, Abram pictured the temple of El Most High in an impregnable fortress at the top of a majestic mountain. Now he saw the city of Salem atop a modest ridge not even the highest in the area. Compacted by surrounding ravines on all sides but the north, the whole of it was less than a quarter the size of Ur. Its walls were equally unimpressive.

Barely ten cubits high, thought Abram. *One could nearly scale it with a roofers' ladder. The towers not much higher, and with no crenellations to protect archers. No threat to Pharaoh, this city. Perhaps that is why it stands.*

> Salem was presumably built here to be close to two springs, Shiloah at its southwest end and Gihon east of its north end. Unfortunately the city wall could not encompass these springs because they were on an elevation too low to be defensible.

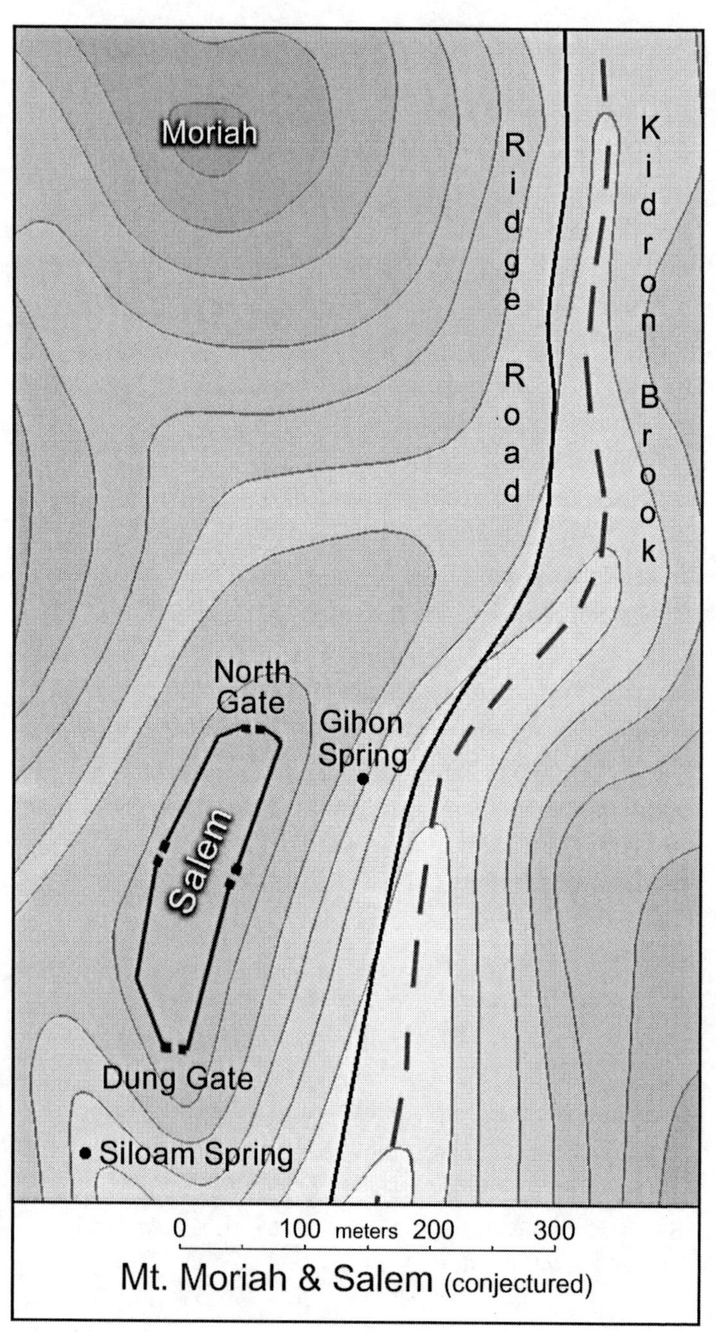

Mt. Moriah & Salem (conjectured)

The tallest building was in the north quarter, bearing no distinctive features but a lack of windows. Still, being highest, *it must be the temple,* thought Abram. Theological disappointments were again piling up.

He entered through the north gate. Expecting a straight avenue to the temple, he was again disappointed to find a hodge-podge of markets and humble dwellings all adjacent in rows. They were nonetheless sturdy and compact. Nearly all of it was of stone and brick. Roofs, when visible for lack of parapets, were tiled – no thatch or bare wood to catch fire. And it was clean. Refuse collectors and street-sweeps were nearly as prevalent as vendors. *A city built by merchants for merchants,* Abram thought. *No beauty to cause envy – but function only. These people hide their wealth in a thousand holes.*

The temple of El Most High was consistent with the rest of Salem – a place of business. Its gate was thronged with patrons bringing offerings and departing with receipts. Abram tried to peer inside but his vision was blocked by a wall. On this wall were two stone bulls sculpted in relief. These appeared to be the temple's only indications of holiness, besides the odor of incense and a column of altar smoke rising from its center. To a man who once looked out from his patio to the majestic Ziggurat of Ur, this hardly counted as a temple at all.

Abram spent one of his goats to lodge himself and his animals at an inn.

Melchizedek was a tall and robust alpha male. At the biological age of sixty-five, he was the hereditary king of Salem. Childless, he would appear to be the last of his dynasty. As judge of Canaan, however, he ruled by popular consensus alone, which was maintained purely by theological and political savvy. Whether he held that office by true spiritual excellence or just superior salesmanship was a question that even the wisest of all men couldn't answer. So he didn't give it much thought. Melchizedek cared only about doing his job. Yes, he enjoyed the benefits of power, but was not greedy for more. His focus of attention was on the peace and prosperity of Canaan. Religion was merely one of the factors in the mix.

In an office full of tables full of documents, and surrounded by priests and scribes, Melchizedek spent his days juggling what might be juggled, and granting audience to those who made it through his filtering system. Now, dressed in casual day linens, he incredulously pondered news told by his herald.

"The king of Haran sends an embassy to inform us that Sin was slain by Baal… ten years past. And he sends it because Sin is a son of El?"

"Yes, Holiness," replied the herald, "but he asks for neither troops nor money."

Melchizedek glanced at his cup-bearer, Jebus. "This is the dung of bulls."

"Perhaps not, Holiness," replied Jebus. "Baal has slain sons of El before."

"But Sin is no son of El," objected Melchizedek.

"If I err not," said Jebus, "the Holy Tablets say that El begat both the sun and the moon."

"On the fourth day of beginnings," confirmed a scribe.

Melchizedek stroked his belly-length beard. "I assume this man brought gifts?"

"Yes, Holiness," replied the herald. "A ewe and three she-goats."

"Search him for daggers and send him in." Then to a scribe, "Who reigns in Haran?… Look it up, quick."

In a few minutes the double doors creaked open and the herald re-entered.

"The ambassador, Abram of Haran."

Abram entered and started to kneel. Melchizedek motioned for him to stay on his feet.

"Welcome to Salem, O Abram. I pray you send my gratitude and best wishes to King Gomer – may his liver rejoice."

"I thank you, Son of El."

"Truly a misfortune it is of El-Sin. I wore sack cloth for a moon, but some years have passed."

"Forgive the delay, Son of El. I have visited the cities of Ebla and the north of Canaan to be sure I informed the servants of all the els."

"Mmm. That would take some time," agreed Melchizedek. "I am sure the els would not have it done over hastily. Does King Gomer wish to speak of any other matters?"

Abram hesitated. "No, Son of El. That is all of it."

"All of it? Forgive me, but I could see it if your king had sent you here to tell me that he is the new Son of Sin, but if Sin be dead, that title would profit him naught. So I am at a loss."

Abram nodded in agreement. "I too find it strange, Holy One – the ways of kings."

"Truly? Well uh… I thank you again, ambassador. I pray you send my, uh… already said all that, did I not?"

"If your Holiness will permit," ventured Abram, "I and my people are here on more than the king's business. We are also pilgrims."

"Of a truth?"

"Yes, Son of El. We have heard that El is different from other gods –els. I mean–"

"I see it," interrupted Melchizedek. "Different in what way?"

"Well… number. One is all, and all are one. So to deal with the highest of all could make things simpler."

"Yes…" coaxed Melchizedek.

"And I hoped perhaps that might cause less… trouble of heart."

"Religion gives you heart trouble?"

"Yes… exceeding much."

A silence fell on the room until Jebus perceived it as tacky. "Surely, you are welcome to stop in for a tablet study."

Melchizedek raised a hand. "I thank you, Jebus. That will be all." Then to Abram, "Religion can give much trouble to a young man. But most men your age have put all that behind them."

A priest offered, "We have counselors."

"Get out!" ordered Melchizedek. "All of you! Abram, you stay. The rest of you, out! Now!"

The entourage hastened to comply, bowing, shuffling backwards, and closing the doors behind them.

Melchizedek twirled a lock of his gray beard around an index finger until he became aware of doing it, then quickly extricated the captive digit. "Come here," he beckoned politely. "I pray you sit."

Abram did so on a bench across the table from the judge.

"I shall ask you a few questions, Abram. And I truly hope you grieve me not." The judge folded his hands on the tabletop. "Why be you here?"

Abram somehow heard the question on a higher level.

"I hoped you could tell me that."

Melchizedek rubbed his eyes and temples. "I mean, why came you to Salem?"

Abram hesitated, not to think of an evasion, but rather to guard against revealing more than was called for. "Different things. I had to leave home, for I quarreled with my brother, and he owned the land."

"In Haran?"

"Yes. Before that we came from Ur, right after…" His eyes glistened over.

Melchizedek understood. He spoke softly. "Why think you that you will find what you seek here?"

"Truly, I thought it not. But where other can one seek?"

Quite unaccustomed to candor, Melchizedek rose abruptly and walked to a window. He understood Abram perfectly. In his youth, he too had once questioned a starry sky. Abram also rose, so as not to be seated while the judge stood. Looking out the window Melchizedek clasped his hands behind his back and rocked nervously.

"Give up," he said firmly. "It is not here… or anywhere. Slay the hope, or it will eat you alive."

Abram went numb. The answer. At last. *Strange,* he thought, *that it did not carry the force of authority one would expect from the Son of the Most High. But then, if gods be lies, what force of authority could be expected?*

"I thank you," said Abram. He bowed to the back of his host and started toward the doors.

Melchizedek sensed that his disciple had not been sufficiently converted. With a flash of insight, he asked, "You have no children, have you?"

Abram stopped and turned. "No."

"Nor I. Mine died young. I was bitter at first. Angry.

But now…" Melchizedek shrugged. "This world is not a good place for children – makes them ugly. Follow me. I wish to show you something."

Melchizedek picked up an oil-lamp and lit it by a torch on the wall. He then walked to the back of his office, drew aside a heavy brocaded wool curtain, and entered a dark room. Abram followed. The room was without windows, cool and musty, having only small ventilation holes near the ceiling. As Melchizedek lit several lamps in wall niches, a library was revealed, stacked with wooden shelves to above eye level. These were full of clay tablets and a few papyri.

"Do you read?" asked the judge.

"No."

"Start not. For a truth-seeker it is like drinking salt water for thirst."

He pulled a plank out from a shelf revealing a dozen or so clay tablets, old and cracked. "These before you are the Tablets of Noah. Know you who Noah was?"

Abram shrugged. Melchizedek continued.

"In the north lands he is called Ouranos – sometimes Utnapishtim – or perhaps three different men escaped the Flood; I know not. But these tablets hold the deeds of men from the first man to the days of Noah. They also contain words of El Most High – laws to tell men what to do and not do. They are the most holy lumps of clay in all Canaan, perhaps the whole Earth. And I am their keeper."

He slid the plank back into its place. "But I have trouble of heart as you do, and the trouble is this. I know not if Noah truly wrote these things. If he did, I know not if he lied. And truly if he believed every word of it, I know not if he was right. Moreover, even if he was right, that was many years past. I know not if the laws then should remain laws now."

He rubbed his hands together and spoke in carefully measured words. "But I must pretend to know all of that, for the people demand it. If I fail, they will harken to another who will. Mine is a job for a good liar. And I am that; I am dung. But I am content to be dung, for my job must be done, and not a man lives in Canaan who could do it better than I."

Abram felt the air sucked out of him. He could do nothing but gape in astonishment. Melchizedek approached and touched his shoulder. "I said all of that but to say this. I could not begin to do this job, had I not given up on that thing you still clutch."

Abram made eye-contact in hopes of hearing more, but Melchizedek turned away. "And ask me not what that is, for I wish not even to speak of it. So other than that... any questions?"

Abram hesitated. "Will you now slay me because I heard it?"

"No." Melchizedek walked out of the library. "No one will believe you. Men believe the lies that feed them. The tastier the lie, the more it is believed. Our whole world could be built on the bones of forgiven liars."

Abram followed him. Despite his host's avalanche of pent up honesty about his dishonesty, Abram could not restrain indignation. "Forgiven by whom? A greater liar? Is El Most High a liar too?"

Melchizedek leaned close to him and spoke barely above a whisper. "We live in a world full of perfect shtupping assholes. If you were the Most High, would you tell them the truth?"

"Yes!"

"No, you would not." The king turned away and lectured into the air. "Whatsoever you tell them, they would make madness of it. No, you would back away and let them find it for themselves."

"What if they could not?"

Melchizedek walked back to his chair and sat.

"Then you would tell them what they could bear at the time, and not a word more. And hope to heaven they write it not." He leaned forward. "For once they press it into clay, the tablets become bigger than the els. The words become greater than the purpose of him who said them." Then weary of his own profundity, he slumped back. "Still, without them we have naught."

Madness or naught flashed through Abram's mind. He lost focus.

Melchizedek saw that his guest had no more to say. "Guards!"

The doors flew open.

"Send Jebus back in. We are finished." He turned his palms upward. "That is it, my pilgrim. That is all I can offer you. You are welcome in Canaan for as long as you wish."

Jebus and the rest re-entered. As they returned to their positions, Melchizedek had a final directive to the herald.

"Give the ambassador a note of my blessing. Also give him back his animals. He has paid too much." Then quietly to Abram, "Pilgrim, you are the first person I have ever truly talked to. It has been a joy."

Abram blanked. Forgetting all protocol, he turned and walked falteringly toward the doorway. It was a strangely long walk. Finally outside, he heard a voice behind him.

"Abram."

He turned, to hear the king's parting words.

"You asked for it."

The doors closed.

A guard handed Abram's sandals back and directed him to a bench on which he might sit to strap them up. At the herald's instructions a clerk filled in the blanks of a certificate of blessing and rolled the king's seal across the bottom. The herald then handed the papyrus square to Abram and escorted him out. Abram exited the palace into a blast of sunlight. A guard politely pressed leash ropes into his hand – a sheep and three goats – a full refund.

Abram sleepwalked in the direction of the fewest people and leaned against a convenient post. Politically the mission had been a complete success. Still, he felt a need to sit down and stare at a wall. While thus absorbed, the sounds of the marketplace pattered senselessly in a corner of his mind until he was brought back to geographic awareness by the words, *Tablets of Noah*. Someone distinctly said, "Tablets of Noah." He got up and followed the sound. It led him to the street of the letter makers.

Among the stalls appeared one with a stack full of clay tablets and papyri inscribed with cuneiform. A long-bearded man in a scribe's robe hawked his product at one end of the stall, as a woman, probably his wife, recited their contents on the other. Abram was first drawn to the hawker.

"Tablets of Noah here. Word for word the same they are, copied by the hand of temple scribes. Clay or bulrush, as you wish. Keep in your home the very Word of El Most High. Frighten away those evil demons."

Then to the other end where the woman either read or recited from memory – hard to tell.

> "And El took the blood of Goshun, the slain, and gave it to Astarte, his wife. And from the blood of Goshun, mixed with earth, Astarte made Adam, the first man. And El put Adam in the forest of Eden. And El said to Adam, 'Of all the plants in the forest you may eat. But never never eat of the haha plant. For in the day I find that you have eaten of the haha plant, I shall gut you like a gir fish.'"

Opium poppy was called joy-plant by Sumerians.

Abram turned and walked away. *The story is changed to please the teller, and each new story is put forth as the original. What a perfect pot of dung!*

LUZ
the retraction

After spending the night at the inn, Abram rode back to base camp. He tried to hide his inner agitation behind the face of a successful negotiator. "All is well," he proclaimed, holding up the token of blessing from Melchizedek. "We shall be welcome in Canaan."

Celebration ensued, but Abram was in no mood to join it. He took Zimran aside. "Pick three strong men and come with me."

Taking along the ewe he had brought back from Salem, Abram led this detachment up a wooded hill until they were out of sight of the camp.

"Build an altar here. Care not for beauty. A pile of rocks, no more."

Upon completion of the task, Abram sent them back. Alone at the new altar, he slaughtered and burnt the ewe. Then assuming the traditional prayer posture, but with a clenched fist pressed tightly into his other palm, he waited pouting for the right words to come.

"Most High God... or El – whosoever you be. I no longer ask to hear you. I repent of it. I wish to give up. *Let me be a common man!*" End of prayer.

He scattered the embers and crushed them out. *Can a man repent of asking a god to speak to him? Is it permitted? Will he be offended? Or was he offended for my asking in the first place?* Abram feared thunderbolts. But none came, neither that day, nor in the weeks to come.

Pasture land around Luz was decent and not over crowded with competition. Armed with Melchizedek's note of blessing, Abram worked his way to favorable trading status with the local sheiks. During the olive harvest of late autumn Havah died. Probably completely unrelated to Abram's prayer – she just died. She was old. She died. They had a funeral; Sarai led the mourners; they buried her. Abram saw no message in it. In fact, this gave him the perfect opportunity to exercise his right as a common man to see absolutely no spiritual connection between his prayer and her death. The timing could not have been better.

One morning Abram awakened suddenly from a deep sleep and sat up.

Sarai knew him well enough to ask, "What?"

"Dream," he muttered groggily.

Sarai put her arm around him and repeated the wifely, "What?"

"It was of you."

"Me?"

"Yes," said Abram. "You were a giant. You walked

around and stepped on houses and things. Everyone ran from you. Then you were naked at Shechem and swollen with child. You lay down on your back and put one leg over each of those hills. Then you shot forth babies like riled up ants from a mound, and they ran all over the land."

Sarai's eyes widened. "Might the voice of a god be in this?"

Abram sat up. "What! No! Naught of gods in it."

"Alas," said Sarai. "I would have hoped it to mean that the god of this land bears us no ill will, and I will no longer be barren."

"Gods talk not to men," snapped Abram, "much less to women. And if they ever talked to any, they would surely not talk to me."

Sarai dared not respond to that, but after a few days of mulling it over, she came to a decision.

"Abram, I have thought."

Abram flashed uncontrollably on, *You asked for it,* and braced for an incoming missile.

Sarai continued. "The law of our fathers says that if a wife is barren, the man may go in unto her handmaid. I know you desire children. For this, I offer you my handmaid… Musha."

Abram felt Musha's eyes upon him. He glanced at the tent, where she quickly ducked out of sight. Though Musha was a cow-faced milque toast in her thirties, Abram was touched. He smiled at Sarai.

"Bless you, my dove, but I could not. Perhaps if I could… No. I love you far too much for that. We shall bear this burden together."

They embraced.

Under perfect circumstances, Abram might have succeeded as a common man. But real circumstances being far from perfect, either by dumb luck or divine tampering, he was again to be tossed into the realm of supernatural suspicions – though not easily. Besides Havah's death, one other totally unrelated event happened in this same time period – or rather, didn't happen.

With the first cold weather, Eliezer stared intently at the west horizon. "This is not good," he said.

"What?" asked Abram.

"The rain is late."

And it remained late.

> This was the late autumn rain, former rain by the Semitic calendar, so essential to germinate the wheat and barley seeds already sown in anticipation of it.

By winter the forecast became as clear as the sky and all Canaan prepared for famine, storing grains in sealed jars and gathering up edibles normally reserved for livestock. They also began slaughtering off their sheep, because sheep eat grass and weeds, and the grass and weeds would soon be dried up. When the spring wheat crop failed, Canaan felt the first stages of famine.

Eliezer had no difficulty convincing Abram to move closer to the Jordan, as it might soon become the only source of free water. Unfortunately for them, the rest of Canaan's nomadic herdsmen had the same idea, and though Abram arrived early, he could not hold his grazing rights against the well established local tribes. Their network of family ties soon squeezed out the newcomer to the least favorable land.

"First my mother and now this," whimpered Sarai over a dreary meal of sycamore figs and carob pods with cakes of drought tolerant barley. "Surely the gods must hate us."

"It is not my fault!" snapped Abram.

Sarai was taken aback. "Who said it was? Truly Abi, I have never seen you so–"

"You said your mother and the famine were both against us. Who is us if not *us?*"

"All Canaan I meant. What? Do you think I meant the gods would punish all Canaan for some sin of yours?"

"They are not gods. They are els."

"Els are gods."

"That is what I meant!" Abram cooled. "Forgive me, I pray you. This bad fortune has me all…"

"And what sin?" continued Sarai.

"What sin of whose?"

"What sin has Canaan done to anger El so greatly?"

"I know not," grumbled Abram. "What am I, a priest?"

"Know you what I think?"

Abram popped a carob pod and looked at her sideways for as long as he dared before asking, "What?"

"I think it is Melchizedek."

"What is Melchizedek?"

"The one who sinned. I would wager on it."

"Many think that."

"I know, but I thought it first before I heard it from others. If the gods – els – be angered at a whole people, it must be either the people or the ruler, yes?"

Abram remained irritated. "Why must it be *sin* at all?"

"What other?"

"I know not. Let us eat in silence."

The next day Abram held a conference.

"We are the least of all the tribes of Canaan. Even the Amorites have a place at the river, but Akkadians have none. If the famine continues, we will be the first to die." He turned to Eliezer. "What can we do?"

"We eat the goats, then eat what the goats eat. I have lived on thistles and locust beans."

"We are not beggars," said Lot firmly. "We are soldiers. I say we cross the hills and look for some spring or well and take it."

"And after we take it, how will we hold it? These clans are tied together like fishnet."

"Eliezer is right," said Abram. "We must not become hated."

"Canaan has had drought before," said Eliezer. "They but dig the wells deeper. If all things fail they turn to Pharaoh."

Abram asked, "Is not Egypt smitten by the same drought?"

"Egypt is watered by a great river," said Eliezer. "It needs not the rains. Pharaoh stores up enough grain to feed the whole Earth."

"Perhaps we should go there."

"Beware, my lord," said Eliezer. "Gyps love not foreigners, least of all shepherds. They are cattle men. They will pay low for your livestock until you have naught left to sell but your children."

Abram now tapped into a reservoir of his father's business sense no longer kept dormant by spirituality. "What do they import?"

Eliezer thought. "Almonds, olives."

"Something that is not eaten," said Abram.

"Wood mostly."

Lot was brilliant. "We trade sheep for wood."

"The best forests are in the north," said Eliezer. "And wood is heavy. Dimashki and the coastlands ship logs by the sea. We cannot fare well against that."

"That is pine and cedar," said Abram. "What of this wood nearby?"

"They use acacia when they can get it," said Eliezer. "oak, terebinth."

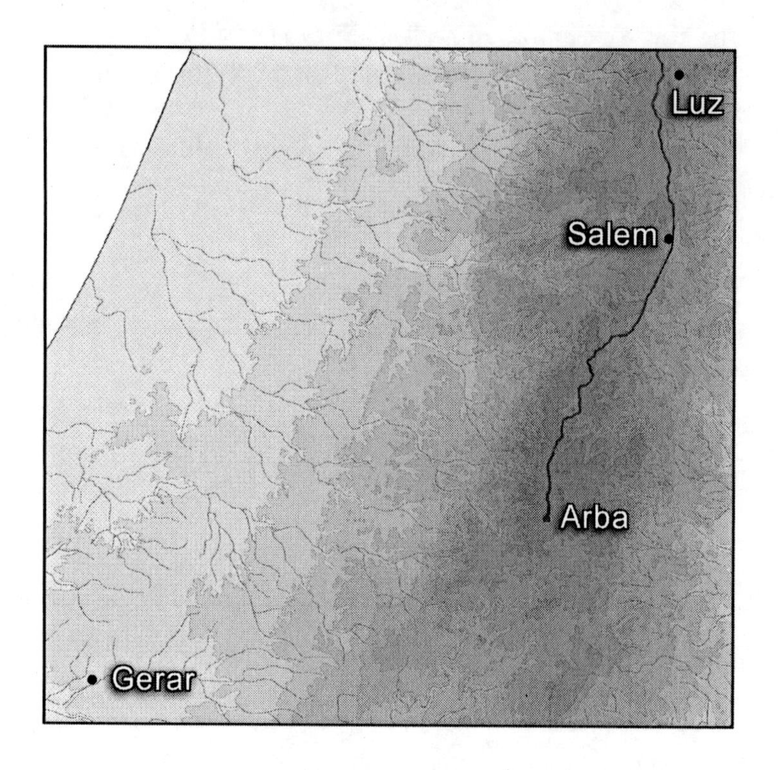
Luz
Salem
Arba
Gerar

GERAR

the alternative

On the road again, southwest again. The sheep had been replaced by donkey-carts and camels laden with side packs full of lumber. From the rocky and wooded hill country they descended gradually to flat and nearly stoneless plains full of dried up wheat fields, thistles, and scrawny tamarisks. Stopping at a well, they paid the owners two goats to water their animals. While resting under palm trees, Eliezer offered a bit of advice.

"Gyps are uneasy outside of Egypt. But in their own land they are lord over all. If they love a thing, they take it."

Abram asked, "Be they without laws?"

"Their laws protect the higher from the lower. Adultery is punished harshly, for the rich can buy all the women they wish. But murder is no great crime, unless it be the murder of one's better."

"Harken my friends," said Abram to his men, "no adultery with rich Egyptians."

They chuckled.

"I mean," insisted Eliezer, "keep your women well covered. They can get you slain."

Lot asked, "How much farther to Egypt?"

"We are in Egypt."

"I thought you said this was Amalek," said Abram.

"It is," replied Eliezer. "Amalek is under Pharaoh. The king of Gerar is but a vassal. And he is a greedy swine."

"How much farther to Gerar?" asked Lot.

Eliezer pointed to a black ripple below the otherwise flat western horizon. "There."

> Gerar, like Haran, was a caravan town. The main purpose for its existence was to facilitate the movement of merchandise. Unlike Haran, it was multi-cultural, and therefore ignored religious differences to the best of its ability. It had suffered enough attacks to have built defensive walls, and like Megiddo, these walls had been torn down and rebuilt so many times that they had become a patchwork of ambivalence waiting for the next change of orders.

Abram, Eliezer, and two servants led one donkey-cart full of acacia to the gates. Amalekite men dressed in clothing of mixed Egyptian/Canaanite style also moved toward the gates. They were neither soldiers nor uniformed officials, but appeared no less confident of their right to block the entry. Abram stopped the cart.

"Behold it!" he said. "Fine acacia from the hills of Canaan. If you love this, we can get you more."

The men surrounded the cart, still in ominous silence.

"Or," continued Abram, "my lord can take his carts somewhere other, and tell his Holiness that king Abimelech cares not for trade."

Abram nodded in the direction of the rest of his tribe visible on the horizon. The men looked as directed, then turned to a burly hulk of a man for guidance.

The man forced a polite smile. "Welcome to Gerar," he said, backing out of Abram's way.

Wasting no time, they headed straight for the royal commerce center. Later that day, Abram and two servants brought the cart, now full of grain sacks, back to join Lot and Zimran at the main party.

Abram motioned excitedly for his men to gather around.

"This could be sweet. They hate sheep, but they love wool. But they have not wool for they hate sheep. We trade the grain for woolies, which are dung cheap in the valleys these days. We shear them. We trade them to the mountain men for wood. Then we haul the wood and the wool back to Gerar."

Lot asked, "Will the prices hold?"

"I wager it, until the famine is over or the rest of Canaan becomes wise."

"Where is Eliezer?" asked Lot.

"Learning the market."

Next day, leaving Lot in charge of camp, Abram let Eliezer guide him through the more scenic streets of Gerar, followed by Sarai and a few other women, all dressed in loose fitting black linen and veiled. Behind them a donkey pulled a cart full of lumber, attended by herdsmen. Eliezer proved invaluable.

"By law you cannot trade wood save through the royal exchange, but we can get better prices on the side. Everybody cheats everybody here, and everybody knows it. But as long as the cows deliver, none ask where they graze or who has milk in his beard."

"What?" asked Abram. He had not been paying attention. There was some culture shock to get over. "What does that child clutch to her breast?" he asked.

"Gyps call it a mau," said Eliezer.

"Have they bred a rat with a rabbit?"

"It is more like a small lion. It makes a whining sound – 'mau, mau.' Terrible meat on them but they can be tamed if caught young. Women love them."

Speaking of women, here they were unveiled in a public market place, walking alongside men, and conversing so casually that one might not know which of them was lord. Some even argued over prices at the stalls. *God's feathers! Some even paint their faces to appear as lusty as men.*

Sarai could endure the gaze of gawking children for only so long before dropping her veil. The other women followed suit.

Unlike Mesopotamian and Canaanite shops, which advertised their wares by samples of merchandise, the shops of Gerar relied more on pictures. One shop in particular stunned the Akkadians with what appeared to be pornography.

"It is a house of circumcision," said Eliezer. "I will explain it later."

"What happened to *them?!*" whispered Abram, quickly looking away from a tall Egyptian clad couple with *black skin!*

Eliezer calmed him. "Nubians from the far end of the earth. Burnt in fire by the sun god, and ill humored about it. You may call an Amorite an Amo to his face. And you may call an Egyptian a Gyp behind his back. But a Nubian is always a Nubian."

Arriving at the royal trade center with the cart, Abram repeated the transaction of the previous day. The supervisor was also commander of the army, a native Amalekite named Phicol. This tall and scar-faced patrician took Abram aside with a friendly arm around the shoulder.

"By law you cannot trade wood here save through the king. But I can get you a better price on the side," he winked. "Between you and me, hey?"

Abram inadvertently glanced at his beard for milk spots.

It was truly sweet. There was no government monopoly on wool trade; that was topping on the cake.

A year later the famine showed no end in sight. Every cloudy day brought hopes to Canaan and sometimes a drizzle, but not nearly enough. Abram and his tribe put on weight and wealth as the woodbine receded north and east. And of course, prosperity brought its own problems.

Abram and Lot conversed privately.

"Let us sell the tents and move to the city," argued Lot. "Should not merchants live as merchants?"

"The weather can change at any time," countered Abram. "and with it our fortune. When it happens I wish not to be surrounded by foreigners. Moreover, these Gyps have an evil spirit about them – beardless men and brazen women with painted eyes."

"And lips," added Lot. "Truly, I rather enjoy it – to look at."

"Our women also enjoy it, and more than but to look at. Have you not seen how quickly they are taken by this shameless fashion? Truly, why put a veil on them if they are just going to paint their eyes? Sarai herself begins to forget her place."

"Not *my* women," boasted Lot.

"Yes, and why? Because they love you? Or because you smack them like dogs? And think not that the men are blind to it."

Lot shrugged. "The men do the same."

"Not *my* men," boasted Abram.

"Not in your sight surely, but behind your back. A man does what he must. You know that."

"Tell me not about *must*, Lot."

"Then you tell me. What *must* we do? We have not our fathers' god behind us to keep order."

"We serve the gods of the land."

"Truly?" exclaimed Lot. "Do we serve *El?* Which one? You now shrink at the very mention of a god, or el, or whatsoever. Your Shabbat prayers are dry as dust. Say what you will about old Suen; at least he kept the women straight."

Abram had no response. He just stood there mute until Lot walked away. For the first time in their lives, Lot actually bested him – and at Abram's own game – the moral high ground game. Could it be that without a god, his tribe had become nothing more than a business enterprise?

On a cloudless autumn afternoon three strangers arrived at camp, men on donkeys coming from the east. Upon identifying themselves as envoys of Melchizedek, they were directed to Abram's tent and welcomed with wine and cheese while the women prepared a feast.

"I am Gabriel," said their leader, "a messenger of his Holiness."

The other two were not introduced, which meant they were servants – bodyguards by their appearance. No one traveled alone in the Bronze Age if he could possibly help it.

"You are a hard man to find," said Gabriel. "I sought a pilgrim."

"Times change," replied Abram.

"Of a truth," replied Gabriel. "I have been sent to tell you that his Holiness believes he has wronged you, and he seeks to make it right."

Abram was shocked. "His Holiness truly owes me naught. If anything, I owe him."

"I would agree, but he thinks that he may have offended you – or if not you, then possibly the Most High in some of the words he said to you."

"What?" asked Abram.

"He said you would ask that. Alas, he knows not."

"Nor I," said Abram. "What does he wish of me?"

"Naught but to tell you he repents of what he said."

"He said many things. What?"

"All of it," said Gabriel. "That is the one way he can know he repents of the right thing."

"And if he repents of all," said Abram, "how knows he anything?"

"If the famine continues, his repentance was in vain. If the famine ends, then he has found its cause."

"But how will he know which of the things he said was the offender?"

"He will not," agreed Gabriel. "But he need not care. He cares only about ending the famine."

"And if the famine ends, what am I to learn?"

Gabriel smiled. "That would be between you and the Most High."

After a good meal, Gabriel and his guards departed.

Abram checked the horizons for clouds. All clear. Still, the visit had an ominous feel. He summoned Eliezer.

"We must seek new trade. Find what these Amalekites want and how we can serve it up better than those who do so now. Or when the famine ends, we end with it."

And so as clouds returned to the Canaanite sky, Abram became a common smuggler. With cold weather, the rains came. But all droughts come to an end, god or no god, and such events need not be interpreted as messages, or divinely caused in any way. Abram had already tried that way of thinking. He had invested the best years of his life giving it the fairest trial any god could possibly require, and he found it to be superstitious nonsense. El Most High was disappointment most high. Now Abram was past that level; he was a businessman. Though without his former competitive advantage since the famine ended, he was still in the game, and still highly respected in an appearance-loving society of common men.

With the end of the winter rainy season came Abimelech's birthday and its party. In Gerar this was the social event of the year – and completely secular – no priests allowed. If you invite one, you would have to invite them all, and that would be unrealistic. The only way to keep from offending sectarians in a multi-cultic society was to offend them all equally.

Phicol, being master of ceremonies, invited Abram and any guests he may choose to bring. Abram gratefully accepted without hesitation, not quite knowing what he had gotten himself into. Upon leaving the royal exchange, he asked.

"Birthday? What be that?"

"An Egyptian custom," replied Eliezer. "They celebrate the day of one's birth as a time of rejoicing."

"What if one is born in a year of thirteen moons?"

"In Egypt they count years by the sun, not the moon. It appears to work fairly well."

"Good then. Lot and Sarai love a festival."

"Uh, my lord. I would not advise that you bring Sarai."

Sarai learned of this party, not from Abram, but from other women, and from them she also learned that she would not be invited. That evening she dismissed Musha early and closed the tent flap.

"Why not?" she demanded, now the liberated wife of a common man.

"Eliezer says it is dangerous," replied a conciliatory Abram.

"What thinks he? – that some Gyp will slay you and run off with me in the king's palace with Phicol and everyone watching?"

"Phicol himself perhaps."

"Truly!" exclaimed Sarai. "And lose one of his best providers?"

"I am not so dear to him now that grain is cheap and wood is costly."

"Will the other merchants bring wives?"

"Some, I would wager," replied Abram.

"Those with ugly wives, no doubt. 'Hello everyone. This ugly woman behind me is my wife.'"

"Those who feel safe may bring wives."

"Oh speak truly, Abram. I am not a fool. You desire to try on some fresh young buttocks. Go ahead! Go to your cursed shmuck party." She stormed out of the tent.

Abram sighed, shrugged, got up, and followed her. "Wear the brown wrap-on… and a drape-over."

"A drape-over!"

"Yes, and a veil."

Upon learning that Sarai would be attending, Lot suddenly lost interest in the party. He would remain at camp while Abram, Sarai, and Eliezer made the required appearance.

This was easily the most elegant affair any of them had ever experienced. The palace courtyard was adorned with purple mandrakes, pink tamarisk, and white crocus and saffron flowers. It was bustling with the polite and proper activity of a formal event. Bulky winter dress made class distinctions easily recognizable. However, a few wealthier merchants were nearly matched jewel for jewel with the lesser nobility. Women outnumbered the men three to one, but fairly equaled them in collective age. Eliezer wheeled in a handcart full of white sheep fleeces and was promptly directed to the gift table. Prior to Abimelech's grand entry was an informal time to mingle and schmooze for all merchants, nobles, officials, and government spies.

"So many odors!" exclaimed Sarai. "How can a nose smell them all?"

"Gods be praised we are outside," said Abram.

Eliezer whispered, "Some of these men drive caravans directly to the Nile. Shall I–"

"Not but if they approach you," cautioned Abram. "And be clouded. The king has ears all over this courtyard. Go."

Eliezer peeled off and soon saw a cluster of his equals gathered around Phicol's squire. He joined them in hopes of cutting a juicy one from the herd.

Abram nabbed two wine cups from a passing servant and handed one to Sarai. She delicately lifted her veil to take a sip.

"Abi," said Sarai.

"What?"

"Do you see one other woman here in a veil?"

"Uhh, yes," Abram pointed. "There."

"That is a dancer."

"And beautiful, is she not?"

"She wears a veil but to take it off. Abi, truly." Sarai lowered the veil and pouted. "Now still, I wear the plainest dress in the yard."

Phicol was buttressed by several bubbly young nymphs clad minimally in Egyptian high fashion. While conversing with Canaanite gentry, he made eye-contact with Abram and raised his cup. "To the famine! Els grant us another."

Abram responded in kind. "And soon."

Phicol motioned him over to join them. Abram leaped to it, leaving Sarai to tag along and be as ignored as Phicol's nymphs.

"Abram, this is Akbar; he owns olive groves near Shechem. Egypt grows not olives. Akbar, this is Abram; he runs caravans."

As the men engaged, Phicol's girls checked out Sarai's dress. Giggling and whispering among themselves, they soon became bolder and gathered around her. One then whispered in her ear, but the Egyptian accent left Sarai clueless. She nodded and smiled politely hoping they would go away, but they began to tug on her to go with them. She looked to Abram, who looked to Phicol for explanation. One of the girls gleefully chattered something in Egyptian to Phicol. He tilted his head back and laughed. Then to Abram – "Ah, the ladies care naught for man talk. They wish to make their own joy." He slapped one on the rear. "Go, go, rejoice."

Abram gave Sarai a nod, and she went away with the girls.

Musicians plunked and tooted their instruments into relative agreement. Servants brought in pillows tossing them around the periphery for people to sit on. The center of the court was cleared for the locally renowned identical twin Twinkling Brothers of Tanis to entertain those who failed to score profitable conversations. Dancing, juggling swords, and performing impressive feats of Egyptian magic, they were nevertheless a warm-up act for the belly dancers.

Phicol, having secured a hefty percentage for his brokerage services, left Abram and Akbar to hammer out the details. This took about half a wine cup, and Abram scanned the court for another deal. *So many little things to remember. No wonder merchants hire men of letters to keep it all straight. Perhaps that should be my next move.*

Cruising the floor for prospects, he was stopped by a stunning Egyptian woman dressed like a rich man's wife.

"Fill my cup, handsome?"

"Uhh, you are lovely, dear, truly, but I have a wife here at this very party and *God's feathers! Sarai, what did you do to yourself?"*

Phicol's girls broke out laughing. Sarai whirled around to display the pleated white linen.

"It is called a kalasiri. Love it?… Mind not." She took his arm. "Let us go enjoy the entertainers."

"Be you mad?" exclaimed Abram.

"Abi, they have plates of brass so flat and polished that I could see my own face as in a pool of clear water."

Eliezer approached. "Abram, be you mad? Sarai is–"

Abram raised his brows and nodded in her direction.

Eliezer was quick. *"Gods of Gomorrah!* Let us leave, now!"

A gong was struck. The palace doors opened and a flock of beautiful girls poured out and formed two lines down the stairs. Abimelech, decked out like a sarcophagus lid, made his grand entry between them to the blast of impala horns. All faced him and knelt.

"Rise!" he commanded graciously. "I beg you rise, my children. Rejoice."

All stood and cheered. The three frustrated fugitives found themselves wedged in the front row.

Abimelech engaged Phicol and some nobles in conversation, but soon caught sight of Sarai.

Eliezer took command. "Quietly make your way back toward the entry."

"This is not my clothing," said Sarai. "I cannot leave with it."

"Abram!" called an authoritative voice.

Abram turned to see Phicol motioning him over. He started in that direction, but of course, Phicol motioned for him to bring Sarai along.

Abram returned to her and took her arm. "Try to look foolish. Not too difficult, hey?"

The three approached as directed to the smiling, pasty-faced Abimelech.

"So this is the famous man of wood," he said, causing uproarious laughter at his wit.

"My Lord," said Phicol, "I present Abram of Salem."

"El be with you," grinned Abimelech, and extended a hand for him to kiss. "I hear you are a friend of Melchizedek."

"Slightly over spoken, Majesty. I attend his court in certain seasons."

"No doubt at the birth of your first-born, hey?" said Abimelech.

"I have not had the blessing of children, Majesty."

Abimelech glanced at Eliezer, "I see," then looked at Sarai. "And is this lovely creature then your servant?"

"No my lord." said Abram. "Truly she is–"

"His sister, Majesty," blurted Eliezer. "Sarai is his sister."

Abimelech took a few seconds to recover from the affront, then asked Abram for confirmation. "Your sister?"

"Uh, yes, Majesty."

"Ah! How fortunate!...for you, Abram, to have such a beautiful sister, and for you, my dear, to have such a connected kinsman." Then back to Abram. "You chose the right place to show her off." He winked. "Do you love riddles?"

"Oh yes, Majesty," said Abram, forcing a smile.

"For what does the Amorite need more land?"

"Uhh... we have often wondered the same, Majesty"

"To escape the odor of his fathers' carcasses."

"Ha ha ha ha ha ha ha ha ha ha."

"Forgive us." Abimelech and Phicol walked away.

Sarai turned to Eliezer. "Why did you say that?" Then to Abram, "And *you!*"

Abram grabbed her arm. "Go change out of that thing, now!"

"Abi, El's bells! Phicol knows I am your wife. If he wanted you dead, he would have slain you long ago."

Abram looked to Eliezer. "What think you?"

Eliezer sighed. "The harm is done, if harm it be."

Servants brought out low tables for food, as people seated themselves on the pillows around the periphery.

"They are serving *beef!*" said Sarai excitedly.

Dinner by fire light in a king's courtyard seated around a dance floor full of Egyptian beauties – it would have been the high point of their lives under normal circumstances. After several courses of delicious dinner, Sarai went to change back into her own clothing. Soon she returned, still in the Egyptian outfit, holding her brown dress under her arm and looking troubled.

"They said it was a gift from Phicol–"

"We cannot accept it," interrupted Abram.

"–and he would be insulted if I refused."

Eliezer grabbed Abram's arm. "Let us go. *Now!*"

They politely made their way out of the courtyard, then walked as briskly as propriety would allow. Half way to the livery stable Phicol's girls along with the Twinkling Brothers came running after them.

"Hallooo there! My lord wood man," came an effeminate yet male voice.

"Too late," said Eliezer.

The three turned to face it.

"Abram of Salem?" asked the twins.

"Yes."

"His Majesty has gifts for you," said Twinkle-One.

A girl approached Sarai with a beautiful necklace.

Twinkle-Two: "His Majesty wishes the company of your sister for the evening."

Twinkle-One: "His intentions are, of a truth, honorable beyond question."

Twinkle-Two: "May these ladies escort her to the king's chambers?"

Eliezer cut in abruptly. "Tell His Majesty that Abram is most honored."

Sarai looked to Abram. He hesitated, then nodded affirmatively. Sarai left with the girls.

Twinkle-One raised his arm in a dramatic flourish. "We beg you accept these humble tokens of gratitude from His Majesty," he said, but indicating nothing as to what those tokens might be. The Twinks then stood beside each other, spread their arms gracefully, and bowed.

Abram turned and stamped off.

As they rode home by star light, Eliezer thought the better of trying to converse with him.

Abram got no sleep that night, and dozed restlessly in bed until noon. Stepping out of his tent into a cloudy day, he sniffed the air. *Smells like rain. At least Melchizedek will fare well.* He walked away from camp to get clear of its distractions.

At a time like this, any common man might be filled with thoughts of his wife – memories of their times together. But in Abram these thoughts were eclipsed by questions – mostly flowing from the same nagging question that had plagued him since the fall of Ur. Why?

What can a man make of this? Terrible happenings, whether to a man or a kingdom – be it all madness? Should I believe it to be the work of gods, or fate, or fortune, or but my own foolishness? No way to know. But the chance that I am punished for wrong doing, that is most troublesome. Whether for willful evil or but errors of thought, punishment means a punisher – some great and terrible Bastard with a stick… Forgive me – some great and terrible King with a stick, who seems to have spies everywhere to peep at me – spies inside my very heart to shout out any tiny crime of thought, yet somehow hide their eyes from every good thing I do.

But once again, curse it all! I have tried that way of thought – tried it perfectly – at least as perfectly as I could at the time, for as much as I knew at the time. But now I have seen more. I know more. I can be held to account for more. Can a man not rid himself of these foolish god-thoughts and not become what he hates, perhaps even... evil?

Whether from sense or superstition, a mind once magnetized has difficulty facing any direction but Godward. Abram conceded to the clouded sky. "What do you desire of me?"

"Abram of Salem?" came a voice, causing a slight bladder accident.

Abram whirled around to see an Egyptian clad messenger from Gerar.

"His Majesty wishes to see you."

The king's atrium was crowded – if not physically, then certainly socially. Abimelech and a bevy of harem girls reclined on large pillows as bodyguards graced the corners. Sarai, dressed in her brown wrap-on, stood to one side. A priest of Amon sat near the door, serving no apparent purpose but to observe the proceedings. And now Abram stood in the center.

Abimelech, bald without his wig, but still pasty without his cosmetics, was obviously angry. "Did I not ask clearly whether this woman were your wife?"

"Yes, Majesty."

"And did you not say that she was your sister?"

"Yes, Majesty."

"Ah!" he raised his hands in justified exasperation for the benefit of the priest. "Why did you not tell me that she was your wife?"

"Truly, Majesty," fumbled Abram. "I feared you might slay me."

Abimelech took an exasperated moment to recover. "What kind of man do you think I am?… I am a god-fearing man! I commit not adultery – nor murder, be it not perfectly deserved. Now I have sinned. And I must pay the price." Abimelech stood. He wore a loose-fitting linen gambaz. Walking toward a table, he was slightly bent, apparently from a pain in the groin. He picked up a goat-skin full of silver, and delivered it to Abram.

"Majesty, I could not."

"You can, and you will," assured Abimelech. "It is the law."

Abram took the bag.

Abimelech now turned to Sarai. "And you, dear lady. I feel that I also owe you something."

Sarai lowered her head. "My lord truly owes me naught."

Abimelech grinned demonically. "Ah, but I do, dear lady. I truly do." Turning to his bevy, "Hagar! Behold your new mistress."

Hagar, a busty teenage Egyptian dancer, did a wide-eyed take.

Abimelech smiled at Sarai and wrinkled up his nose like he had just over-tipped a serving wench.

Four donkeys exited Gerar in single file, carrying Abram, Sarai, a sobbing Hagar, and Hagar's possessions.

They set her up in a side tent with Musha – not the most ideal of companions, but at least here Hagar could learn the duties and demeanor of a servant. While this was going on, Sarai cooked supper. She and Abram had not exchanged a single word since the party. All through the meal both were pouty and silent. Finally, Abram led off.

"How did he know that you were my wife?"

"He asked, and I told him."

"He asked? Why asked he?"

"He said he had a bad dream."

"A dream?"

"I wager he dreamed that I was your wife."

"So this happened this morning?"

"Yes."

Abram mulled it over. "And he asked for that one cause and no other?"

"He spoke of no other cause."

Abram chose his question carefully. "Know you of any other cause?"

"Perhaps I displeased him."

"In what way?"

"I know not," said Sarai, looking him straight in the face. "Perhaps he loved not the way I give straight answers to straight questions. Do you wish to learn any other thing… brother?"

The subject was never mentioned again.

It rained that night. The Gerar phase was definitely over.

When they packed up to leave, the tribe was three times the size it had been when they arrived, and loaded with possessions. Eliezer suggested that they buy land and become gentry. Lot preferred to buy city shops where they might retail their own livestock. Abram again favored preserving mobility. And whether by persuasion or just rank, he had his way. They would return to Luz. Abram felt uneasy about his past actions there, and wanted to rectify something.

10 LUZ
the contract

It was sowing season when they arrived at Luz. Abram took a bit of pride in knowing that much of the wheat and barley planted had come from his tradesmanship – never mind the receded woodbine. He rebuilt his old stone altar and offered up a fine ewe. But facing the flames, he could think of little to say. He repented of his shady transactions at Gerar, not because he regretted doing them, but just to avert possible punishment. The best he could do was to apologize for not regretting it, but still this did not feel like the main issue.

So what if I behaved like a common man? If the Maker loves not common men, why did He make so many of them? What did Melchizedek say that had brought famine on Canaan? No. That was Melchizedek's trouble. My trouble is to learn what this "el" desires of me. Truly, I feel no guilt for anything I said at this altar two years ago. I but repented of a prayer to hear a god. Is that a sin?

I found the results unpleasant... grievous... maddening! So I gave up. What more can be asked of a man? Perhaps I gave up too much.

Abram shrugged. "Whatsoever you wish." Possibly giving up in the other direction would appease the silent Observer.

Judging by its results, *whatsoever you wish* seemed to smooth things out between Abram and Whomever might be on the other end of it. Things started going well – possibly too well in certain areas.

One spring day with flowers covering the fields and the almonds in blossom Zimran caught Abram alone and asked, "What think you of this Eliezer, Abram?"

"Looks to be a good man so far."

"I mean, think you that he will ever be a man one could fully trust?"

Abram heard something else under the question. "Have you a daughter with child?"

Zimran scratched the back of his neck. "Not yet."

Though not fully prepared for marriage, Eliezer had only one other option – leave the tribe without financial compensation. And though his actions had put all dowry bargaining out of the question, he knew that this would probably be the outcome when he first lifted the flap.

> Strangely enough, there was nothing religious about Semitic marriage at this time. They just made a business agreement in front of a group of witnesses. Later the contract would be enforced with an oath, that invokes a god, that brings in religion, that introduces liturgy, that evolves into a ceremony, that gradually usurps the whole show into a holy and sacramental institution. But for now, a contract sufficed.

Since he and Zimran were both ex-slaves and of inaccessible if not unknown parentage, the marriage was taken as between equals.

With the tribe circled around the participants Abram presided. “Eliezer of Dimashki, take you Betula, daughter of Zimran, for your wife?”

“I do.”

“For the rest of your life, if she die not first?”

“I do, yes.”

“And you pay for her food and other needs from this time forward?”

“I agree.”

Abram turned to the other party concerned.

“Zimran of Haran, find you this agreement satisfactory?”

“No dowry,” muttered Zimran.

“Surely,” said Abram, returning to Eliezer. “And you demand no dowry or other pay of any kind?”

“Yes, I do not,” said Eliezer.

Abram turned back to Zimran. “Enough?”

Zimran nodded in consent.

Abram continued. “And for your part, Zimran, demand you no bride price, but for one she-goat?”

“I do… not so demand.”

“And swear you that the woman is virgin to any man?”

Zimran knit his brows.

Abram clarified, “but perhaps this one?”

“I do.”

Abram turned to Eliezer. “ Enough?”

“Yes.”

And back to Zimran, “Bestow the ring.”

Zimran handed Eliezer a copper nose-ring for his bride.

"My friends," said Abram, "I declare you father and son in the eyes of all here present. You may drink beer."

Lot put forth two large cups finely strained beer between them. Each took a cup, linked arms, and raced for the bottom. Zimran finished first, but whether honestly or by the traditional courtesy of the younger man only Eliezer knew. They smashed the cups on a rock.

"Good fortune!" shouted the crowd.

The return to Luz may have been spiritually cathartic for Abram, but it was not the best political move for a tribe of that size. Friction with the Luzites over grazing land was unavoidable. That autumn when some of his shepherds returned to camp bloodied, Abram called a conference.

"No trouble," said Lot. "We are the most powerful tribe in the area. We can return any bruise ten fold."

"But then they will run to their sheikhs," said Abram, "and we will have all Luz against us."

Lot scoffed. "The sheikhs are no different from the merchants at Gerar. A few well placed gifts will get us ahead of the game."

Abram became irritated. "I no longer wish to get ahead of the cursed *game*! I have *been* ahead. I wish but to get to where I belong."

Lot was confused. "The strong belong where they will."

Abram raised his voice. "I wish to find some place to live where I can love my god… uh, where I can love my neighbors and they love me. Is that so hard to see?" He turned to Eliezer. "We need more space. What think you?"

"South," said Eliezer.

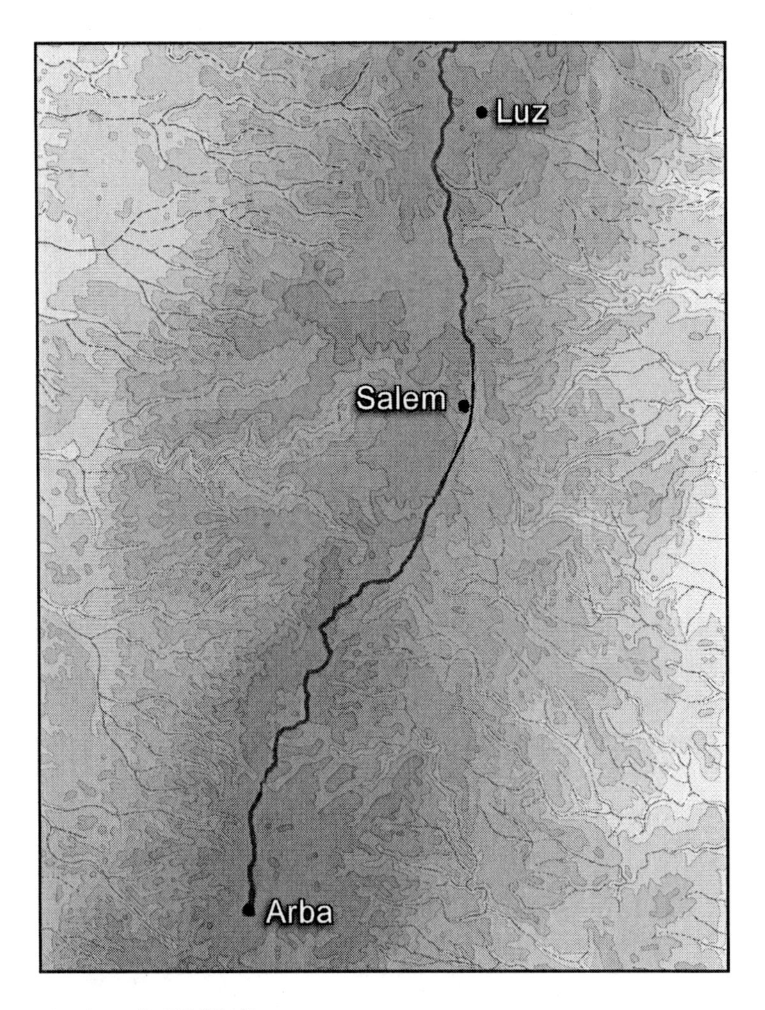

ARBA
the split

As the grape harvest began they followed the Ridge Road southward through rocky hill country. After passing Salem it was mostly uphill through oak forests now in orange leaves. Two days' journey brought them to the highest mountains of the region.

"I am told that the city of Arba is up there," said Eliezer.

"You are told?" said Lot. "I thought you have been everywhere."

"I have," said Eliezer. "Arba is the middle of nowhere."

"We need not go to it," said Abram looking down hill to his left. "I see fine pasture land. Think you that we be welcome there?"

Eliezer laughed. "With a tribe this big, what does it matter?"

They detoured eastward down the hill, and made camp.

> Arba was not visible because it lay in a depression at the top of the highest mountains of Canaan. The location would never have been chosen for habitation except for springs. Not on a major trade route, this quiet community served as a center for sedate farmers and herdsmen in the surrounding countryside. Many foreigners ended up here to get away from it all.

Abram courteously inquired as to what land was already claimed and took up permanent residence east and down-stream of it. It was some of the best pasture land in Canaan, arable and cut with wadis draining to the Dead Sea. But here with no external adversity, his men found that they couldn't get along with each other. Aside from ideological differences between Abram and Lot, the tribe was simply too big.

"We must divide the people." said Abram.

"I know," replied Lot.

"Which way do you desire?"

Lot nodded southeast. "The valley."

Eliezer felt a word of caution in order. "Umm… Lot, be aware. The cities of that land are outside of Salem's rule and custom."

"So I have heard," replied Lot. "Sodom and Gomorrah – they are full of strangelings. But they have abundant salt, and they most surely eat meat."

It was an amiable separation, but not easy. Most of the people would have rather stayed with Abram. Zimran and Eliezer flat out insisted on it. But after dividing the livestock down the middle, economic considerations gave Lot his fair share of workers. So Lot went southeast and Abram remained, but they still kept in touch and quickly developed commercial relations, the hills of Arba having resources different from those of the Dead Sea valley.

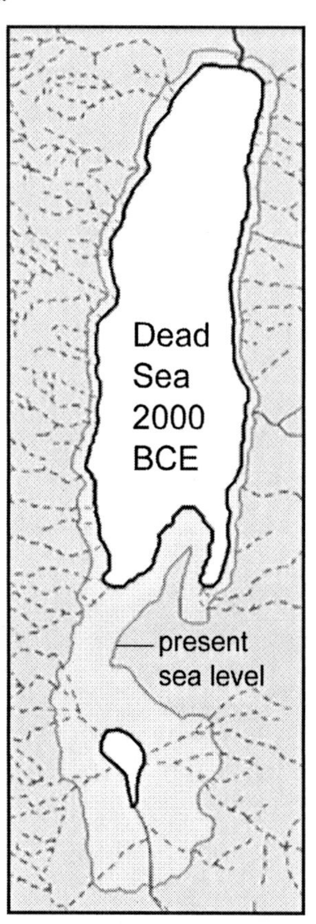

The level of the Dead Sea was lower in 2000 BCE By how much is unknown. This leaves a wide range of possibilities for the locations of Sodom & Gomorrah.

Living east of Arba was a pleasant time for Abram. Boredom being outside of Bronze Age vocabulary, he saw it only as peaceful – doing little more than routine chores, making friends among the other foreigners, including even a few civilized Amorites. The life of a simple law-abiding citizen was all he ever wanted – at least it was good enough. And he would take the necessary steps to preserve it. Every spring and fall he made the three-day journey to Salem with a generous offering.

"To what el do you sacrifice?" asked the priest at the registry.

"Whatsoever," replied Abram.

The priest raised his brows.

"Most High." Abram smiled. "Make it Most High."

It was going along swimmingly. Then came a day of foreboding.

The tribe had gathered around the tent of one Jokshan, a herdsman of Abram's. The man was about to become a father. Soon from inside the tent came the cry of an infant.

"It is a boy," came a happy woman's voice.

All cheered. A ram's horn bleated to announce the event, and of course a party.

Finding Abram once again alone on the periphery, Eliezer approached him. "Bittersweet, is it not?"

"You unmask me, friend," said Abram. "I hoped my envy better hidden."

"Envy?" said Eliezer. "Perhaps you hear me not. That was Jokshan's first-born son; was it not?"

"Yes."

"You must know that he is to be passed through the fire."

Abram shrugged. "So be it. We will pass him through fire."

"Abram," said Eliezer directly, "To pass through the fire means to pass through death. The boy is haram."

"He is what?" asked Abram.

"Haram," replied Eliezer. "He is to be sacrificed. Law of the first fruits."

"What?!"

Eliezer raised his palms. "I told you this long ago."

Abram was incredulous. "We have had other children born in Canaan!"

"Girls," agreed Eliezer. "Girls are not counted. Nor second sons. None but first-born sons."

Abram gritted his teeth, rubbed his head, and walked away from the crowd. The word, "*whatsoever*," echoed in his mind. It was the old god-hassle all over again. He knew the feeling of it – like a big white-bearded face in the sky staring at him. Obey and become evil in your own eyes; disobey and be thrown out of your community.

"Whatsoever I wish?" said the grinning god-thing in Abram's mind. *"Let us see if you truly mean it."*

Curse you… No. No, thought Abram. *Never curse the god-thing, or the god-thing can make it even worse.*

Somehow it always comes down to two choices: give up or move on to the next two choices. And even if you give up, you just slide back into another set of cursed choices. And such mad choices! What ever happened to good and evil? That I can work with. But this madness or naught – god or heart– what can I make of it? Is there no way to get god and heart on the same side?

Abram wrestled with it, made a decision, and walked back to Eliezer.

"So who will know this was Jokshan's first-born son?"

"Everyone here, surely," replied Eliezer.

"Jokshan!" called Abram, and motioned for him to approach.

The man responded to his boss's voice.

"Know you of the law of first fruits?" asked Abram.

"Yes," replied Jokshan.

"Know you that it reaches also to the sons of men?"

"What mean you, my lord?"

"If a man's first-born son is born in Canaan, that son is to be sacrificed to El."

Jokshan, who had come with Abram from Haran, gaped in disbelief, but Abram calmed him.

"Fortunately for you, however, this son is not your first-born. You had another son, did you not? It was born at Megiddo, if I recall" Abram threw an arm firmly around Jokshan's shoulder. "But that son died. You remember that, do you not? And your wife will most surely remember it also. Hear you?… Tell me if you hear me."

"Yes," replied Jokshan. "I hear you."

"Go in unto her and bring it to her remembrance, will you?"

"Most surely, my lord." Jokshan hurried to his tent.

"Uhh… Abram, my master and friend," said Eliezer, "exceeding dangerous it is to cheat the gods, even lesser gods. To cheat the Most High is truly foolish, most truly when the neighbors learn of it. And they will." Eliezer was right, politically if not otherwise, and Abram knew it.

"Wait," said Abram. "You said Sodom and Gomorrah are outside of Salem's rule, true?"

"Yes."

"So be it," said Abram. "I can trade more than merchandise with Lot." He walked back to the group.

"This is not good," muttered Eliezer.

A few days later Jokshan, his wife, his daughters, and newborn son were packed up and saying their good-byes.

As they left for Lot's camp, Sarai turned to Abram. "So if I ever bear a son, it is haram?"

"Yes," said Abram.

Right on schedule, Abram appeared at the Salem temple, this time with more than the usual number of offerings on ropes. But gone was that former air of spiritual confidence, always so resented by those who don't have it. Waiting in the registration line, he felt like a sheep trying to sneak through a pride of sleeping lions.

A young man carrying a woolen-wrapped infant in his arms walked somberly past the registration tables. Abram now recalled that he had seen such men before at temple, but had previously paid no attention to them. He watched as the man asked directions from a guard and followed him out of sight.

"Your name?" asked the clerk.

"Abram!... son of Terah."

"Ah yes, I should have remembered. And you are of Arba, yes?

"Yes."

"And your offering is to El Most High?"

"Yes." Abram handed the ropes to a priest.

"Have you prayer requests?" asked the priest.

"No. I thank you." Abram turned and walked away.

"Abram."

Abram whipped around.

"Your token," said the clerk, holding up his papyrus receipt.

Abram took the receipt. Something about the sound of his name being called from behind had made him jumpy.

12 ARBA
the error

Upon arrival at camp, Abram noticed Zimran and Eliezer having an animated discussion. *What now? Disputes over pasturage?* But when the two saw Abram approaching, they immediately stopped waving their hands and went silent. Abram's ears burned.

Eliezer smiled. "Welcome back, my lord. How went the journey?"

"Journey was fine," said Abram. "Of what were you speaking?"

"Naught," replied Eliezer. "Family matters."

Zimran looked away.

"Zimran," said Abram. "Of what were you speaking?"

Zimran sighed and scratched the back of his neck. "We spoke of, uhh… good and evil – all that."

"Truly?" said Abram. "My own thoughts have been on the very same. What kind?"

"Kind?" said Zimran.

"Good and evil to men? To nations? To gods? What?"

Zimran continued to fidget. "Well, Eliezer here thinks sin and evil are the same–"

"They *are* the same," blurted Eliezer.

"And I say they are the same in one way but different in another way."

"Hmh," grunted Abram, "how be they different?"

"Well first, they are the same in that they are both offenses."

Eliezer and his hands could not keep quiet. "And I asked him what be the difference between a sinful offense and an evil offense, and he could not answer."

Zimran also unlocked his hands. "I said they were the *same* that way, mush-heart. The difference is who is offended."

"So?" said Abram. "Is not a sin against a man the same as an evil against a man?"

"Hah!" agreed Eliezer. "The very same said I!"

"Sin is an offense against a god," explained Zimran. "Evil is an offense against a man."

"Not always," said both Abram and Eliezer.

"The words are used foolishly," said Zimran. "But an offense against a god is not always the same as an offense against a man."

"When is it not?" asked Abram.

Zimran and Eliezer went silent. Then Zimran carefully picked out his words. "Well, perhaps a god might tell a man to slay a man. Then to slay that man is not a sin against that god, but it remains an evil against that man."

All three of them fell silent.

"A worthy piece of thought," said Abram. "Then you would say that not all evil is sin?"

"Yes, and not all sin is evil," agreed Zimran. "If that

same man refused to slay the other man, then he has done good to that man."

"But he has sinned against the god who commanded him to slay," interrupted Eliezer.

"My very meaning," said Zimran. "Not all sin is evil."

"But wait," said Eliezer. "If that god is the Most High, surely any sin against the Most High is evil."

Zimran threw his arms up. "Again you mush the words together, youngster. Evil is against men; sin is against gods."

"Says who? You but made it up."

"Moreover," Abram trumped in. "It was not my son. It was Jokshan's. And I never commanded him not to sacrifice it. I but showed him another way to go."

"Ah," said Eliezer. "Then the sin is Jokshan's."

"Jokshan is Akkadian," insisted Abram.

"But his first son was born on El's land – El Most High."

"Jokshan knew not of the Firstfruits Law – nor I – that it reaches to sons of men."

Eliezer folded his arms. "And now that you know it, will you leave Canaan? – or perhaps stop knowing your wife?"

"Insolent whelp!" said Zimran. "Shall I thrash him, my lord?"

"No, no," said Abram. "He is young. Give him space."

Though Abram had successfully muddled the issue, he had not dodged the philosophical arrow. Under it all remained the fact that he believed he was disobeying the god to whom he was accountable, and he did it anyway. Should he be punished? Fortunately that question can remain dodged, because Abram now followed up with an act for which punishment would be justly deserved.

After a long and private conference in their tent, Abram and Sarai came to a fateful decision.

"Hagar," called Sarai. "Come in, I pray you."

Hagar entered.

"Sit down," said Sarai, politely.

Hagar sat.

Sarai folded her hands and leaned forward. "Abram and I have spoken of... things. As you know, I have been unable to bear children."

Hagar listened, wide eyed and attentive, as Sarai explained the Akkadian custom of surrogate motherhood. The Egyptian was soon pregnant. It was neither fully Abram's idea nor fully Sarai's. Together they contrived a plan to put the Gyp out in front and let her take the divinely legislated hit. Of course, the baby could be a girl, but that was a necessary risk. This gambit was an insurance policy that may or may not prove to have been wise, depending on future events. And like all insurance policies, it had its price.

"Abram," called Sarai. "Come in, I pray you."

Abram entered.

"Sit down," said Sarai, politely.

Abram sat.

Sarai folded her hands and leaned forward. "The field is seeded well, is it not?... And no further seeding will be needed... will it?"

Abram was forced to nod in agreement.

Sarai continued. "And where in truth we all know the zeal of the farmer for a once-planted field, the shepherd will abide with his sheep. Will he not?"

"Most surely," mumbled Abram.

It was easier said than done. Though Abram had the good sense not to initiate an advance, Hagar was not so disciplined. Pregnancy by the chief had gotten her new found respect in the tribe, and she tended to forget her place. Places were very important to Bronze Agers.

"I saw that look!" said Sarai.

"What look?" asked Abram.

"That look you gave her."

"I gave her no look!"

"Well, she truly gave *you* one!"

"But I gave it not back!"

Ah! Then you saw it!"

"Saw what?"

"The look she gave you."

"Oh, *that* look. That was no look."

"That was a look."

"Look. If you love not the way she looks, do as you wish with her. She is your servant."

And so, Sarai drove her out of camp, pregnant and alone. Fortunately it was summer, and she had no trouble finding fields to glean.

Abram could have prevented this entire unfortunate scenario. He could have set up Hagar on the far end of the camp with some workers and simply kept her away from both of them, but he let it happen. He and Sarai had both become morally weak – and stupid. This jeopardized their whole reason for getting her pregnant in the first place. Abram had become exactly what he had sought to avoid being– a maker of stupid and immoral decisions.

Why? How? he screamed in silence. *Because I promised this El "whatsoever you wish," but failed the test when he took me up on it? Because I chose to follow my heart over against an evil law? Because I thought my knowledge of evil better than his? Ah! That one smacks of truth. But then why then did my Maker make me to think what the Most High wishes me not to think? Is my Maker an enemy of the Most High? I thought they were one, or at least not enemies. So terribly difficult – this god business.*

With the autumn rains, Hagar wandered back into camp, claiming that an angel had told her to. By now she was too swollen to be attractive, so Sarai left her alone. Or possibly it was because she had learned to play humble. Or maybe the angel told Sarai to back off. Always best to be fair about these things.

Abram sat on a rock and stared at the muddy ground. He could have stared at the horizon, but so many false hopes come from there. *Ground is good. It changes not the rules on you. You can count on it. It will always be there. Dirt and dung and thorns and rocks will always be there. But the rest… so terribly difficult.*

Sarai approached and sat beside him. "Be you troubled by anything?"

Abram heaved a sigh. "I fear a storm approaches – a storm of bad news."

He had become a competent spiritual weatherman. On a cloudy day as Abram supervised the blocking and opening of wadi trenches, one of his goatherds arrived, out of breath from running.

"Abram! Come quick!"

Oh yes, missiles can come from the horizon too. Abram got up and trotted in his direction. Reaching the top of a rise, he saw about fifty people approaching slowly from the southeast – men, women, and children, without provisions and many of them apparently injured.

He ran down the slope, and found some of Lot's herds-men among them.

"We have been attacked," said an exhausted man.

Jokshan is dead, was Abram's first thought. His sec-ond, "Where is Lot?"

"I know not," said the man.

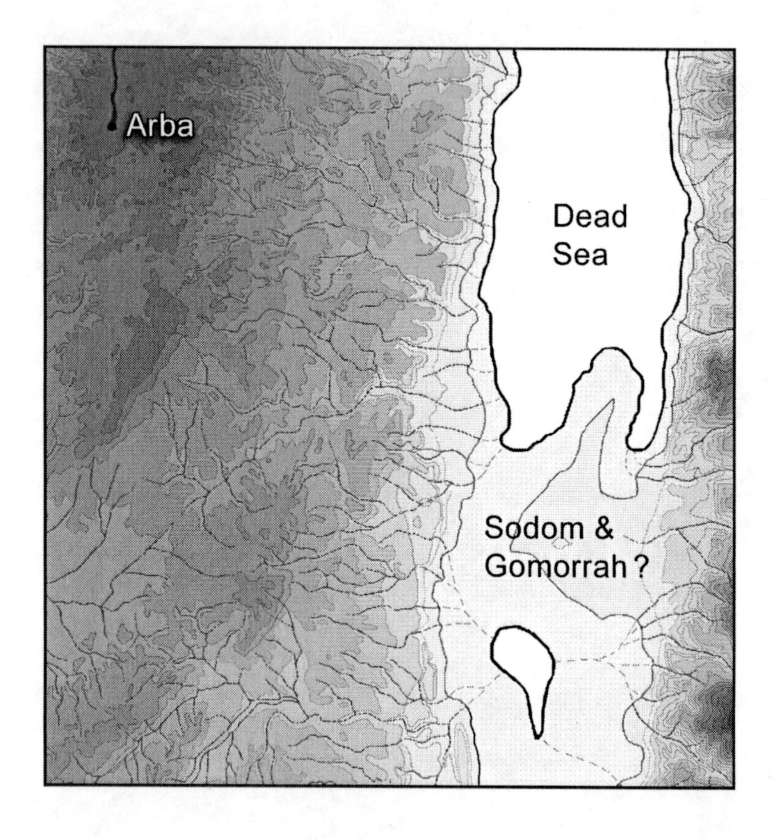
Arba
Dead Sea
Sodom & Gomorrah ?

SODOM
the price

Sodom was a small walled city on the south end of the Dead Sea. The walls were more for looks, and to thwart voyeurs, than to keep out invaders. Who would want to invade it? Though much of the valley was fertile from wadi irrigation, the land around this lowest place on earth was good for nothing but salt-tolerant crops like mallow, balsam, and barley – and hemp. They loved their hemp. But the salt was full of metals and barely palatable. They made more money selling asphalt found in blobs on the sea and in pits around it, all stinking of gas, sulphur, and sun-heated bitumen.

> Some Torah passages indicate the north end.

> Hemp is purely speculative. Evidence exists of cannabis in Asia & India at this time, but not in Canaan. Opium would have been more likely, but not as cool.

Why would anybody even want to live there? Precisely because normal people didn't! In a world held together by unquestioned authority dominated by stone deities, there had to be someplace for closet liberals to risk exposure.

Sodom and its suburb Gomorrah were the first artist colonies. They attracted those who knew they were odd for one reason or another, and preferred the company of fellow misfits to that of the mind-regimented differo-phobic masses. Lot, though sexually straight, had suffered enough religious disillusionment to be more comfortable with dissenters than with the orthodox. Even Abram had to empathize with them, despite his affliction with sanity – or possibly because of it.

Abram and several of his men mounted up and rode for Sodom. The gates were pushed in and broken, but not burnt. In fact, none of the surrounding farmland was burnt, nor was the city devastated – just plundered hastily by an army with apparently more important things to do. Riding through the streets, he shouted Lot's name until he got a response from an old woman in the market square.

"Lot was taken prisoner – his family also."

"For what? Ransom?"

"For slaves, I wager. Many were taken."

"Who has done this thing?"

"The high king of the east, Chederolamer."

Abram got as many details as possible and hurried home.

Arba was as cold as its snow-capped mountains to these refugees, lending only what hospitality was required by custom and not a bit more. Tents and blankets were offered liberally, but never lodging. The foreigners on the outskirts took up most of the burden, but even they were hesitant to let the strangers get too close.

Abram, being the most powerful kinsman of a war prisoner, was appointed their spokesman. At a town meeting of community leaders he presented their case and warned of possible danger.

"Sodom was attacked by Chederolamer and some other kings of the east. Their army is near four thousand. After Gomorrah they continued southward into Edom. When they return, perhaps they go back the same way, or perhaps they come west to Arba."

A Salemite army captain, quite out of place among the Arbaite elders, spoke. "They will not dare enter Canaan."

Abram objected. "They have already dared more."

"Fear not," replied the captain. "We have near twice their number at towns north of here. If they enter, we shall pin them against the Salt Sea."

Abram was taken aback. "How could you assemble so many soldiers so quickly? Is this but a happy accident?"

"Far from it," said the captain.

The king of Arba spoke up. "You must see, Abram, this is not our fight. Sodom and Gomorrah are under the east kings."

"Then for what be the army?"

"To discourage betrayal," replied the king. "You see, five of the east cities stopped paying due tribute to their lords. This is known by all. Many moons ago Chederolamer sent an embassy to Salem and bought a peace agreement while he punished the rebels."

"You knew of this?"

The king shrugged. "Sodom and Gomorrah are not the most savory of neighbors."

Abram turned and stomped out of the meeting to keep from losing composure.

To take up the sword, or not to take up the sword, that was Abram's question. A question difficult for any man, it is even more difficult for one who has raised the sword in the past and done shameful things with it. The alternative: to take ransom money and reward criminals for a job well done, and hope they behave honorably in return. Such a serious decision to make, and all this with the dust of ruffled god-feathers still hanging in the air. Abram dared not risk a life-shaping decision without first making every effort to atone with Old Number One. "Been-there, done-that" all you like, a miffed Fate Holder may have been the whole reason for the dung storm.

In a secluded spot, Abram had his workmen pile up rocks for an altar. He didn't feel he could trust the priests at Salem to get it right, or even target the right god. His own clumsy but sincere fumbling for words gave him more confidence of being heard than all their holy hocus-pocus.

Abram sat under a tree waiting for the workmen to finish the altar. In his hand he held a rope tied to a sheep. Occasionally he would glance at the sheep. Occasionally the sheep would glance at him. Occasionally they would glance at each other.

"Silence!" he snapped. "I made not the rules."

Slaughtering, butchering, and roasting the animal all according to ancient ritual, Abram was suddenly struck by the apparent absurdity of it all.

Why would a god wish for men to do this? They cannot eat it. Well, truly the odor is sweet. If it smells good to men, perhaps it smells good to the gods. That was as close as he could get to making sense of this strange ritual. Pressing his palms together in the traditional prayer posture, he waited for words to come. All that came was anger. Only in the effort to restrain it could he find anything to say.

"I am back. You wished it; here I am. What?"

Hearing or imagining an answer, he continued. "So be it, I repent. But repent of what?" …

"Tell me not to repent of anger. It but makes me angrier." …

"Yes, I said, *whatsoever you wish.* Yes, I meant that I would do whatsoever you say." …

"Yes, I disobeyed." …

"No, I am not sorry. I think I did right." …

"I know you can make me sorry. But if you wish me to say I am sorry when I am not, I refuse." …

"So be it, then I refuse not. Shall I say I am sorry when it be a lie?" …

"But tell me and I will say it. I will say whatsoever lie you wish me to say. What lie do you wish to hear?"

Silence on the other end. Abram stood there waiting for a reply. None came.

"Perhaps we should speak of other things." …

"I would speak of Lot." …

"I wish to go get him. But I wish to know that you desire me to go get him." …

"So how do I get you on my side?…or get me on your side? …without the evil part?" …

"Law of the first fruits. Killing babies." …

"Well it looks evil to me!" …

"I care not! It looks evil. And it makes you look evil. And if you are evil, I hate you." …

"I hate you because you made me to hate evil, so if you wish not for me to hate evil, then slay me and be done with it!"

Another silence.

"Or make me to hate what you wish me to hate. Make me to think what you wish me to think. But either make me what you wish me to be or slay me, curse it!"

Abram stood there waiting – not exactly for a reply this time because he hadn't really asked a question. Still there should be some response. No response. *Perhaps because I spoke it as a command. But it was a perfectly righteous command. So be it. Perhaps it would be better as a request.*

"How is this? If to be good in your eyes, I must become evil in my own, then I request that you end my life. Acceptable?" …

"That is the best I can do. And the best I can do is the best I can do is the best I can cursed well do!" …

"So, what of Lot?"

More silence. Abram grabbed a burning stick and smashed it over rocks in a hail of sparks. He wanted to kick the altar over – to dive onto it and die – to explode. *"Aaaaaaaaah!"* he yelled. Then falling to the ground he tried to cry and failed even at that. *What can a man do when he is furious at his god? Grab some air and squeeze hard?*

He sat up, leaned back against the altar and waited for his mind to settle. Nothing had been resolved. But something had been accomplished. He had done his best to get right with God, and he knew it. That knowledge could not be taken from him by anyone – *Anyone!*

The next day he held a meeting with his men and the refugees.

"We cannot fight them," he said. "Arba will not help us and Salem is bought off. The best we can hope for is to bargain for those most loved."

A toothless old codger named Moab was among Lot's former herdsmen who made it to safety. Abram chose him to negotiate with the enemy. He was the oldest and least valuable to anyone concerned, including himself. Probably the invaders would not kill him or keep him as a slave.

"Find out how much they demand," ordered Abram.

"Think you to buy them back?" asked Moab.

"Yes."

"How many?"

"Ask for prices," said Abram, "First for Lot, and then for his wife, and then for his daughters."

"What of his men?" asked Moab.

"Yes, surely. Them too. But let not the captors learn which you desire most. Ask the prices of many. Tell them you are of Sodom."

Moab nodded his understanding of the situation and departed.

Abram turned to one of his men. "Follow him at a distance. If he runs away, let him go. But tell me." He glanced at Zimran and Eliezer in silence, knowing they all thought the same thing. *We could all be hirelings soon.*

Abram spent the next days taking inventory of his assets, calling in all payable debts, and preparing for the worst. As mentioned, he had made friends south of Arba among the other foreigners. One of them, Mamre by name, now paid Abram a visit.

"I and my brothers had kindred at Hazazon," said Mamre. "The city has been put to the torch by Chederolamer. The Hittites too had kindred there. We would join you in battle, if you could but show us a way to win."

"How many men have you?" asked Abram.

"Some two hundred among us all who would fight. Add yours and what is left of Sodom, we have over three hundred."

"Against four thousand?" scoffed Eliezer.

"Thirty-five hundred by now," said Mamre. "And fewer as battles continue."

"Still, three hundred against that?" objected Eliezer.

"Three hundred plus the five kings of the rebels," said Abram.

Eliezer muttered, "Truly, we have them surrounded."

"Wait until Moab returns," said Abram. "He will have seen things that may help us."

After Mamre had departed, Zimran leaned toward Abram. "Know you that Mamre is an Amorite?"

"I know," replied Abram.

"And what of it?" said Eliezer. "Amos are good fighters, and they avenge their kindred."

Abram exchanged a quick glance with Zimran. No point in revealing any more than necessary.

Abram thought back to his prayers at the altar. Was this a case of divine meddling or not? If so, was it a message of forgiveness, or would it turn out to be one of retribution? There was no cause for confidence.

By the time Moab returned from Edom, a panel of generals was anxious to grill him.

"Ten minas of silver they say. That for Lot."

"You have done well," said Abram. "But tell us where the enemy is and all you learned of them."

"After Sodom they went south, they did, to Zoar, then to Bozrah. They now press along the Kings' Highway toward the south sea."

"Did they burn Zoar and Bozrah?" asked Abram.

"No," replied Moab.

"A thing of note," said Abram to Mamre. "They burn not Sodom or Gomorrah. And they burn not Zoar or

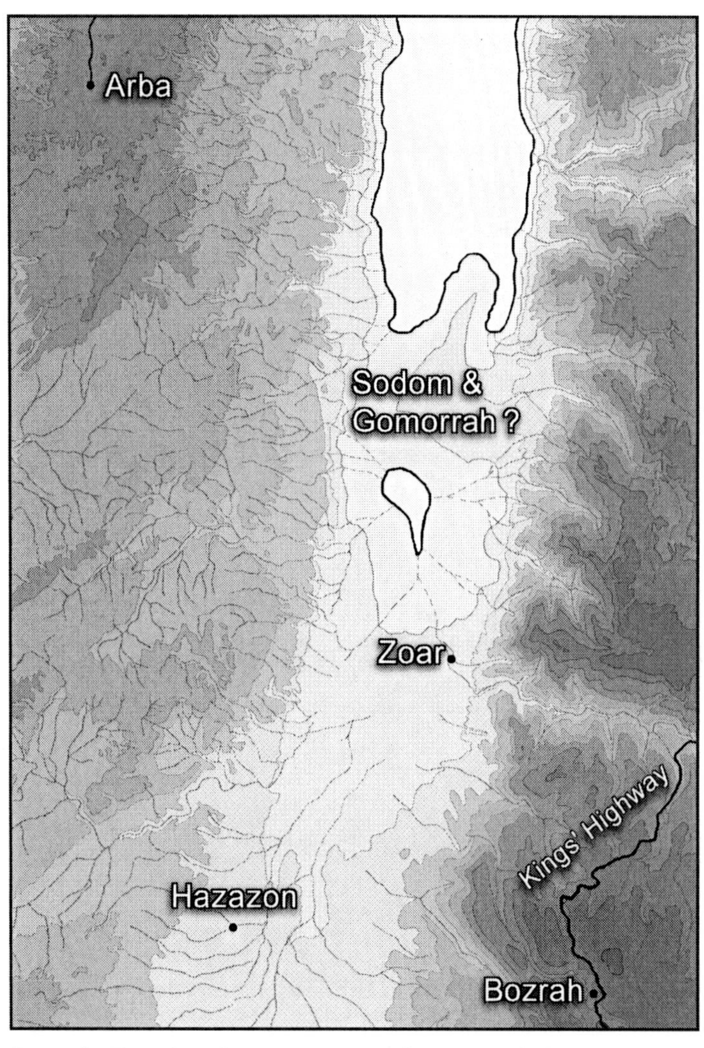

Bozrah. But they burn Hazazon far west of the highway."

"What think you?" asked Mamre.

"Have they cause to hate Hazazon above other cities?" asked Abram.

"No," replied Mamre. "The king of Hazazon was not of the rebels."

"My wager," said Abram, "they burn not the cities they seek to plunder again as they return north. They need those cities for provisions."

"What then?" asked the Hittite chief. "Shall *we* burn them?"

Mamre balked. "Not if we wish to live with them afterward."

"We warn them," said Abram. "We tell them all along the trade route that Chederolamer shall return. And this time he will have no cause to spare them. They must hide their animals, and burn their fields."

"All their fields?" asked Mamre.

"All that are ripe, but not those that are green."

"What if they hear us not?" asked the Hittite.

"Then we speak firmly but politely, with torches ready."

14 WAR
the redemption

Despite having only three hundred men, Abram chose to divide them. A hundred mounted Amorites rode to Sodom, and thence northward up the Kings' Highway east of the Dead Sea, politely warning all in their path of the terrible horde behind them. Aiding in the destruction of anything that could be used by the enemy, the Amorites also ambushed supply detachments. Abram and the rest did the same at Zoar and Bozrah, then backed off to wait.

It worked. Chederolamer had to send his allies on foraging parties westward into the Wilderness of Zin. These could not be restrained from raiding cities all the way to Amalek – very bad politics. He was over-extended and now had to return, not knowing what to expect along the way. All of the five kings whom he had chased to the middle of Edom now became aggressors. Chederolamer's retreat was orderly at first, but after his army passed Sodom Abram and his two hundred fresh troops joined the pursuers. From there, the pace quickened.

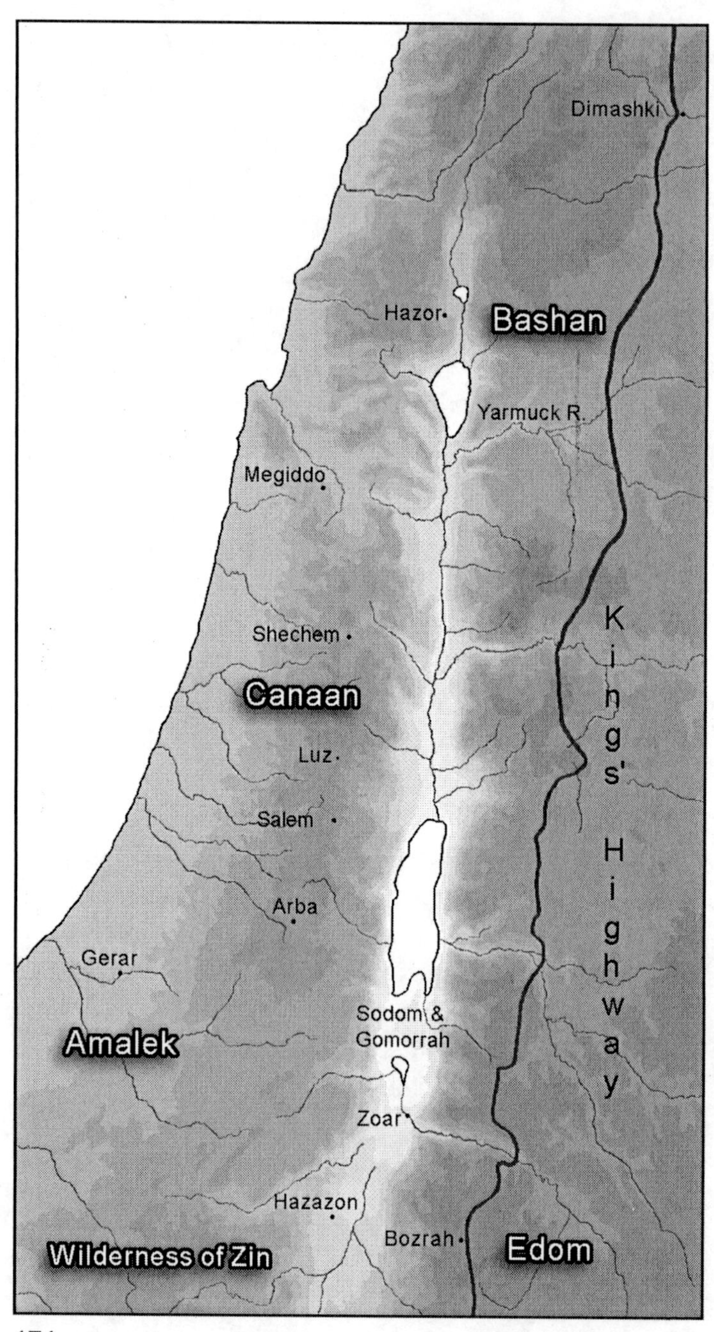
Dimashki
Hazor
Bashan
Yarmuck R.
Megiddo
Shechem
Canaan
Luz
Salem
Arba
Gerar
Amalek
Sodom &
Gomorrah
Zoar
Hazazon
Bozrah
Edom
Wilderness of Zin
Kings' Highway

When they got to Bashan, the remaining hundred Amorites rushed out from the oak forest, and the chase became a rout. The hostages were left chained together in a ravine, and abandoned. Their rescue only slightly slowed down the pursuers.

Of course, there were many bloody battle scenes with gobs of gratuitous gore and a tearful and touching reunion, but so what? What did it all mean? Was this evidence of divine meddling? The most one could give it is a maybe. If so, what was the message? Abram was being rewarded, but for what?

Because I did my best? he thought. It appears that I am now forgiven for those unfortunate deeds so long ago against the Amorites. But does this mean I am permitted to disobey a law of the Most High because it feels evil? That question had not been addressed. And at every lull in battle, it rose to Abram's consciousness.

Their objective achieved in Bashan, the victors continued to chase Chederolamer all the way to Dimashki just for the fun of it. Now loaded with booty, they returned southward along the same route. News of every part of their success had rippled through Canaan at the pace of a hurried donkey.

> Pilgrim turned warrior saves kinsman,
> rescues neighbors from invaders –
> make that *evil* invaders.

Nothing shows the favor of the gods more than military victory. All Canaan now saw Abram as divinely blessed. And this sentiment was not lost on Melchizedek. The son of El would make it clear which god was to be praised.

Tired soldiers marching with tired pack animals behind leaders on tired donkeys, the returning victors re-entered Bashan. At the Yarmuk River, they found three mounted men waiting to greet them.

"They are from Salem," said Abram, recognizing the messenger, Gabriel, and his two servants. The three rode up alongside the leaders for some casual saddle talk.

"His Holiness wishes to convey his joy at your victory."

The five kings nodded politely.

"And to you, Abram, he wishes to convey great joy at the recovery of your kinsman."

"Truly?" replied Abram. "I pray you convey to his Holiness my joy at his joy."

"His Holiness wishes to welcome you home with a great feast at Salem."

"For me alone?" asked Abram. "Surely his Holiness thinks not that my hand alone won this victory?"

"Surely not," replied Gabriel. "Bring Lot and your friends and your entire band… less, of course, the armies of the east kings."

All had a good laugh at that one.

"Tell his Holiness we will be most happy to attend," replied Abram, "we and our comrades, the Amorites and the Hittites."

"His Holiness will be overjoyed," said Gabriel.

"And the Sodomites and the Gomorrans," added Abram.

Gabriel winced.

"I thank you, Abram," interjected Bera, king of Sodom, "but I and my people have much to repair."

"You are my friend, are you not, Majesty?"

"Most truly."

"Then surely you have been invited by the judge of Canaan to a feast. Would you dishonor both him and me?"

No sound but that of hooves on dirt disturbed the next few seconds. Then Gabriel thought of a fix.

"The kings of Sodom and Gomorrah are truly welcome, but without their armies."

"What think you, Majesty?" asked Abram. "Can you trust his Holiness without your army?"

The king of Gomorrah now spoke up. "I would be happy to lead them back for you, Bera. An invitation from the most holy judge of Canaan is not to be snubbed, least of all the first one ever."

"But truly I have these spoils to guard."

"Bring your treasure with you," said Abram. "I promise you no evil shall befall it."

Bera looked at Abram and shrugged in compliance.

Abram smiled at Gabriel. "Tell his Holiness we most gratefully accept his invitation. Expect about four hundred."

Gabriel nodded, pursed his lips, and departed westward with his servants. Lot got a hearty laugh out of it. The rest kept it down to a suppressed grin.

"If we must leave for Canaan," said Bera, "best to do it here. The Jordan deepens farther south."

That evening they celebrated their last meal as allies with song and laughter, but not long past sunset. They were just too exhausted. The next morning Abram and friends split off to the west.

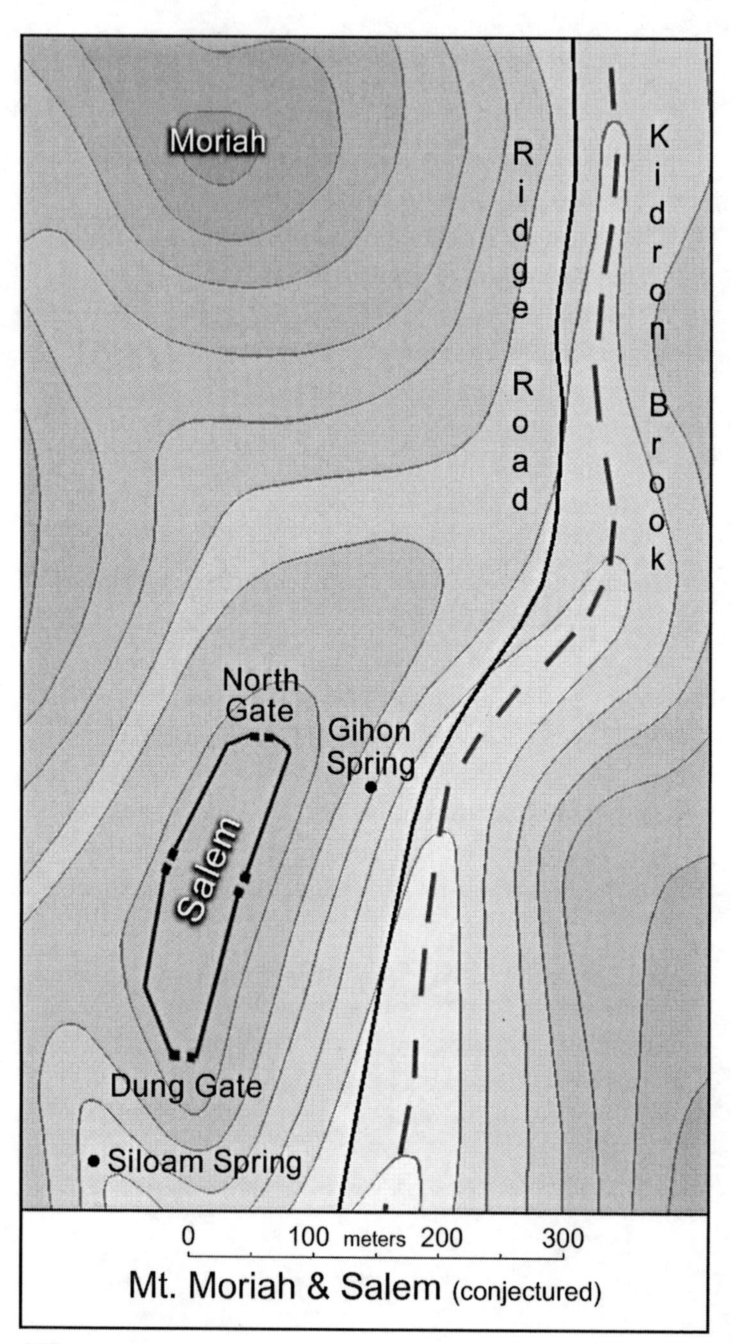

Mt. Moriah & Salem (conjectured)

15 SALEM
the homecoming

"Four hundred!?" exclaimed Melchizedek.

Gabriel shrugged. "I can return, Holiness, and tell him Salem is not prepared for such a number."

"No," grumbled the king, "we have a place for them... outside the city."

"One other matter, Holiness. He intends to bring the king of Sodom with him."

Melchizedek scratched his nose and fidgeted. "He intends?"

"I told him you said he could bring his friends – without their armies."

"Did I say that, Jebus?"

"As I recall, yes, Holiness."

Melchizedek bit the inside of his lip. "When did the king of Sodom become his friend?"

"On campaign, it would appear, Holiness."

The king slumped into his chair. "Truly if I said it, I said it."

A spiritual leader must lead in spirit. Melchizedek's expressed exuberance for the celebrity of the day must equal, or exceed popular sentiment. And having fulfilled all prior business agreements with the losers, he was not obligated to mourn for them. At his direction, a festival ground was set up outside the north gate on the saddle of land between Salem and Moriah. It was enough to accommodate not only the four hundred, but half again as many Canaanite high rollers.

Comparing it to Abimelech's birthday, there was everything but the entertainers – the same music, pomp, good food and liquor, but the spirit was completely different. These people were not here to pay obligatory respects to a power broker; they were here voluntarily to celebrate and get close to something noble – a rarity in any age.

Still, all this shimmering virtuosity was no reason not to charge for seating, or to ignore theatrical pragmatics. Melchizedek was careful to save his own entry until after applause had died down for the rescuers and rescued – and after they all had a drink or two.

The high point of the day was the meeting of hero and head of cult. It took place in the center of a large circle of cheering spectators, Abram kneeling and Melchizedek forbidding him to, both as required. Visible to all, but audible to none, judge and hero were free to speak candidly, as long as they smiled.

"You are the man of the day, O pilgrim."

"You could have made this war unnecessary," said Abram.

"Perhaps," said Melchizedek. "My decision was a wager of judgment. You know not the weight of this office."

"Do you wish to meet the king of Sodom?"

"Knows he of my part in this?"

"Doubtful," replied Abram. "If so, not from me."

"Still, you should not have brought him here."

"A wager of judgment."

Melchizedek maintained his smile. "The Most High looks to be with you for now, but lean not heavily on it."

"Do you still believe one should give up?"

"You frighten me, pilgrim. Not good. You stand on dangerous ground. Now hug me while we still love each other."

They embraced. Bystanders cheered again. It was a moment worth milking, and Melchizedek did not waste it. He raised his staff to silence the crowd.

"Blessed be Abram of El Most High!"

Throwing an arm around the hero and leading him back into the crowd made it clear that the meeting with Bera would have to wait. Other introductions took precedence. Only after they were no longer on stage could the judge appear to chide Abram for not introducing the king of Sodom sooner.

Seating arrangements for dinner made for another minor glitch. Melchizedek traditionally sat in the center. But having the "ungodly king" on either side of him would raise eyebrows. So they placed Abram as a buffer between them, and added two seats on the other side for the kings of Shechem and Arba.

Dinner conversation under the head canopy consisted of Abram giving a blow-by-blow recount of the entire operation. Melchizedek kept it moving along gracefully with intensely interested questions, the two kings on his other side chiming in with jovial quips. The king of Sodom was ignored except when Abram deferred to his perspective on certain points.

At the conclusion of dinner, when things started winding down, the Canaanites were still eager for more of the new star. The call for a speech grew from sporadic muttering to a ground-thumping chant. Abram, of course, declined until Melchizedek was virtually forced to beg him to address the crowd. Upon agreeing, Abram stood. He had to raise his hands to quiet their applause. He loved it.

"First, I must honor our allies, who prodded me to action by their courage, and who fought by our side: Mamre the Amorite and his brothers, and all the Amorites and Hittites of Arba."

The named parties heartily cheered themselves as the Canaanites applauded.

"Also the five kings of the east cities who took the heaviest losses, and inflicted the same upon the enemy. None save one could be here today; I salute His Majesty, King Bera of Sodom."

Applause was cordial and restrained.

"As you can see from the baggage trains, we all did well from the enemy. And from my spoils, I now dedicate a tenth part to our honored ruler, his Holiness, the judge of Canaan."

All applauded until Melchizedek graciously shushed them. But Abram was not finished.

"For what would we do without his fearless protection?… his just and righteous judgment of disputes?… and his timely warning when danger may come?" Turning to his host, Abram raised his goblet. "To the judge!"

All raised goblets and cheered. Melchizedek smiled through clenched teeth and took it.

After a pleasant night's sleep in the orchards of the Kidron Valley, the hung-over but happy allies formed ranks and proceeded south. Abram now had time to ask a question that had been on his mind. He turned to Lot.

"Do you remember an Akkadian named Jokshan? I sent him over to you."

"The one with the newborn?"

"Yes. What became of him?"

"Slain in the first attack."

"His wife also?"

"Yes."

"And his children?"

"All dead."

In two days of leisurely journey, they reached Arba and detoured eastward descending into the green hill country. After a pleasant noon-day meal it was once again time for Abram and Lot to part. King Bera, too, had a farewell to offer.

"We of Sodom and Gomorrah have different gods, for we are truly different people. Many think we have no knowledge of good and evil. I wish to correct this error. Abram, to you I give not a tenth part, but the whole of all we took from the enemy, and my deepest gratitude."

"Majesty, truly you will need this to rebuild your city."

"I insist."

"Your Majesty's grace abounds," said Abram. "Let the Amorites and Hittites take their portion, but I fear that if your children's children think you made me rich, they may come back for it."

All laughed.

"Would you deny me this honor?" asked Bera.

"I would truly honor your Majesty, but I made a vow.

Before I chose to war, I promised the Most High that if He grant us victory, I would take no profit save my due portion. My servant, Eliezer, heard me. Is this not true?"

"Most true, Majesty," responded Eliezer, "not a thread, a shoe latchet. I myself heard him clearly at the altar."

This was sufficient. The king delivered two thirds of his winnings to the Amorites and Hittites. Abram gave Lot a parting embrace, then faced Bera. Moisture in the king's eyes revealed more than he would have preferred.

"You have bestowed abundant grace upon my people, Abram. Perhaps more than you know."

Still, neither man felt comfortable enough to extend his right hand to the other.

"El be with you," said Bera. He and Lot then departed southward with their entourage. Abram and his allies turned west.

ARBA
the fruition

Upon arrival at camp, Abram's homecoming was picture perfect, a tearful Sarai rushing to him with a warm embrace. But this was interrupted by Hagar. The girl was beaming with joy and held an unmistakable bundle at her breast. She pushed forward proudly and presented it to Abram.

"A son. El hears me."

Abram did not look at the child. He kissed Hagar's forehead and stroked her hair, then realized that the girl was too happy. Turning to Sarai he asked, "Have you not told her?"

Sarai lowered her eyes. "I thought you would wish to"

"*You* tell her!" snapped Abram. He gave the child back to Hagar and walked away fuming. *Must I fight a war and also suffer this?*

Sarai asked Hagar to hand the child to Musha, but by now, the Egyptian was suspicious and resistive. None of this went easily.

Abram waited near his tent, determined to get this business over with as quickly as possible. The sound of Hagar's wailing chilled the air. Musha came out of the tent cradling the infant. She held him out to his father, but Abram forbade her.

"Prepare for journey," he ordered.

He would not sleep in his tent until all matters of necessity were resolved. Taking Musha and an assistant with him, Abram immediately set out for Salem with the child. The three day journey remained silent except for the occasional cry of the infant.

Arriving at the temple with his bundle Abram informed the guards of the nature of his business, and was directed to a small waiting room in the back of the courtyard. He entered and sat on a comfortable leather chair which had been provided for patrons. On the wall was a painting of a man kneeling before a great bull and offering up an infant. Next to it a painting of the same man smiling in rays of sunlight and surrounded by many children. *Government,* thought Abram. *Religion... government... religion.*

A pleasant-faced old cleric entered and opened wide his arms. "The blessings of El upon you and your house, Abram."

"This is my first-born son."

The cleric smiled broadly. "El be praised! Many of the people have prayed that your wife might conceive. They shall have great joy at this news."

"Give them my thanks, I pray you," replied Abram, "but my wife is still barren. This child is of a concubine."

The cleric's smile suddenly dropped. "Oh... unfortunate!" he said, to Abram's surprise. The smile snapped back into place. "But in that case, you will be happy to know that your son is spared."

Three days hence, Abram and Musha were back home. He returned somberly to his tent, carrying the wrapped infant in his arms.

Hagar's wailing had silenced, but it still showed on her face. This turned to squeals of delight as Abram handed the child back to her. She held him protectively and huddled in a corner, still not sure that the next moment might bring another reversal.

Abram sat down beside Sarai without making eye-contact.

"Sons of bond servants are not allowed."

Her face sank into the palm of her hand. It might not have been so bad if they hadn't both known they deserved it. But Sarai would not accept guilt easily. Storming out of the tent angry and teary eyed, she walked briskly straight for Eliezer's digs.

"Eliezer!" she called. "Why told you not the truth to Abram?"

He came out. "What truth?"

"That sons of bond women are no good for haram logs!" she sobbed.

Eliezer slapped his forehead. "El's beard! All this time, it was but for *that?*"

Hagar called him Ishmael. As the heir apparent, he was treated with more than the usual respect by everyone except Sarai, who tried valiantly to suppress her hatred of the boy – and his mother – and Abimelech – and herself. Fortunately for all, she had the nobility to become a very sorrowful woman, instead of a bitch. This time Abram had the good sense to give Hagar and their son separate living quarters away from his own.

In this awkward but acceptable condition, the tribe spent the next five years.

17 ARBA
the three men

In the heat of a summer's day Ishmael and some little girls were playing outside in center camp. Abram watched from his tent, perplexed at their behavior. Ishmael was wearing the sleeve of a discarded linen tunic over his arm. Holding the arm up at forty-five degrees, with the sleeve drooping over his fist, he chased the girls around, all of them giggling and squealing. When he peeled it back, revealing his bare arm, they stopped running and came back to him.

"Sarai," said Abram, "what be that game Ishmael is playing?"

Sarai glanced out of the tent. "Oh, Hagar taught them that. It is the shmuck game."

"The *what?*"

"Egyptian men have no skin over their… acorns… as everyone knows."

Abram nodded and looked back at the children. "Strange people, those Egyptians. But why would Hagar teach that to Ishmael? Think you she plans to do such a thing to him?"

"As I hear it, she wishes for *you* to do it."

"What? To *Ishmael?*"

"Who other?"

"Bloody butchers!" huffed Abram. "Surely if the Maker had wished for man to be bob-staffed he would have bobbed it himself."

"Oh Abi, be not so Akkadian. Truly, it *is* cleaner… So says Hagar."

One of the children stopped playing and looked northward curiously. The others did the same. Abram came out of his tent to see what had captured their attention.

Three men riding donkeys slowly approached the camp. *Gabriel?* thought Abram at first. But no, these men were different. They were dressed in black and wore their turban tails pulled across their mouths like desert dwellers – or bandits. But only three of them riding into a camp of thirty-some adult men? Hardly bandits.

"Children!" called Abram. "Play somewhere other."

Abram whistled a caution signal, and several men came out of their tents and awaited further instructions.

The three rode up. Their clothing was fine woven and without patches. Their demeanor revealed subtle signs of confidence normally associated with noble rank. One, the apparent leader, removed the cloth from his face. Abram didn't recognize him. He was a tall, well-groomed man in his forties.

"El be with you. We would speak with Abram."

"El be with you. I am Abram."

"Melchizedek sent us," said the tall man.

No Canaanite would have called the judge by his personal name.

"Sarai," called Abram, "we have guests."

Seated on mats opposite Abram under the front canopy of his tent, the three kept their eyes on Abram as if sizing him up. The two shorter ones remained masked. Sarai silently provided food and wine.

"I pray you forgive my friends," began the tall man, shaping a piece of bread and scooping some relish from the communal dish. "They will happily dip bread with you, but they would remain unknown."

With impeccable manners, the tall man brought the bread to his mouth. In nearly comedic contrast his two associates passed theirs under their masks.

"We know you and honor you, Abram," said the shorter of them, then biting into his bread.

The tall man continued. "We are servants of certain powers from the east. And these powers have cares in the areas of Sodom and Gomorrah. I am told that you also have cares there."

"Go on," said Abram.

"Another invasion will come," said the tall man dispassionately. "This time no prisoners will be taken. As we hear it, your one care in the area is for your brother. If your brother were to leave Sodom, then you would have no care in the area. True?"

"Truly he is my nephew," said Abram.

The tall man continued. "We desire to learn what would be your price to quietly get your nephew out of Sodom, and to have no more care in the area."

"And how know you," said Abram, "that I will not warn the kings of Sodom and Gomorrah of your plans? – also the other three kings who are their allies?"

"The kings of Sodom and Gomorrah have been warned, and warned again. As for the other kings, they are among those who gave warning. Two of their envoys now sit before you." He nodded to his masked associates.

The short man spoke up. "This is not for payment of tribute, Abram."

"Then for what be it?"

"You cannot guess?" said the tall man.

Abram guessed. "What be it of Sodom and Gomorrah–"

"Their deeds are an abomination before all gods of the Earth!" blurted the third man, abruptly breaking his silence.

"Their deeds are what they have always been," said Abram. "Why be the gods so angry now?"

The short man leaned forward raising his palms. "So long as they abode within their own cities, we saw them not. But now they have begun to come out."

"How prideful," said Abram.

The third man, still angry, spoke again. "If men do what is shameful in secret behind barred doors, we would not care. But we will not have them show it openly."

Abram snorted. "So because they set your teeth on edge, then you would lock them up, or slay them."

The tall man offered a fact without emotion. "It is written in your own Tablets of Noah that such men must be stoned to death."

The third man remained irritated. "How can we tell our sons why two men kiss in the street?"

Abram shrugged. "We all kiss in the street."

"Not like that!"

The short man: "And some say their boldness was kindled by you yourself."

Abram's mouth fell open. *"Me?!"*

"Your friendship at Salem five years past," said the short man.

Abram was stunned to silence. Could his good intentions have led to this? But the third man gave him no time to reflect.

"What do you tell your children of Sodomites?"

Abram hesitated, then parried clumsily. "We have no children."

"Well we have!" slammed the third.

The tall one calmed him. "Forbear, I pray you," he said, rising to his feet, "Abram, I can see that you are not a man to talk price. But get your kinsman out of there. Sodom and Gomorrah have been declared haram."

The two masked men also rose, and the three started toward their donkeys. Abram rose and followed them trying to think of an argument.

"Many good people live in Sodom."

"Then get them out also," responded the tall man.

The three mounted up.

"What if fifty be there?" asked Abram.

The tall man smiled. "Find fifty and we shall spare the city."

The third man fired a parting shot. "You, my good man, will have a son."

A laugh was heard from inside Abram's tent.

The man continued. "If the gods be just, that woman, your wife, will bear a son, and you will learn the sorrow of a loving father in an evil world."

The three rode back northward. Sarai came out of the tent and stood beside Abram.

"Who were those men?" she asked.

"They said not."

And it mattered not. What mattered was warning his nephew.

SODOM
the two men

When Abram had sent Jokshan and his family to Lot, he had received in return the family of one named Benammi. This Benammi, being a straight-laced fellow, had always felt uncomfortable living near Sodom and was therefore the perfect candidate for exchange. Since he knew where Lot lived, Abram chose him to deliver the warning. Benammi then invited a young herdsman named Korah to accompany him.

Now Benammi did not trust Sodomites in any way. So rather than ride donkeys and park them with local livery, he chose to walk. On the dusk of the third day he and Korah approached Sodom's west gate.

The gate was attended by a group of soldiers, partly in uniform, but with flares of obviously individual design. They looked more like cronies hanging out than gate guards. As Benammi and Korah got within earshot, this group went silent. The sergeant at the check table was plump for a soldier and had what appeared to be breasts bulging over his… *her* chest armor. Sarge greeted them.

"Ho."

Benammi kept his eyes glued to his/her face. "El be–," he began, but thought better of it. "Ho."

Sarge was chewing a piece of spiced tar, popular in the area.

"What seek ya?"

"We are here to visit Lot," said Benammi, "the nephew of Abram of Arba."

He/she gazed at them calmly – chewing.

A figure in the shadows commented, "I thought they were brothers."

"Lot loves to say that," replied Benammi.

Sarge continued chewing for a few seconds before asking, "You family?"

"We work for Abram," replied Benammi.

Every time it was Sarge's turn to speak, he/she seemed to pause for a few seconds. "Know you where they live?"

"Yes," replied Benammi.

"Where?"

Benammi fumbled, "He has a butcher shop on the market square… this side, next to the shop where they do skin pictures – pictures on skin."

After a pause another anonymous voice said, "He is not there no more."

"He moved?" asked Benammi nervously.

"Lot is there," said the voice. "Tattoo man moved."

"I am sure we could still find it," said Benammi. "–Lot's place."

Sarge glanced around to get a consensus, then decided, "Leave the swords here."

Benammi and Korah delivered their swords, then inched toward the entry.

"Not yet," said Sarge, nodding to a pair of patrolmen.

The patrolmen approached Benammi and Korah, smiled, and began to pat them down – slowly and looking into their eyes. Finding nothing unexpected, they backed away. Sarge gave a hand motion indicating that the visitors may enter. All eyes followed them past the gate until they were out of sight.

Sarge turned to the patrolmen. "Follow. If they do anything strange..."

The patrolmen did not need the order completed. Following Benammi and Korah at a distance, they sped up and slowed down as needed to keep sight of them through the crooked streets.

The two stiffs stood out like monks at a carnival. Painted faces turned to stare as they passed by. Benammi kept focused on his goal, but Korah checked out the surroundings.

"They follow us," he said softly to Benammi.

"How many?"

"Two at the least."

They sped up. The two patrolmen did the same. They passed by a group of soldiers conversing outside of an inn. The patrolmen motioned to the soldiers to follow them. Benammi and Korah now broke into a trot. The followers did likewise. Others began to follow. Benammi and Korah began to run. Coming into the home stretch, they announced their presence.

"Lot! Lot!"

Lot's apartment behind his shop on the market square was upper middle class and modern; it had a door. Lot now heard them and opened it. Benammi and Korah rushed past him.

"Shut the gate!" shouted Benammi.

"The strangelings are after us," cried Korah. *"Shut it!"*

Lot turned and saw a crowd approaching. He slammed the door and barred it, then turned back wide-eyed.

"What?"

"Abram sent us," panted Benammi.

"Lot," called one of the patrolmen, clearly audible through the wide cracks around the door, "we must talk to those men."

"Send them out," demanded the other patrolman.

"Do it not!" begged Korah.

Lot turned to Benammi, "What be this about?"

A patrolman, thinking the question was to him, replied, "We must know who they are."

"They work for my brother," replied Lot. "What be this–"

"We need but to know their business here."

Lot asked Benammi, "Why be you here?"

"Message from Abram."

Korah felt a defense necessary. "We but walked down the street."

Lot spoke through the crack. "My brother sent them."

"So be it," said a patrolman. "Let us take them to the chief of watch. We will bring them back forthwith."

Korah jumped behind Lot. "They wish to have mischief with us."

Lot spoke again through the crack. "They are my guests."

"Lot, send them out!" demanded a patrolman. "Or we shall bring a troop here."

"As you wish," said Lot. "Back away from the door."

Benammi joined Korah behind Lot. *"No!"*

"Do it not!" begged Korah.

"All is well," said Lot. Then turning to his two daughters huddled in a corner, "Come here, girls. Come here, my dears."

Lot's daughters timidly complied. He gently guided them to the door. "Tell the nice men outside that you wish them to go away. They will hear you." Then to Benammi and Korah, "Unbar the door."

The men did so. Lot pushed his screaming daughters out, and pulled the door shut.

"Bar it!"

Benammi and Korah did so.

"Take my daughters!" shouted Lot. "They are virgins!"

"What!" said the patrolmen.

"They are all yours," said Lot.

The crowd backed away in shock, then simultaneously fell into laughter. One of the patrolmen spoke through the crack.

"Lot, uhh… truly it is not like that."

But Lot was not fooled. "These men are under my roof, and they are not that way."

The people outside reacted with either dumb-struck incredulity or uncontrollable laughter.

The second patrolmen turned to the first. "Truly, if you were a spy, would you lodge with this dung-heart?"

It was sufficient. The patrolmen stepped away from the door.

"Pay them no heed, friends. They are but fools, all of them."

The crowd dispersed.

"Papa!" cried the daughters, "Let us in."

Lot opened a window and peeked out. It appeared safe. He unbarred the door and the girls rushed in. Then barring it again, he turned to Benammi and Korah, "Some wine?"

The envoys delivered their message and spent the night. Next morning Lot personally escorted them out. This time, instead of staring at them, the townsfolk turned away in disgust.

In Sodom, as in any community of self-centered individualists, the worst thing you could do to a person was ignore him. At the gate, even the guards looked away. Not bothering to reclaim their swords, Benammi and Korah hastened out of the city.

Back at camp, they reported to Abram in such excitement that he could barely sort it out.

"Truly my lord, we barely escaped with our lives."

"And our virtue intact."

"They desired us in that most unholy manner."

"But the hand of El was upon us."

"Your brother was valiant in our defense."

"Nephew."

"Stood right in the gate way, he did. Held them all at bay."

"Would have sacrificed his very daughters to protect us."

"Then in the morning he led us straight through them."

"But he need not have."

"For El had made us invisible."

"Struck them all blind, he did."

"A miracle."

Abram took it all in. "So, you told him, yes? – of the invasion?"

"Oh. Yes, most surely," said Benammi.

"Good. I thank you."

Benammi and Korah never could quite agree on the details, but they had done their job, and they had spoken well of Lot, and the Most High was given credit for their success. These were, after all, the things that really mattered.

ARBA
the fulfillment

At the end of a crisp autumn day Abram arrived at his tent. Sarai and Musha sat beside a fire, Musha cooking, Sarai sewing.

Without looking up from her work Sarai announced, "I am with child."

Abram took a deep breath, let it out, and delivered the prescribed response. "Glory to El, my dove. That is wonderful."

The women continued their work.

The next day Abram chose Zimran to accompany him on what was ostensibly a search for new pastures. Near dusk, he turned his donkey off the road. "We are not here on business, my friend," he explained. "We are here to get quietly drunk."

Zimran made a fire and prepared a sheep shank for dinner. Abram lifted a goatskin of strong wine and took a large mouthful.

"Many years ago at Haran by the light of a crescent moon I did a foolish thing."

"Surely that is dust in the wind, my lord."

"Not that," said Abram. "I speak of another foolish thing on another night – a night when I asked a god to hear his voice."

Abram then told Zimran what he had dared tell no one – the full history of his spiritual incarceration. After roast mutton and a quarter skin of wine he finished his tale with Sarai's pregnancy.

"But all this may be naught," said drunken Abram. "I may be mad. Here is the whole of it. You find yourself in a world where people tell you that a great and mighty Person rules it, but you can not see Him. But He can make your life happy if He loves you or grievous if He loves you not. And He loves you only if you obey Him. And then these people tell you what He has told other men long ago, and they show you some tablets to prove it. But the tablets prove naught, because you know not if the writer lied. Nevertheless, the tablets hold many commands – what to do and not do. Most of them look wise, and you agree that people should obey them. But some are frightfully strange, and some look truly evil. What do you do?"

Zimran, whose part in the conversation consisted of little more than grunts and shrugs, now offered one of each. Abram continued.

"I will tell you. You can throw it all away and do what you wish – hope to heaven it is but a lie. Or you can throw it away and do what appears good to you. But after you throw it away, why do what appears good? Who will reward you for it? The world? Hah!

"Or you can go the other way. You can believe it all

and do what this God of Tablets commands. Surely He must know good and evil better than you. So whatsoever He tells you must be right. Care not for how it feels.

"Most men choose one of these two ways and somehow live with it. But if you have tried them both and found madness either way, then what?" He looked at Zimran. "Then what?"

Zimran rubbed his head. "Abi my friend, this is far beyond me."

"I know, I know, my friend. But I needed your ear."

They slept it off and returned to camp the next day. It would be neither wine nor counsel by which Abram arrived at his decision, but simple fear and a reasoned response to it. He would flee the jurisdiction of this seemingly evil god. He would get out of Canaan. In a week the tribe was packed up and heading south.

On the second day of journey the vineyards and olive groves were gone. The terebinth woodlands began to give way to junipers and tamarisks. In the middle of the third day Abram looked east and saw two large columns of smoke rising from the Dead Sea valley.

Benammi tried to offer a word of comfort. "Truly my lord, they deserved it." He quickly clarified the comment. "The men of Sodom and Gomorrah, I mean – not Lot and his family."

Abram's clenched his teeth and looked away. He could not help wanting to smack the man.

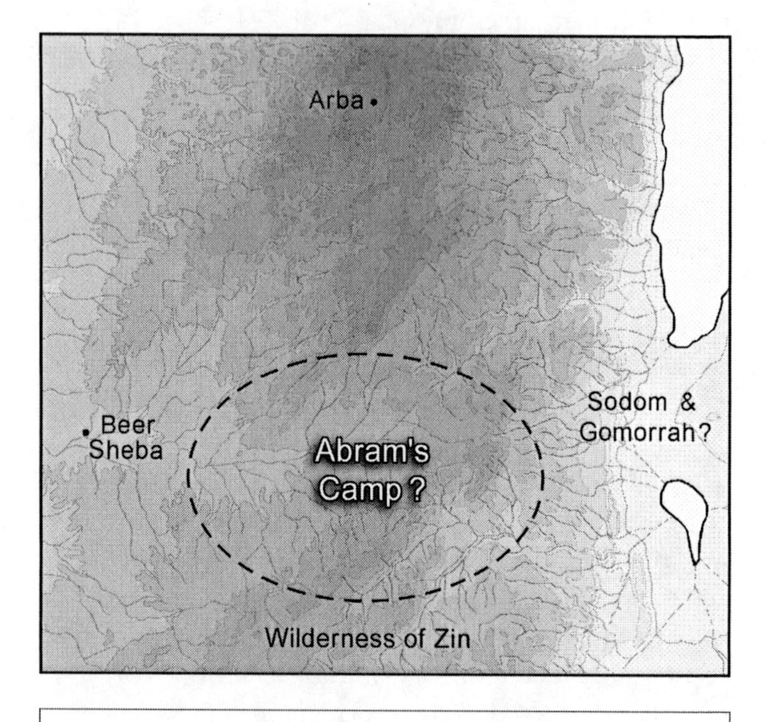

The Torah says the location of Abram's camp was Beer-Sheba, but this is probably a late interpolation. Archaeological evidence would date the well at present-day Beer-Sheba no earlier than 1200 BCE.

20 WILDERNESS
the evasion

On the fourth day, the junipers and tamarisks gave way to thistles and the people began to murmur. Eliezer rode up along side of Abram.

"My lord, if we go much farther, naught remains save the Wilderness of Zin where the only green is wormwood."

"Be this land outside of Canaan?"

"I told you," said Eliezer, "Canaan has not borders. It is but a region. Out here no man can say if you are in it or out of it."

Abram sighed. "Then let us seek low ground and dig a well."

Getting out of Canaan for the birth of a first-born was not unheard of, but not common either. The surrounding areas, except for Amalek and Egypt, had the same sacrificial custom, often more hideous than a quick execution. Still, a man might take his pregnant wife to a foreign city, and let her bear her first child unnoticed. When they departed, it would usually be to a new location. If they returned home with a first-born son, they would face the contempt of all who had paid their dues.

Among the Abramites, however, few would feel contempt for their lord, and none would show it. But it was a dreary eight months for all on the edge of the wilderness. Trading expeditions were few, and every family planted gardens. The well was busy every waking hour and needed constant deepening.

"It is a boy," came Musha's voice from the birthing tent. Somehow Abram and Sarai both knew it would be. Without the traditional bleat of ram's horn, the men celebrated, but with mixed emotions. Sarai called him Isaac – "laughter" – a self-effacing commemoration of her response to the masked envoy who had prophesied the event, and was now regarded as either a seer or an angel.

Of course, no one could convince Hagar of that. To Hagar, Sarai's "laughter" was nothing but a spiteful barb directed straight at her. No longer the mother of the heir apparent, she was moved with her five-year-old to a remote corner of the camp. Now they were spare parts – back-up equipment to be kept around in case of emergency.

Four years passed, each diminishing the status of Hagar and Ishmael in the tribe. Neither could help the resentment generated in them by the popular newcomer. Nor could Ishmael help but show it.

On a summer day Isaac ran away from Ishmael crying to Abram and Sarai.

"What be it, Isaac?" asked Sarai.

"Ishmael threw dung on me."

"Truly not," said the smirking boy. "He fell in it."

Punishment would only make Ishmael more resentful. Abram dreaded the thought of expelling the child. And though Sarai would have loved to get rid of the Egyptian and her whelp, she had no desire to repeat the mistake they had made ten years previously. But the problem could not be checked and would only worsen. They exchanged a glance that meant they both knew it.

Hagar and her possessions, now fewer than when she arrived, were loaded into a donkey-cart along with her son. Abram mounted another donkey and led the cart northwest toward Gerar. Hagar had always boasted of having many friends there. But as they approached a small oasis community she slid out of the cart and snatched the reins away from Abram.

Her parting words: "You owe me." Then turning, she led the donkey toward the palm trees without looking back. Too old to survive on beauty alone, she could at least trade her domestic skills.

Ishmael, seated in the back of the cart, now faced his father with a bewildered look. Abram timidly waved good-bye, knowing that his son's bewilderment would one day turn to hatred.

Upon returning to camp, Abram found two families packed up and heading north. One of them was Benammi's.

"What be this?" he asked Zimran.

"People love not this place, Abi. And that matter of Hagar and the child…" Zimran shrugged. "More will leave."

He was right. Some left by night with more than their share of livestock. The hero of a decade ago was now just an ordinary boss who inspired no one, and couldn't pay enough to justify the living conditions. Once again, inaction would only make it worse. They would return to Arba where Abram was still loved and Sarai still barren – or thought to be.

Isaac then needed to learn a new identity.

"You were born in Edom," said Abram to the boy standing at attention before him. "You are my second son, but not with Sarai. You are the son of Hagar, the Egyptian. Your older brother is Ishmael. Now let me hear you say that your mother is Hagar."

Isaac's lower lip pooched out, and a tear rolled down his cheek. Sarai rubbed his curly black hair and hugged him.

"It is but play," she cajoled. "This is what you must tell people when we get to Arba. You can do that; can you not?"

Isaac nodded in assent. It would take some drill, but he would learn. He had to.

"One thing more," added Abram. "You must look like the son of an Egyptian. You remember how Ishmael looked when he was naked? How his… thing was different – his pisser? I must make yours like that. It will hurt, but not for long."

Isaac began to whimper uncontrollably.

Sarai wrapped her arms around him and cooed into his ear. "There there, my dear one. You must learn to be a man. Papa will show you how it is done."

Abram perked up. "Huh?"

"Will you not, Papa?"

"Uhh… Surely."

21 SODOM

the reunion

As soon as Abram had healed, the tribe again packed up and prepared to migrate. Now much reduced in size, possibly remerging with Lot's band would work out. Abram detoured eastward.

In a few days over nearly roadless hill country they arrives atop a chalky limestone cliff above the Dead Sea valley. The ruins of Sodom and Gomorrah had not been rebuilt. Indeed, they were barely recognizable as city ruins. These had not been deep-rooted cities to leave foundation stones for posterity to rediscover. They were cities of the surface, built of wood and wicker, colored cloth, and wisps of things like their inhabitants, holding no illusion of permanence, or hope for it in this life or beyond. Those who happened to survive would melt into the scenery, pretending to be whatever the locals wanted.

Abram descended into the valley and camped near the ruins just to take it in.

"What happened here, Papa?" asked Isaac.

What could he say? That certain men did certain acts that were offensive to other men, because those other men didn't like having to explain those acts to their sons? The irony was ridiculous.

"El punished some bad men here," was the best answer he could offer. "And call me not Papa. Call me 'my lord.'"

Korah approached. "We found Lot, my lord."

"Where?" asked Abram.

"He lives in a cave in the hills."

"Is he well?"

Korah knit his brows and looked down. "He is in health."

"What?" demanded Abram.

"He is exceeding… peaceful."

Though Lot had fled the disaster in time, being a Sodomite refugee had won him no respect at Zoar. They had pillaged his livestock so much that his tribe disintegrated. Some of his former servants now lived in caves nearby as his neighbors and equals. Without enough grazing animals to justify the nomadic life, they had settled down to grow whatever the soil would bear – including hemp.

Leaving Zimran in charge of camp, Abram took Eliezer and several herdsmen with empty carts prepared to bring Lot and his family back into the tribe. Upon seeing him, Abram winced. In the ten years since they had parted, Lot had aged twenty. Still he was, as Korah said, peaceful. They embraced.

The garbage dump was still smoldering. It was obvious that Lot and his daughters had done a fast clean-up in preparation for their arrival, but the place still smelled bad. And though he noticed no hemp growing on the way in, there was more than the usual amount of rope laying around. Lot had set up a dining area under a canopy in his front and only yard. One of his daughters served, while the other remained in the cave, with two toddlers.

Both of Lot's daughters were veiled – strange behavior at home among friends and family.

"You must try Edomite beer," said Lot. "The best I have tasted since Haran." It was merely a distraction so that, hopefully, no one would notice that he had no wine to offer. The guests were not fooled. Like many veterans, Lot seemed to need to tell his war story before any other conversation would be meaningful.

"It was terrible. They hit Sodom at dawn. We watched from the hills. They chased people down and slaughtered them – women, children, dogs, everything. Never have I seen such hate. It was like…" He trailed off into a blank zone.

"And where is your wife?" asked Abram.

"She… chose to stay behind."

"What?"

"Well truly, she ran off with some salt picker a long time ago. Sow. Left me with the girls. Men, I tell you, never marry outside your family. You never can tell. Never."

Abram shot a glance at Eliezer to see if he was offended. Eliezer showed only pity.

"Be that as it may," said Abram, "at least you and me are back together. So… I see you have grandchildren now, hey?"

"Yes, of a truth. Two boys – Moab and Benammi. Say, how fares Benammi?"

"We lost him some moons ago," said Abram. "He left. Long story. Where be their husbands?"

"What?"

"Your daughters. We can take them and their husbands too if they wish to come."

"Oh, they are… uhh…"

"Not dead, I pray?

"Alas, they remained in Sodom. I warned them, but they laughed at me."

"Alas," agreed Abram, hanging his head. Then something seemed strange. He glanced back at the daughters with their toddlers. "Hmh. Truly those children are not three years old. How is it that their fathers died five years past?"

"Uhh…" Lot squirmed.

Abram reassured him. "Truly my nephew, if they have married anew, no ill judgment shall befall them from any in my tribe."

Lot blanked out again, then recovered. "Well, uhh… truly, the girls have no husbands. That is a long story too. Heh heh."

Abram and the rest remained silent until Lot realized that there was no escape.

"Well, of a truth, the girls thought, without dowries, no man will marry them. And me being without sons, of a truth, they would have none to care for them when they get old. So one night they got me drunk, of a truth… two nights as I recall."

Abram felt everyone's eyes turn to him. He jumped up and backed away to get his bearings. Looking for a scapegoat, he stomped over to the daughters, now cowering behind their veils. *No. Make it not worse.* He turned and paced a few meters away, his back to the men.

Lot had always been disdainful of women. Being the youngest male of the family, he was outranked by his aunts up to the time he married. Abram always hoped Lot would outgrow it, but apparently he had not. Abram simmered, then returned to the group.

"Let us go."

His men got up.

"Go to the carts. I will be there forthwith."

They complied.

Abram faced Lot alone. "Forgive me," he said.

"Of a truth, Abi. El's cow! It is not like I am a bad man or whatnot… We both done one or two things we are not all that proud of."

Abram turned away. The comparison disgusted him, mostly because he could not thoroughly dismiss it. He turned back.

"You are right – truly right. But I cannot have you in my tribe."

Both men stood there avoiding each other's eyes.

"Do you need money?" asked Abram.

"No, I need not your money."

"If you do, I will be near Arba."

Abram turned and walked back toward his carts.

"It is all lies, Abi," shouted Lot. "You know it, and I know it."

Without looking back, Abram got into a cart. "Let us go! Now!"

The long, silent ride home was just one more occasion for a thought-wallow.

Lot may be right. It may all be lies. Good and evil is such a bear! Such a dog! How can a man know if anything is truly good or evil? By the way it feels? What if it feels differently to different men? Perhaps father was right; it is all naught. But then what? What can you do from there? Whatsoever you wish? What be even worth wishing from there?

No! Murder is bad. Theft is bad. They must be bad… Says who? Oh think not about who. That question leads you right back to… Abram felt His obnoxious grin filling the sky.

"Either Me or chaos," came the soundless taunt.

"Silence!" muttered Abram, then cleared his throat to mask it in case anyone heard.

Back at camp he informed the tribe that Lot would not be joining them. The question "why?" was thrown at him from all sides.

"He… has a home and gardens. His daughters have sons. Better they remain where they are."

Zimran tried to comfort him. "At least you did your best for him, my lord."

Abram's jaw tightened. He nodded politely to Zimran and turned toward his tent.

Did my best for him – did my best. Did I truly? No. I did my best for the tribe. The tribe is greater. Cannot have a hemp-chewing daughter-shtupper in the tribe. Surely I did right. Why? Because it was right? Or because I wished not to lose my workers? Am I truly a good man? Or but a lover of self? I no longer know even that much.

Sarai rescued him from his mind. "What of Lot's wife? She is well, I hope?"

"Alas," said Abram. "She chose to remain in Sodom."

"Oh no! What became of her?"

"Turned to a picker of salt."

22 ARBA
the acceptance

Again east of Arba, Abram was welcomed by his old friends. It was so good to be Abram the hero again. Everybody's polite; nobody cheats you. But gradually all that subsided – not just the natural cooling down of enthusiasm one would expect, but more than that. Friends were becoming distant, and strangers were becoming rude – like they knew some dark secret. And there was only one secret they might know.

Abram watched Isaac chase toads in a wadi.

"Abram," called Eliezer, "that messenger from Salem is here."

Abram hastened away from the incriminating subject. He and Eliezer walked back to his tent where he found Gabriel and his two guards waiting.

"Gabriel, my friend, I pray you stay. Sarai, we have guests."

"You are most gracious, Abram, but I must return quickly. I have but a brief message from his Holiness." Gabriel stepped away from his guards and motioned for Abram to follow him. Abram and Eliezer did so.

"The message is for your ears alone," said Gabriel.

"I have no secrets from my servant, Eliezer." Not quite true, but good politics to say it.

Eliezer responded in kind. "The man has his orders, my lord." He walked away and disappeared behind a tent.

Gabriel leaned toward Abram. "His Holiness says, 'rumors.'"

Abram waited for more, but Gabriel had no more.

"Rumors?" asked Abram, "Rumors of what?"

"He said naught but that."

"Know you of what he spoke?"

"I know naught but what I am told, my friend."

"Have you any thoughts on it?"

Gabriel smiled politely. "I also think what I am told."

"There is a skill I have yet to master."

"He will ask me what you said. What shall I tell him?"

Abram blanked. "Tell him… I am grateful for the warning."

"As you wish," agreed Gabriel. He turned and went back to his guards.

As they mounted up and rode away, Eliezer came around from behind the tent. "Grateful for the warning! From what be this?"

"What?" asked Abram.

"You could have said, 'Rumors? What rumors?' or at least, 'Those rumors are lies made up by my enemies.' 'Grateful for the warning' tells him you know the rumor he speaks of, and you deny it not. Abi, you are a better player than this."

Abram had no response. He was losing not only the will to fight, but his entire grasp of the situation. What was he fighting for? Whom was he fighting? What does he win if he wins? What does he lose if he loses? It was all coming apart.

Abram felt a need to work his way down to some kind of stable foundation before he fell head first into it. The god question simply had to be addressed and dealt with. He had already tried priests and prayer, obedience and disobedience, listening and not listening. What was left? When all else fails, read the manual. *Perhaps the Tablets of Noah might shed some light on this.*

Abram loaded a cart with wool and picked out the straggliest sheep and goats for a trip to Salem, ostensibly for trading purposes. Once there, he left his men in charge of business and wandered over to the street of the letter makers. Finding a comfortable resting place, he parked himself to listen to the hawker's wife recite from the Tablets.

Some of it he recognized as spin-off versions of Akkadian stories, some of which were spin-off versions of Sumerian stories– or the other way around. *God! Who knows?* Some of it was uniquely Canaanite. But none of it seemed relevant to his own experience with the El Most High, with whom he had been trying and failing to establish a mutually acceptable relationship. Then suddenly one part stood out.

> "And El said to Adam, 'From the blood of a dead god be you made. For this, lest you forget the price that bought you, the blood of your first-born son shall I demand of you. You shall sacrifice him and burn him until the flesh be consumed.' And Adam knew his wife, and she conceived and bore a son. And Adam named him Haram, and Adam sacrificed him as El had commanded."

That part he hadn't heard before. And it made his neck bristle. *Could that be it? Could it be that to slay your first-born son could possibly give you peace with the Most High? Foolishness! But wait. If the Most High commands it, then it cannot be foolish. But wait again. If that were true, why had not the Sumerians learned it? And the Egyptians? Why are not the Canaanites master of the earth, if they alone know how to appease the terrible Fate Holder?* Just more damned questions.

"Abram?" came a voice behind him.

Another near bladder accident! *Why do people do that?* He whirled around.

Gabriel jumped back. "Forgive me! I meant not to startle you."

"No, forgive me, I pray you."

"This is from his Holiness," Gabriel said. He handed Abram a package. It was a roll of shaven sheep skin about the size of a teraph box, and tied with a cord of purple flax– expensive cord. Not only was Tyrian purple expensive, but flax did not take dye easily.

"What am I to do with this?" asked Abram.

"I know not, my friend. I but–"

"–follow orders, I know."

"El be with you." Gabriel turned toward the palace and departed.

Abram looked up at the limestone walls. In the blackness of a window he saw Melchizedek looking down upon him. As soon as their eyes met, the king moved out of sight.

Abram untied the cord and felt something hard inside the leather. He unrolled it until he saw a flint dagger.

Any questions?

No.

It is clear, yes?

Yes.

He rolled the gift up and tied it tightly, then went back to his men. His cart now full of spices, herbs, and olive oil, they headed for home. The journey gave him three days to prepare his mind. He would do it. He would get everything in order, and do it.

Thought-binge time. *We must be truly sure we do the right thing here. No errors. After we do this, we cannot say, 'I meant well.'*

What be this God Thing? This is no ghostly King made up by men to control other men. This God reaches down with His own hand and moves the bricks – or at least the heart.

But is He mad? First He makes us to love sons, then He commands us to slay one, so that we cannot help but hate Him. But we cannot show that we hate him or He will smite us. We are supposed to love Him – or pretend to. Why would any god set it up like this? – Most High or otherwise?

But does it truly matter why? I must do it anyway, so why care about why? Of a truth, I do care about why, even though I wish not to. And that means my Maker made me to care about why. Why? Why would He even make things that ask 'why?'

Abram noticed an old and disheveled man sitting on a rock. He held a shepherd's crook as though it were a scepter, but there were no sheep around. As they passed by him, the man let out a gurgly laugh. "Haw!" No apparent reason – he just laughed.

Mad, thought Abram, *moon howling mad… but not unhappy. It must be nice to be mad. Yet I dare not pray to become so. Therefore I likely am mad.* Abram laughed.

Another old man sat cross-legged on a hilltop under a fig tree. He was gazing down at the people on the road. The setting sun was in his eyes, yet he continued to squint at whatever might pass in front of him. Why did he stare into the sun? He could have looked in any other direction. *To see us envy him,* thought Abram. *He wants us to know he is rich and idle. That is why he climbed the hill to sit under a fig tree. The Tablets say Shem sat under a fig tree in his old age. He was fat and happy sitting under his fig tree. So this proud old fool sits posing like Shem under a fig tree so other fools will think him happy.*

Abram laughed again. *Be that all this life has to offer? To become a madman or a fool? And to care not which? Father seemed to do it. Even Melchizedek somehow gave up. Turned them all to vinegar, but they lived. Yes, that must be it. You pose as a common man, and in time you become one. You forget that you were ever real. But I tried that and failed. No! I must try it again. It must succeed, or… they are all lying. Could that be? No, no, let us not think about that. That would be… the maddest of all mad. Let us think about pleasant things… So be it, then let us think about needful things. What are we going to tell Sarai? … There is a thought stopper.*

Abram concluded that he must conform to the rules whether they made sense or not. Still, finding no compelling prohibition against procrastination, he put off the actual doing of it until the next prod – which came shortly.

Sarai got sick. It was the common flu-like sort of thing that usually doesn't last more than a few days. First they treated it with bitter herbs and garlic and prayer. Illness demons hate bitter herbs and garlic and prayer. But these demons were persistent. And before long the whole tribe began to suspect that Abram was out of sync with El.

One morning as Abram was at his tent preparing for the day's work, Eliezer approached. "Abram, visitors."

Eliezer pointed to the north horizon. On a rise, three men on donkeys, sat observing the camp. Though they were too far away to recognize faces, Abram knew Gabriel, by his bearing.

Isaac asked innocently, "Be those the demons, my lord?"

"What?… No," Abram said. "Those are men of business."

"What do they want?" asked Isaac.

Abram stood staring at them, then turned to Isaac. "Tell Korah to load up a cart. We shall go to Salem."

"May I go?" asked the boy.

"Yes."

"Ayyy!" Isaac jumped with elation.

"Tell him to tie on a ewe for sacrifice."

Isaac ran happily to comply.

Abram turned to Eliezer. "It is Gabriel. He is here to collect a debt."

"What will you do?"

"Pay it. Ride with me to Salem?"

"Surely, my lord."

The three visitors remained in place silently observing – not the sort of thing they would have been instructed to do. Gabriel had always been discrete.

Abram went to his tent, where Musha was tending to Sarai with hot poultices. He rummaged through his tool box and pulled out a sheep skin tied in purple flax.

"Harken, my dove. I shall go to Salem to make offering and seek the counsel of the priests. Do you hear?"

"Mmh," Sarai responded. Actually, Musha was better company in time of illness anyway, being wise in health matters from her vast experience in communal laundry days, and occasional midwifery.

Abram picked up a skin of strong wine and exited. "Isaac wishes to come also."

He held the sheep skin above his head so that Gabriel could see it. When the cart was fully loaded Isaac jumped in. All was ready.

Korah, totally unaware of the true purpose of the trip, asked to go along. Abram had no reason to refuse. They mounted up and rode out to the bill collectors. Abram made eye-contact with Gabriel and held it until he was satisfied that they understood each other.

"El be with you," said Abram.

"El be with you," responded Gabriel. "Nice day."

"Do you go to Salem?"

"It so happens," replied Gabriel.

"May we ride with you?"

It was all posturing for the benefit of the ignorant. They hardly slowed down as Gabriel's party joined them.

"The boy's mother is sick," said Abram. "I thought to go to Salem and make a little offering – ask El to heal her."

"May I watch?" asked Isaac.

"Surely."

Gabriel spoke softly. "A high place is but north of town. Beautiful little spot. Green trees. Private. Altar up top. The judge recommends it."

23 MORIAH

the revelation

High places were small religious shrines for the purpose of private devotion. Just about every hill in Canaan had one at this time. They consisted of anything from some artfully arranged rocks to a small enclosure with a statue – but no priests, no lines, no receipts. It was a convenient way to feel pious, either by giving your favorite god a barbecue, or cleaning up previous ashes.

Abram told Korah to gather dry wood along the way. Isaac eagerly helped him. By the time they reached the Kidron valley east of Salem the cart was full of firewood. At the turn-off to the east gate, Abram figured they would part company.

"I thank you for the escort, Gabriel. I am sure we can find the high place."

"We shall see you all the way there," said Gabriel. "This land is full of bandits."

"Gracious of you."

"I am sure his Holiness would approve."

They rode on past the turn-off.

"Do we not go to Salem?" asked Isaac.

"On the way back," replied Abram. "First I would speak to El in a high place."

The hill called Moriah was three bowshots from the north gate of Salem – possibly the highest hill in the area for the next thousand years. As promised, it was covered in trees.

> Solomon would later scrape down this hill to join it to Salem and then build the world's most famous temple on it.

As they loaded the dry wood onto Abram's donkey, Korah noticed that something didn't jibe.

"If you make sacrifice here, you will have naught left for Salem."

Eliezer parried. "We can buy an offering in the city."

After they lashed up the wood securely to Abram's donkey, Korah went back to untie the sheep.

"Leave it there," said Abram. "We shall be back soon." Then to Isaac, "Let us go."

"What of the sheep?" asked Isaac.

"The sheep is for Salem," said Abram. "This shall be what they call a drink offering. The els must drink too, just like we do." He unslung the wineskin from his shoulder, held it up, and took a swig, then smiled at Isaac.

"Do you desire some?... It is strong, but we shall not tell momma." He held it down for Isaac to drink, then chuckled as the boy pretended to like it.

"Good, hey?" Then turning to the group, "Who will drink with us on the day of my son's first sacrifice?"

Korah was surprised that no one else spoke up. "I will!" he said, joyfully stepping forward to accept the wineskin.

Gabriel was second. "The blessing of El Most High upon your family, Abram." He took a drink and passed it on. The skin went around the group and back to Abram.

"Let us go," he said, resting a hand on Isaac's shoulder. They turned and led the wood-laden donkey toward the hill.

The boy was full of questions along the path – religious questions that brought back memories

"Where do the els live, my lord?"

"Call me father, son."

"It is permitted now?"

"Yes."

"Where do the els live, father?"

"Up in the sky."

"Why do they not fall down?"

"Clouds. They walk about on clouds."

"When no clouds are in the sky, be the els gone?"

"Yes, but they still see you, for they have demons all about, who peek at you and tell their masters."

"Why can we not see them?"

"They are made of air."

Abram mused at how easily the lies flowed from his mouth, not because he remembered them from his childhood, but because the truth didn't matter any more. Maybe it never did. Acting fatherly mattered – playing the role. Maybe that was the whole secret to being normal.

To lie to a child is much like to slay Amorites, thought Abram. *The first one or two feel a bit slimy, but then one goes numb. After a while it becomes like a song with a drum beat, and it truly starts to feel good, like a dance – like a shtup on a young harlot, I wager. Like I am but a common man doing that which common men have done from the beginning. I am at last connected to my roots. To slay and to lie are but part of life. Was it not these very skills by which my line of fathers overcame their enemies from the first? Should I not take pride in them? No good, no bad; you do what you must – shtup and slay, eat and dung, learn and lie. And of a truth, it is not truly lying. I but do my part to pass on the traditions that were passed down to me, just like father and his father and every shtupping bastard all the way back to the first father who ever forced a smile and called it love. So what if I get taxed my first lamb to that great Shepherd King in the sky? I can always make more. Small price to pay for this glorious slide down the impaling stake of life.*

The top of the hill was adorned with a variety of fragrant shrubs. Aloes, cassia, and even white bramble were cultivated in a feeble effort to mask the odor of blood-soaked earth. There in a clearing was the nearly rectangular pile of stones – recently cleaned. *How perfect!* thought Abram. *One could not ask for a more beautiful killing table.* Abram led the donkey up to the altar, loosened the straps, and let the wood fall to the ground. He then tied the animal to a tree.

Arranging the wood on the altar, he explained as he went along. "First when you make a sacrifice, you build a bed of sticks. Put the kindling down first, then the smaller sticks on top of it."

Noticing one the size of a short sword, he leaned it against the altar.

"Save the bigger logs like this one for last. Never use up all your wood at the first, for you might need it later to burn up some pieces that did not burn."

"Even for drink offerings?"

"Yes, even then, for the wine will put out parts of the fire, so you must start it up again."

"If the wine be burnt up, how can the els drink it?"

"Well, they told us not that part. They but tell us the parts we need to know. That is how els are. Now the first thing when you sacrifice to an el is, you must gain his ear. You must pray to him."

Abram faced the altar and clasped his hands in the customary position. Blank. No prayer came out. Standing there waiting for his mind to work, his upper lip curled into an uncontrollable snarl. Then throwing his arms wide he shouted.

"Be a righteous god anywhere in this shtup-ing place?"

The echo was not audible, still Abram imagined the thought wave bouncing off every particle in the world. He took a deep breath and let it out. The faint sound of a sheep bleated in the background. "A-a-a-a-a."

Truly, thought Abram. *What more can be said of it? A-a-a-a-a.*

He turned to Isaac with a pleasant smile. The boy looked confused, and needed a little reassurance. Abram rubbed his curly locks and walked back to the donkey to get his tinder kit.

"You see, you must know you got the right el. You wish not to give your offering to any old el. Do you wish to call to him?"

Isaac passed.

"A-a-a-a-a," repeated the sheep, but it went unnoticed.

Abram brought his tinder kit back and unwrapped it.

"Now, I shall trust you with the greatest part – to build the fire. You seen me do that, yes?"

He handed Isaac the flints and sack of dry leaf chips.

"Most joyous!" exclaimed the boy, finally trusted with the fire maker. He knelt on the ground with it and began scooping a cone of tinder together.

"Face into the sun," said Abram. "Always face into the sun when you build a fire; it helps."

Abram picked up the stick he had leaned against the altar.

"A-a-a-a", came the bothersome distraction from off stage.

Shut your mouth, Sarai. It is my duty.

He approached Isaac from behind.

Yes, Sarai, I slew your son. Now lift your skirt and make me another. Call me an animal? What of it? El is an animal – a great Bull with a great shmuck up my ass all the way to my head. And I would be the same to you, Sarai. Wail not of the horror. Life is horror – a long line of shtuppers upon shtuppers – killers of killers – a great mountain of us from the earth to the sky. Now kneel down and take your place in the pile or I will bash your head in next!

He raised the stick.

"A-a-a-bram."

Abram turned.

Meanwhile, back at the cart, everyone but Korah had chosen to sit or lie down and nap. Korah had become thoroughly put out with the group's silence. This was the most depressing group of men he had ever hung out with. Even Eliezer seemed to have caught their antisocial spirit.

"If you honorables wish to go back to Salem, I am sure Eliezer and I can guard the cart."

"Korah," said Eliezer, "we are all a bit drowsy, if you mind not."

Well, Korah wasn't drowsy. He took a bone-comb and

went to groom the donkeys. At least they would appreciate his company.

Suddenly Gabriel jumped to his feet, staring westward. The rest looked in the same direction. There from out of the woods walked Abram leading the donkey with Isaac riding it.

Gabriel turned angrily and stalked off toward his own donkey. His two companions rose and followed. They hastily mounted up without a word and kicked flanks for Salem.

"Rudest men I have ever seen," muttered Korah to Eliezer, who also ignored him.

Seriously in need of an explanation, Eliezer ran out to meet Abram, whose countenance now appeared so peaceful that Eliezer dared not disturb it with a question. Abram handed him a charred ram's horn as though it were made of gold.

"Your questions will be answered, my friend… all of them."

From there, they bypassed Salem and headed for home.

A good thing too, for at that moment Gabriel stood before Melchizedek giving a full report of what he had seen.

"The boy was in plain sight of us all, alive and well."

Melchizedek stroked his beard. "So he took the boy up the hill, but then something caused him to change his heart?"

"My thought, Holiness, he never planned to go through with it. He hoped to trick us, and then hide the boy. But when we followed him to Moriah, he saw that the lie would not work."

Melchizedek paused long enough for Jebus to intervene. "They will most surely travel back by the Ridge Road, Holiness. Shall I dispatch a troop?"

"And do what?" replied Melchizedek. "Seize his son and drag him back to the temple and slay him?"

"It has been done in the past." replied Jebus.

"Yes, and to what end? The people hate the likes of that. It has caused riots even with unknown persons. How much more with a beloved hero?"

"We could at the least arrest him," replied Jebus. "Let the people see him stand with criminals, and have his impiety made known."

"The people have already seen him stand at my right hand. How will it look to stand him now with swine? How will it make *me* look? No. Many know his face, and all Canaan has heard of him. Gabriel, go and spread the knowledge of his deeds throughout the land – not as of my command, but of your own witness."

"Yes, Holiness." Gabriel departed.

"And now?" queried Jebus.

"Now we wait," said Melchizedek. "You see, Jebus, it is not for the judge of Canaan to seek out criminals. It is for the people of Canaan to bring criminals to the judge. And when we hear that this once noble man has fallen into sin, we shall show deep grief and ask the people to pray for him."

"Pray for him?"

"Fervently," Melchizedek smiled. "And when he fails to respond to their prayers, the good people of Canaan know what to do with men who despise divine law. And I shall smell like myrrh and balsam."

The ram-caught-in-a-thicket part of the story is common knowledge, and need not be repeated here. But of course, Abram repeated it all to Eliezer and Korah on the three day journey home, and repeated it several times over with all motivational detail to Isaac, who only then realized how close he had come to death.

24 ARBA
the heresy

Arriving at home they found Sarai recovered and healthy – very important to Abram, not only for obvious reasons, but because her continued illness would have cast doubts on the significance of the entire Moriah experience. The ewe that they neglected to sacrifice at Salem did not escape. They slaughtered it and had a feast.

That night Abram put it all together in his mind, and became possibly the first of a long list of persons to formulate a more rational alternative to a less rational belief system. The following morning he held a tribal conference and laid it out. Carefully avoiding dogmatic statements about what God said, he reported only what he had experienced and how it appeared to him, both at the time and in retrospect.

"That is how it happened, men. For this I have set my heart to serve a just and righteous El… and none but a just and righteous El… whether any man stands with me or not. You are all free to do as you wish. I am now a rebel in the eyes of all Canaan. Any of you still here tomorrow morning will be seen likewise."

Abram stood. The rest stood.

Korah raised his hand. "My Lord, a question. What if no just and righteous El be anywhere?"

Abram paused. "Then I will serve the hole where one should have been."

All dispersed except Zimran and Eliezer.

"Abram," said Zimran, "be you sure you are right about this?"

"No," said Abram calmly. "And I care not. If I be wrong, naught is right."

Abram turned and walked back toward his tent.

Eliezer stomped after him. "Abram!" His subordinate tone had vanished. "What shall we make of this? You care not for right and wrong, but you care for justice and righteousness? What?"

"Come now," said Abram. "Know you not what I mean? Can you not feel my heart in this?"

"Yes, but what then? Will your heart save me when the priests ask me what el I serve? What shall I say? El who may be a hole in the sky? I care not for right or justice or any of it. I care for my skin."

"And I care for all of it," added Zimran. "Right and wrong is the same as justice. You cannot care for one and not the other. You must say it right. I mean… you must say it truly."

"What now?" Abram threw his hands up. "Must I line up all my words like soldiers?"

Zimran nodded. "If men need that to know your meaning."

Eliezer interrupted. "But tell me this. Will you continue to sacrifice to El at Salem? If not, then you must leave Canaan."

Abram thought before responding. "Then I will leave Canaan."

The closest place that didn't require worship of some local deity was back down south in the Wilderness of Zin. So Abram made the decision to once again turn around and go back where he came from. This time, however, there was no hurry. When the people of Arba applied sufficient pressure, Abram would make the move with whomever remained of his tribe.

The next day Korah and all of the Canaanites left – all except Eliezer, and even he had decided to go as soon as his wife could tear herself away from her parents. All that remained beside the Hurian, Zimran, were five households of the original Akkadians from Haran.

On the following day two more families left. That evening in front of Abram's tent, as he and Zimran sat discussing theology and survival, Eliezer came stomping up in an obviously bad mood.

"Forgive me, my lord. May I speak to Musha?"

"Uhh, surely. Musha!"

"In private if you will," said Eliezer.

As Abram and Zimran looked on, Eliezer and Musha stepped out of earshot, and began quietly discussing something. Then Eliezer broke off the discussion and stomped back toward his tent. Abram turned to Musha. "What was that?"

Musha smiled. "He wanted to learn how to know if a woman is with child."

Abram and Zimran looked at each other and cracked

up laughing. About ten minutes later Eliezer trudged back to the theological conference and sat down. Abram and Zimran remained respectfully silent.

"If it be a girl," said Eliezer, "I shall be gone forthwith."

In the next week the tribe was reduced by another household. But on the eighth night the tide turned. In his tent, preparing for bed, Abram was interrupted by Zimran's voice.

"Abi."

Coming out, Abram saw two people approaching from the north. A young man burdened under a large back pack was leading a donkey carrying a fully veiled woman. Getting to within earshot, the man dropped his burden, caught his breath, and without the customary *El be with you*, said, "I seek Abram."

"I am Abram," came the reply.

"I am Medan of Salem," said the man. "My wife." He motioned for the woman to reveal herself. As she drew aside her outer veil, the two visitors became three; she was holding an infant.

"My first-born," said Medan, "a son. May we join you?"

Abram could say nothing. He merely embraced the young man and wept.

As it turned out, this particular heresy had a strong appeal to young couples. And though Abram's tribe was disrespected in the market place and shunned by all clergy, it grew in number and youthful vigor. This influx of spiritual gamblers was no random cross-section of Canaanite newly weds. It contained a high percentage of disgruntled rebels, and even more obnoxious – sincere theological truth-seekers.

"Be the law of the first fruits now abolished?"

"Be it amended?"

"Was it ever a law of El?"

"Did El change his heart?"

"Do we serve El Most High, or some other el?"

There were details to hammer out, and Abram had some lively fireside discussions with Zimran and Eliezer each night.

On the next Shabbat the tribe was seated around the traditional evening campfire. But this Shabbat was not like all other Shabbats. In addition to the new members, eagerly awaiting the pronouncements of Pope Abram, were visiting critics just as eager to evaluate those pronouncements, and report their findings to any curious ear.

"First I must say," began Abram, "that I serve no new el. I serve El Most High… Or I try to. But I believe not that El Most High has joy in the killing of children."

"Yeaah!" cheered some in the inner circle.

Abram continued. "The law of the first fruits was, I think, given by the Most High. But for animals alone, and not for the sons of men."

"Mmmmh," came a murmur from the back row.

A priest's son ventured a question. "What of the Tablets of Noah? Be they lies?"

The inner circle erupted in jeers at the heckler. But Abram raised his hands to silence them.

"I cannot read," he said. "Perhaps you will help me. Do the Tablets of Noah say that El required the blood of *all* first-born sons of men, or but of the son of Adam?"

"Adam alone!" shouted Medan, and the inner circle grunted their approval.

But the priest's son was not content. "Who among us is not a son of Adam?"

"I am not!" came the high voice of a young girl, causing laughter among the Abramites.

But the heckler was undaunted. "We are all in Adam. And what the blessed El demanded of Adam, he demands of us all."

Murmuring followed in all parts of the crowd.

"And where say the Tablets that?" came an unexpected objection from Eliezer.

"It need not be said," replied the priest's son. "It is known from what is said."

"By whom?" asked Eliezer.

"By all."

"By priests!" asserted Eliezer, standing to his feet. "And by those who fear them more than they love justice."

The crowd erupted, this time into noisy controversy. The priest's son rose with his entourage and left in a huff.

Eliezer slumped back down onto the dirt. "Holy dung!" he exclaimed to his pregnant wife. "I truly said that!"

Abram hastily decreed that all fathers of first-born sons must sacrifice an unblemished male of their flock or herd in lieu of the infant itself. But all knew that this token compliance would be unacceptable to Salem.

The next day Abram ordered the tribe to pack up.

Abram's new religion was not yet full-blown monotheism. His god was still just the top god of the region with the same old Canaanite title – El Most High, the meaning of which had not yet evolved to the concept of a Supreme Being. But his nature had now changed. He was not quite as demanding. Moreover, the nature of humanity had changed. No longer were men tools of a Slave-Maker to be used up and thrown away, but children of a Father – possibly even a loving Father, and much more accessible. Closer to truth? Who knows? But definitely a better sales pitch at the grass roots level.

25 WILDERNESS
the visitors

Once again encamped at the well on the edge of the wilderness, the tribe settled in. This time resolved to reside there permanently, they planted tamarisks for shade, dug irrigation ditches, and sowed barley. Wheat-fields, olive trees, and vineyards would follow in years to come.

Here they received visitors almost daily, many of whom asked to stay, and were seldom refused. Korah and family returned at this time and were treated as though their absence went unnoticed. But one visitor was welcomed with great enthusiasm. Mamre the Amorite felt a need to confirm his friendship.

"Slay the fattest of calves," commanded Abram loudly. Then slinging an arm around his old war buddy, "How do you take your meat, my friend?"

"Well cooked, I pray you."

243

After a jubilant feast, Abram and Mamre took a private walk among newly planted groves and vineyards.

"Have you heard that Damashka now has a new king"

"No," replied Abram.

"An Amorite, I hear."

"No! Truly?"

"Most truly. Canaan now swells with Amorites. My own tribe must turn them away."

"How fortunate for Canaan!"

Mamre smiled graciously. "Many of my people lean toward your new religion, Abram. But they also fear the wrath of Baal. I would wager that few of us have joined you. True?"

"True."

"Know you that in our own tents we Amorites boast ourselves the cleanest of all people?"

"Uhh... No, I knew it not."

"This is because we eat not the flesh of swine."

"Truly?"

"Truly. Baal-El has not changed the law to my knowledge, unlike your El Most High, who has now made great changes. If he were to forbid men to eat swine's flesh, then he would seem a great friend to Baal-El."

"Hmm, I see."

"I and my brothers have long ago sent our first-born sons to Salem, and hold tokens to prove it, but we have no great love of Salem's cult." He paused, hoping that Abram would offer some assurance of agreement. Seeing none, he continued. "But truly, the ways of an el are his own, and not swayed by the desires of men. I but thought you might consent to ask him about it."

"Swine's flesh?"

"Yes."

Abram stroked his beard. "I will surely do that, my friend…. Hm, no. No, that will not be needed. Surely a righteous el would love Amorites above swine's flesh. And I have already bet my life that the Most High is righteous."

Mamre smiled and opened wide his arms. They gave each other a manly embrace and headed back toward camp, all business being finished. Savoring the leisurely stroll, Abram felt his protracted guilt from that regrettable night so long ago lifted.

In the customary three days Mamre's visit drew to a close. From the back of his donkey he delivered his parting words.

"One last thing, Abram – a thing I tried to let myself forget. You may have another visitor soon – one Caleb the Hermit. He asked me to give a good report of him and I said I would."

"But you find it difficult?"

Mamre pursed his lips and struggled for words, then released them in a flurry of hand motion. "The man is truthful, truly truthful, the most truthful man I have ever met."

"But?" asked Abram.

"Well… the rest will speak for itself."

Mamre and his entourage rode north.

In a week the expected visitor arrived.

"What be this, a starved lion?" said Eliezer, looking northward at the new arrival.

The lion was wiry and sun-browned with hair and beard encircling his head in long dread-locks. He walked alone clad only in loin cloth and carried a wineskin and small pack of possessions over a shoulder.

Judging him to be about thirty, Zimran said, "That could have been you some years ago."

"I would have at least carried a staff," said Eliezer. "This man is weaponless."

"El be with you," called Zimran.

The stranger made no reply until he could be heard without raising his voice. "El of Goodness, or el of Salem?" he asked.

"Uh, El Most High is whom we serve," said Zimran.

"I care not for his height," said the man. "I care for his heart."

Zimran and Eliezer glanced at each other and then back at him without response.

"I seek a good and righteous el," said the stranger. "Be others like me in these parts?"

"Most truly!" replied Zimran. "We are of the tribe of Abram."

"I would see him," said the man, stepping between them and taking the lead toward the camp.

Getting a whiff of him, Zimran commented to Eliezer, "Not *perfectly* weaponless."

The stranger allowed himself to be directed from behind toward Abram's tent.

"My lord," said Zimran, "I would present a visitor."

"Caleb the Hermit, son of a harlot, father of none," said the man. "You heard tell of me?"

"Yes," said Abram. "Mamre said you were the most truthful of men."

"Men say many things of you, Abram. Be it true you blasphemed the temple at Salem?"

"No! Where heard you that?"

"Be it true you bring no offering to the temple at Salem?"

"True, but I offer to El Most High at my own altar."

"Be it true you refuse to serve El Most High, if El Most High be not righteous?"

"True," said Abram. "Desire you some wine?"

"I thank you, but I have not yet earned it. I take what I earn and no more. I steal not, I lie not, and I do my own shmuck. Got you a place for me?"

"Uh, do you do field work?" Abram immediately regretted asking such a question of this obviously weathered creature.

"More than that," said Caleb. "I read."

"Truly?" said Abram.

"Once sold myself to a priest, I did. Had me copy out them Tablets of Noah."

"Truly?" said Abram again. "I thought they were copied by temple scribes."

Caleb smiled. "Hah! Behind the long beards they are all merchants."

Eliezer had reached into his purse, pulled out a square of papyrus and unfolded it. He handed it to Caleb.

"Can you read this?"

"Year… thirty… and four… of holy of him – of his Holiness Melchizedek… I received… of Eliezer… of Arba… one… she-goat…"

Eliezer took back the receipt. "He reads."

Abram searched for words. "I… am overjoyed that you have chosen to join us, Caleb."

"I shall not call you my lord, for I have no lord save the El of Goodness. Can I call you Abram?"

"That will be acceptable."

"I can start that field work now."

"Surely. Zimran, I pray you show Caleb to a herdsman – or farmer – as Caleb wishes."

Zimran and Caleb walked off, leaving Abram and Eliezer silently wondering what to make of this fellow.

"He can read," mused Eliezer, "yet he speaks like a fool."

"Or a hermit," said Abram. "He is a God-seeker. That can do strange things to a man."

"I will take your word on it."

"But never have I seen one with less guile. I marvel that I should find him a bit frightening."

"Frightens you, does he?" said Eliezer. "He *terrifies* me!"

> Unlike state cults wherein access to divinity is strictly buffered by a hierarchy of priests, a cult which claims that a common man made personal contact with divinity will necessarily attract the attention of those who wish to do the same. Those who appear to succeed at this endeavor will eventually be called prophets.

Zimran pointed out the bathing tents next to the well in case Caleb might like to use one after work. "We bathe once a moon here, needed or not."

"Some men say the odor of man offends them," said Caleb. "I rejoice in it. Keeps the bugs away."

"Keeps everyone away, I wager," returned Zimran.

"My Maker give me this odor. I believe He knows how a man should smell."

"Our Maker gave us these noses," returned Zimran. "If you wish to eat with us, you bathe."

Caleb considered the pros and cons of it while he spent the afternoon pulling thistles from wheat and barley fields. By quitting time he conceded.

Arriving for dinner with hair and loincloth still wet, he

approached Zimran for inspection. "Sniff away, but curse me if I put on false odor like Gyps and harlots."

Abram invited him to dine at the head mat with his inner circle, mostly for fear that the savage would likely crash it, invited or not. Caleb was careful to lick his fingers between scoops to prove he had not forgotten his dining manners. This gesture made it easier to forgive him for talking with his mouth full.

"The main thing what drew me here is, you say the El of Goodness be the same as El Most High.

"I know not if there be an El of Goodness," replied Abram, "but I see cause to wager that El Most High is good."

"Wager? You know it not, but you wager?"

"Yes."

"I hoped for better than a wager."

"I also," said Abram, "but I have found naught better."

"From what I seen, it looks not like the El what has the most power be good. You see it different?"

"No, I agree," said Abram. "But I wager against what I see."

"Heh! Then how be you anything but a fool?"

"If He is not good," said Abram, "we are all cheated, and it would be most wise to slay ourselves. I fear death. Therefore, I choose to bet my life on a righteous El."

Caleb's eyes glistened over. "Can it be that simple?"

Abram shrugged. "What more is needed?"

Caleb bit a large bite out of a mutton chop. "I got to think on this."

Abram took a sip of beer. "Could you teach my son to read?"

"I can teach any man what has a heart to learn."

"Could you teach him to read the Tablets of Noah?"

Caleb fidgeted. "I can do it, but why? If I found what I sought in tablets, I never would have come here. A seeker of truth finds no joy in reading lies."

"So I have heard," said Abram. "But even a truth-seeker is grieved for his lack of such knowledge."

Caleb now took a sip of beer. "Your son would need some beating."

"I will beat him," said Abram.

In the following days Caleb's field work was cut short in the afternoons, and he became a tutor. Isaac's play time was also cut short. The two faced each other sitting on mats and pressing triangles into the dirt with wedges. Other children soon lost their fear of the strange chimera and gathered around. In time they began to bring their own wedges. In a few weeks many of them were eager to show their parents that they could write their names.

Caleb became a full time school teacher, and for the first time in his life, a functioning and respected member of a community. It was not an easy adjustment. In the following weeks his crust began to soften, then suddenly it fell apart.

After a Shabbat dinner Abram prayed as usual and asked if there were any prayer requests from the tribe. The sound of restrained sobbing turned all attention toward Caleb. An old woman – the most pleasant spirited person in the whole tribe – got up and walked to him. She knelt behind him and embraced him. Normally such an act would have been outside the bounds of propriety, but neither Caleb nor anyone else dared forbid her. He broke into uncontrollable weeping.

A whuff of Holy Happenings floated down upon the area like a hush. The breeze stopped; the sounds of the wilderness paused. Even the fire ceased to crackle. Everyone went silent and wide eyed. Caleb slumped into a peaceful stupor.

Eliezer and Zimran turned to Abram. *What be this?* Abram shrugged.

A child whispered to her mother, "Mama, the fire dances."

People gazed into the fire, which now miraculously did what fires normally do.

"Pray, my people," Abram squeaked in a vain effort to maintain the appearance of being in charge. But the Hush overruled him and no one made a sound.

Caleb was the first to find words. "I see!" he blubbered. "Praise El, I see."

The Hush gently lifted.

Abram, Eliezer, and Zimran exchanged glances. *Now what?*

Eliezer coughed, and the spell was broken.

This would be remembered for years to come as The Night The Fire Danced.

The next morning in full view of the breakfast crowd, Caleb took a pair of sheep shears and cut off his flea-ridden dreadlocks. He then trimmed his beard down to scruffy patches and tossed the hair into a pile in the center of camp. Taking a burning stick from a cooking fire, he ignited it.

"Born anew I am," he declared solemnly. "Servant and soldier of El Most High, but not as Salem teaches – as Abram teaches, a righteous El."

An awkward silence was broken by applause from the old woman who had embraced him the previous night, then the rest joined in.

Eliezer raised his cup. "Praise be to El. We now have an army."

"And call me not Caleb no more," he continued. "My name is now Elizedek."

caleb = dog
eli = my god
zedek = righteous

It went smoothly for a few weeks. Everything Abram said resonated with Caleb's – now Elizedek's – life experience, and he echoed it with enthusiasm. Elizedek seemed to get the message better than anyone else in the tribe, in some ways better even than Abram.

One evening as the women prepared supper Eliezer took Abram aside for a private discussion. "We have trouble," he said.

"What?" asked Abram.

"Many of the people seek the counsel of this Elizedek and not us."

"So?" Abram shrugged. "As long as we all say the same things, why care from whose tongue they come?"

"This man is the newest of all, and he is given the honor of an elder."

Abram raised his brows. "Envy?"

"Some of the children he teaches love his words above yours. Did you know that?"

Abram looked away. "I never had a gift for speaking."

Eliezer continued, "Though you say the same things, you say them weakly, but he says them strongly."

"What be this *weakly*?!"

"You say you *think* certain things about the Most High, and he says he *knows* those things. The people love strength."

"So because the people love strength, shall I boast of knowledge when it be a lie?"

"Who would know the difference?" asked Eliezer.

"I would. And if a god watches us, he would also. And if that god be just and righteous, he would cease to love me."

Eliezer leaned close and spoke softly. "Abi, we both know that you have lied before."

"Yes, and I will surely lie again, but not about this – not about the Most High."

"Abi, men have lied about gods since they learned to speak."

"And look what it has gotten us."

"And what will you do instead? Sit in your tent as another does it?"

Abram turned away. "Dung! No wonder priests are such liars. Look at you people. You *beg* for lies."

"Sometimes we need them."

"But look where it leads? Look what it makes of the world – *a cursed pot of dung!*" Abram's rise of emotion at this last statement surprised both of them. He regained composure. "I would not be part of that cause."

"As you wish," Eliezer sighed. "But will you at least tell Elizedek to harness his donkey?"

Abram was conflicted. "I will talk to him."

The next day at Abram's tent, he and Elizedek sat on opposite sides of a dish of goat-cheese. Abram sipped his wine and began with the customary amenities, but Elizedek had no patience for that sort of thing.

"So why am I here?"

Abram took a large gulp and put down his cup. "I rejoice that you agree with me, my friend, but I fear, as many of us fear, that you may take it too far."

"I agree too much?" asked Elizedek.

"No, uh… the *strength* of your agreement."

"Strength?"

"I know not how to say this." Abram fumbled for words. "Of a truth, that is the trouble. We know not, yet you know – or you *say* you know."

"Yes."

"One might ask *how* you know what you say you know?"

Elizedek shrugged. "How do you *not* know it?"

Abram fidgeted. "You cannot know that els are real, but that one appears to you and shows you some miracle. And even then you cannot know that he is *good*. He may do evil as well as good."

Elizedek knit his brows. "You say I know too much?"

"Yes. You say you know more than a man *can* know."

"Hmm." Elizedek scratched his chin. "How do you know what I know?"

"Huh?"

"You say I cannot know what I say I know. How do you know that?"

Abram was at a loss.

Elizedek pressed it. "Sounds to me like *you* say you know more than a man can know."

Abram got up and paced around scratching his neck.

Elizedek became curious. "You born again?"

"What!?"

The only thing this meeting accomplished was to convince Elizedek that he was now a step ahead of Abram, at least spiritually, if not officially. In his own mind he had surpassed his master, not out of ego or lust for power, but in that sincere pursuit of truth for which he had come to Abram in the first place. Nevertheless, the result was pride.

Pride, one of the great sins of later monotheism, gained its negative connotations in early civilization, when tokens of subservience were expected of anyone in the presence of anyone more powerful. No one recognized a distinction between pride and insolence. Nor did anyone bother to figure out that pride is an unavoidable side effect of the belief that you are doing well. Unfortunately however, it can make you careless. Abram's spiritual turf was barely charted, and Elizedek had now moved beyond it into totally uncharted territory. Invisible lines would inevitably be crossed.

Eliezer now brought Zimran with him to Abram's tent.

"Tell him what you told me," said Eliezer.

Zimran began reluctantly. "Abi, my grandchildren now think they know El better than I do. And all because they harken to this Elizedek."

Abram rose from his mat and paced nervously.

Eliezer pushed it. "Something must be done."

"It is a test," said Abram. "Surely it is a test."

"A what?"

"El is testing us," said Abram, "– me anyway. I can feel it."

Zimran and Eliezer glanced at each other.

Abram wagged his finger. "Think not that the tests end. They never end. Will I do what is right or what is easy? Will I pass on the kindness that was passed down to me by Melchizedek, or will I withhold? Elizedek is a truth-seeker – a God-seeker. Surely when men seek the same God they will live together in peace."

"My lord," said Eliezer, "we live in peace because we agree with you. You are our priest."

Abram winced. "God!"

"No, just priest."

"Our high priest," added Zimran.

"Why must you people have priests? What be you – sheep in need of a shepherd? Latch your nose to the Most High, and you will have no need of such nonsense."

Zimran inquired. "Be that your command, my lord – that we all go straight to the Most High?"

Eliezer balked. "You yourself said it was a fearful thing to do."

"I do it," said Abram. "Elizedek does it."

"To what end?" said Zimran. "The tribe now grows a second head. In time it will be ripped asunder."

"Not if we both do it right."

"And if the tribe splits, how do we know which of you does it wrong?" asked Zimran.

Abram had no answer.

Zimran clasped his hands at his chest. "My lord, I know not what gods there be. But I know that you are all that stands between me and them. If you command me to go straight to the Most High, I will do it. Do you so command?"

Abram rubbed his temples. "No. Surely not."

"Then will you remain my priest, or shall I seek another?"

Abram stood silently looking at them, then scratched his beard and paced. "Perhaps Elizedek *would* make a better high priest."

"That harlot's son!" exclaimed Eliezer, forgetting his own parentage. "I would sooner crawl back to Salem and beg forgiveness."

"My lord," said Zimran, "perhaps you should ask Isaac what he learned from his teacher."

"What mean you?" asked Abram.

Zimran continued, "My grandchildren have learned from Elizedek that the Canaanites are evil."

"I also have heard children say it," said Eliezer. "Some say the El of Salem is evil."

On the following day Abram called Elizedek in for a talk. Ignoring the wine and cheese brought in by Musha, both men remained standing.

"My son tells me that the cult of Salem is evil. Learned he that from you?"

"Truly," replied Elizedek, "just as I learned it from you."

"I *never* said that! Not once!"

"Forgive me. I learned it not from you. I learned it from the Most High hisself. You but gave me the courage to speak it."

"Elizedek, we cannot say these things to the children, even to the adults. Salem will surely learn of it."

"As it should have long ago. Truth should be spoken everywhere by everyone."

"They will bring an army down on us! Do you not see that?"

"I would die a thousand times for truth."

"You are not the only one here! They will declare the whole tribe haram!"

"Be these the words of Abram? You sound more like Eliezer."

"I care not who I sound like!"

"No, you care for truth, if I remember right."

"Yes, but…"

"To slay babes is evil," Elizedek said calmly. "True or false? The el of Salem commands it. Can the el of Salem be good? No! He must be evil."

"It is not the el. It is the priests."

"Ah! Then you agree. The priests are evil."

"No! They are but mistaken."

"Then stand with me and shout it."

"I will not bring destruction on my tribe!"

A man who sought truth met a man resolved to embody truth. In this world their romance could only end in divorce or death. Elizedek was brought up on charges of false teaching and corrupting the youth (that one always seems to get in there). And though Abram couldn't honestly convict him of either, he nevertheless expelled Elizedek from the tribe on grounds of irreconcilable differences.

But a man like Elizedek would not be silenced. He was soon preaching the El of Righteousness in the market place of Arba.

"Harken, you crop eared hedgehogs! Awaken, you sleeping cattle! Gone be the days of evil els and evil men what serve them. The time has come for *new rules*."

Before the sun set he was arrested on charges of blasphemy – not against the els, but against the Sacred Tablets. Heresy was so infrequent that they had not yet coined a specific word for it. Nor were the priests of Arba certain as to the appropriate penalty. Therefore, Elizedek was shackled and taken by the roshdath (chief of law) to Salem for judgment.

26 SALEM
the heretic

Jebus stood at an east window of the palace hoping for the next gust of cool afternoon breeze. Looking down at the Kidron Valley, his eyes were drawn to a young family of three exiting Salem's gate. A man on a donkey led an ox cart packed full of household goods, and his wife and child. Jebus noted that the child was a girl, then looked closely at the woman. Sure enough – pregnant. *Could they not but wait to see if it is a boy?* Jebus walked away from the window. *Naught to gain by telling Melchizedek. Just another leaf in the wind to him.* The king now sat calmly at his work table figuring budgetary matters.

His judgment has never been so wrong, thought Jebus. *This evil could have been nipped in the bud. Now it takes root and grows. In time it could threaten the holy throne itself. But naught can be done – naught by law. The new cult is outside of Canaan's rule. But, as Melchizedek foresaw, he is blamed by none. Few even care. Out of sight is out of heart.*

It might have continued like that, except for Elizedek.

Granted audience with Melchizedek and Jebus, the roshdath of Arba made his case.

"This man is truly evil, Holiness, in the sight of all els, even of the Most High, for he teaches against what the els have taught."

"What does he teach?" asked Melchizedek.

"Truly, that the law of first fruits is evil, and that men should make sacrifice to no el save the El of Righteousness."

Melchizedek and Jebus chuckled. "El of Righteousness indeed," responded Melchizedek. "And who is this 'El of Righteousness?'"

"The man says it is El Most High, the El of old, but not as revealed in the Holy Tablets. Rather new and strange as taught by Abram the blasphemer."

Jebus turned his eyes toward Melchizedek to see his response. The judge remained motionless except to tighten his lips into their smallest possible configuration.

"What be this villain's name?" asked Jebus.

"Elizedek he calls himself," replied the roshdath. "A no-account harlot's son of the wilderness."

"Did Abram send forth this man?" asked Melchizedek.

"It would appear not, Holiness. For Abram himself sent a messenger to speak against the fool, sent him to the king of Arba, he did. This Elizedek, it seems, was so shameful that even the other blasphemers cast him out."

"Where is he now?"

"In the Salem dungeon. Bound and gagged, lest he foul the air with the bile in his heart."

Melchizedek stood. "I will see him."

Jebus also rose. "Shall I send for him, Holiness?"

"And soil this floor with the feet of a blasphemer?"

Melchizedek removed his priestly mantle and wrapped his head in the manner of a commoner. "No. I shall go to him – quietly. Stay here, Jebus. I wish not to be known."

Melchizedek and the roshdath exited the palace through a side door and proceeded toward the dungeon.

"What know you of the Abramites, roshdath?"

"Blasphemers they are. So it is said."

"Have they made any trouble?"

"None but in the talk of those who speak of them, Holiness. We have seen little of them since they moved south."

"And what of the talk?"

"Some say they steal newborn boys in the night, or even worse – that they piss upon holy tablets."

"Have any been reported missing?"

"Tablets?"

"Boys."

"No."

On arriving at the dungeon, they found a bevy of priests already interrogating the prisoner.

"I thought you gagged him," snapped Melchizedek.

The roshdath shrugged. "Truly we did."

Melchizedek removed his head covering. Upon recognizing him, the priests immediately made way. The prisoner was tied with cords, and sitting on the floor against a wall. He had obviously been slapped around, but was not seriously injured.

"What said he?" asked Melchizedek.

"Enough to stone him ten times over," replied a priest.

"And worthy as much of laughter as stones," added another. "It would appear that we are all killers of babies and sons of witches."

Jebus then arrived and uncovered his head.

Melchizedek grabbed his arm and whispered through clenched teeth, "I told you–"

"None knew me, Holiness. I was wary."

Melchizedek could not afford to scold Jebus in public. He walked back and glared down at the prisoner. "Is Elizedek your true name?"

The man did not look up. "Truer than that me mother give me."

The judge continued. "And be us all sons of witches?"

"That and worse. For you serve an evil el."

"Hold!" commanded Melchizedek, to prevent the priests from slapping the man again. "Is El Most High evil?"

"No, and He will not let you fools call Him evil."

"We call Him not evil," countered the judge. "We say He is the greatest of all that is good."

"You say also He commands you to slay babes."

"None but firstborn sons."

"And you call that good?"

"I call it obedience."

"To a good el or an evil el?"

"To El Most High who made all things."

"Why would El Most High have made the hearts of men, and then commanded men to slay their sons?"

Again Melchizedek's lips tightened into a nervous sphincter. Jebus made use of the silence.

"And what of the Tablets of Noah, which tell us that El Most High commanded that very thing?"

Elizedek snorted. "I spit on them."

A smack across the prisoner's cheek came too fast for Melchizedek to prevent it.

"Hold, I said!" Then to Elizedek, "Learned you these things from Abram?"

"I learned these things from my Maker."

"Does Abram teach these things to his tribe?" asked Melchizedek.

"Would that he were so bold. On the right path, he is, but has not the stones to follow it to the end. Fears for his people, him. Me – I got naught to lose."

Jebus huffed. "Your life."

Elizedek laughed heartily then glared into Jebus's eyes. "Think you it be some kind of joy to live among you dung-fountains?"

Melchizedek was finished. "Put the gag back on him. Leave it there but to feed him. Soldiers remain here. Priests come with me."

He led the clergy outside to a corner of the patio and addressed them quietly. "I wish him not beaten, but he must die. Let not his eyes see morning."

"Holiness," interjected an elderly priest, "if I may. This miserable wretch holds an opportunity for us. If the people learn that Abram spawns vermin like this, they will surely support the destruction of the whole Abramite abomination."

"I agree," said Jebus. "This could be the blessing we have prayed for. Give him a public trial and let all Salem see what filth comes from the teachings of Abram."

"No," countered Melchizedek. "The man is not of Abram. Abram cast him out."

"But he learned his blasphemy from Abram," said the old priest.

"From his Creator, he says," corrected Melchizedek.

"But," intruded Jebus, "he says Abram is on the right path. Surely Abram's poison will breed more like this, even if Abram loves them not."

Melchizedek scratched his beard nervously. "This

could turn against us."

"How, Holiness?" asked the old priest. "If we succeed, we rid Canaan of this treason of heart. If we fail, what be lost?"

A younger priest was emboldened. "Surely, we need not fear that this bush-man could win over the people?"

"Surely not," scoffed Melchizedek.

"What then?" asked Jebus.

Melchizedek broke into a sly grin. "Exceeding good, my friends. My thoughts truly. But now, if it fails, you cannot say it was born of my heart."

The priests all laughed at the judge's apparent ploy, none of them being quite sure who won the game.

It was decided that they would first put Elizedek on display at the dung-gate on the south end of the city, and let him run his mouth. Priests would be present to ask him the right questions so that his blasphemy and ties to Abram would be made clear. From there, the trial would be a mere formality. Elizedek would be stoned, and the crowd would demand the eradication of the Abramite heresy. So went the theory.

The town pillory had been built near the dung-gate for public denouncement of social malefactors. These included all from petty thieves to murderers to the most depraved of adulteresses. The condemned would be tied to one of several vertical posts firmly planted in the ground and the nature of his crime proclaimed by any interested party, or at least twice a day by the town crier. First to be entertained by this spectacle were the refuse disposers plodding to and from the city dump outside the south wall. If they liked the show, a crowd would gather.

As Elizedek was being fastened to the post, a dung-hauler pulled up his creaking ox-cart and stopped.

"For what be this one, rabbi?"

A priest responded, "Blasphemy."

"What said he?" asked the dung-hauler.

"Truly that El Most High is evil."

"Lying pig," blurted Elizedek.

"Forgive me," said the priest. "You say it so much better."

Elizedek addressed the dung-hauler. "The Most High be not evil and He commands not evil deeds."

"What evil deeds?" asked the priest.

"To slay babes!"

The priest spoke loudly so as to attract attention. "Ah, then he who commanded the Law of Firstfruits must be evil."

Everyone in earshot turned to listen.

"Yes!" said Elizedek. "But it be not the Most High what commanded that."

"Then who was it?" asked the priest. "One of His sons? Baal? Perhaps His wife!"

All laughed, attracting a greater audience.

"Fools like you commanded it, chaff basket."

"Ah," said the priest, "then we are fools but you are wise. Mind not that you are the one tied to a post."

All laughed again.

The priest continued. "Think you that any man can speak for the Most High, blasphemer? Who anointed you? Who poured holy oil upon your head? I am anointed by Jebus who was anointed by his Holiness, and so on through all judges back to Shem the son of Noah. Who anointed you?"

"The Most High anointed my heart."

More laughter.

"No," said the priest. "What man? Speak his name."

"Truth needs no man's anointing," said Elizedek.

"Who be you to speak for the Most High?" came another voice.

"A lump of dirt with a soul. What need I be, dung merchant?"

"I am no dung merchant! I am a *priest!"*

Elizedek froze, then broke into uncontrollable laughter. "No man need permission to speak truth. These priests have permission, but they use it not, for they fear that him who gave it might well take it back."

A dung-hauler dipped a ladle into a pot on his cart. "Surely the man needs anointing, rabbi." All cheered and applauded as he poured brown liquid over Elizedek's head.

"See what they make of you?" shouted Elizedek. "Fools like themselves – servants of an evil el. I bring you a righteous el and you pour filth upon me."

The dung-hauler spat. "You bring us vain dreams, blasphemer."

Elizedek yelled, "If a righteous el be vain, then slay all babes! Slay yourselves! We all be fools for living."

Though most of the crowd laughed, a few heard something disturbing. "What righteous el?"

A priest jumped in. "Good people, the serpent tricks you with words. Surely El Most High is righteous. He cannot be otherwise. And He who gave life can surely demand it back."

"He can slay any man at any time," said Elizedek. "Why would He command men to slay their own sons?"

"It is not for men to ask els why," said the priest. "It matters only that He has commanded it. And we have that very command in the holy Tablets of Noah."

"Tablets Of Nobody," said Elizedek. "Pack of lies.

For He be no bull, and He be not talking bull's dung."

The crowd gasped. By now their number was close to a hundred and growing.

"You heard it, Salem," cried the priest. "He calls the Holy Tablets bull's dung."

"Have some man's dung, blasphemer," shouted a refuse-hauler, slinging a trowel of it at Elizedek.

The crowd laughed and applauded.

"Who sent you, blasphemer?" shouted the priest.

"The Most High."

"Liar! Where learned you this filth?"

"I learned no filth. I learned these pearls of wisdom from the Most High. And you swine be unworthy of them."

A brown lump smacked into his chest. It was followed by another.

"More!" shouted Elizedek. "It smells better than all of you."

The crowd obliged enthusiastically with an indiscriminate hail. Laughter ceased and rocks were soon added to the missiles.

The first sight of blood alarmed the priest. "Hold, good people! Let the law slay him."

But it was too late. They would not be stopped. Nor would Elizedek. "More, you fools! Death cannot harm a righteous man."

Religious zeal whipped the crowd to frenzy and Elizedek to ecstasy. "You can slay me, but you cannot silence me!"

"Who sent you?" yelled the priest, but he was ignored by all.

Elizedek's parting words: "I will be back!" He had no idea why he said it. It just sounded right.

The difference between a whacko and a prophet – assuming there *is* such a thing as a prophet – is often blurred. Historically the only difference depends on their post-mortem write-up. And here Elizedek would lose. His words would never be recorded, and his name would soon be forgotten.

The conspiracy, however, was rescued by a priest who suggested that the body be sent to Abram in a cart. From this, the crowd was only too eager to jump to the conclusion that Abram had sent him in the first place. The priests, figuring that no one would be the wiser, went along with it. And thus was the Abramite heresy popularly condemned, and the news brought back to the judge's chamber.

"Fools!" Melchizedek slammed his fist down on the table.

"Who?" asked Jebus.

"All of them," he fumed. "And fortunate for us, is it not? Otherwise, who would pay for all this? But mostly the blasphemers, truly. Yes, them above all. We have the revealed word of El Most High in the Tablets of Noah! Think they that they can but make up an el out of air and happy thoughts? Or think they that El no longer cares what He said to our forefathers? – that He makes up new laws as He goes?" The judge grabbed his cup-bearer by the shoulders and lifted him nearly off the floor. "Tell me, Jebus. How is it that men see not how full of dung they are?"

Jebus didn't know.

"Summon all the armies of Canaan to Salem forthwith."

"All of them?" asked Jebus

"All that can be spared."

Jebus gathered his wits. "Holiness, we could destroy this cult easily with a few hundred men."

"If you were a soldier, would you wish to be left out?"

A scribe spoke up. "That could take weeks."

Melchizedek put on his ceremonial headgear.

"My comrades, this is more than a battle; this is jihad. And by El's beard, we will do it right."

27 ARBA
the decision

Within five days Abram learned of the impending attack. The only sensible course of action was flight, but to where? Edom practiced infant sacrifice, and Egypt was not known to welcome outsiders of any kind, much less religious dissidents. South was the Negev Desert, crossable only through Edom. Still, if they could get to Ezion-Geber at the gulf, there was at least a chance.

But the night before the planned move out, Abram had another one of those obnoxious dreams. It began murkily with Abram struggling to get down from a hill. He then came upon Sarai and Isaac seated at a tent. He told them to rise and flee with him, for something at the top of the hill was trying to get them. They didn't understand, so Abram put them in a cart and pulled them down the hill. But the underbrush tangled in the wheels, and the cart stuck. Abram tried to pull it loose, but the brush turned to purple cords and tangled further. Abram looked to the top of the hill and saw Melchizedek standing at an altar of stacked clay tablets, a flint dagger in his hand. His hair and beard grew out into purple strands that became alive as snakes and began to tangle. But he cut them loose with the dagger. He then lay down on the altar, turned toward Abram, and said, "Fear not the unjust God." Melchizedek then lifted his beard, and slit his own throat.

Abram awoke in a sweat, and retraced the images in his mind, lest they fade from memory. *Do gods speak through dreams? Can they be trusted if they do?*

Seated around the breakfast fire, the men ate silently, waiting for Abram to announce what they believed to be the only sensible decision he could make – to flee. By the end of the meal, he remained deep in thought, then took a large gulp of beer and said, "I shall remain here."

"What!?" came Eliezer's expected response. His shock was shared by all present.

"Once again," continued Abram, "I speak but for my own family. The rest of you may do as you choose."

"And your wisdom is…?" queried Eliezer.

"Some moons back, Korah asked me a question. He said, 'what if no just and righteous God be anywhere?'. My answer was good enough for me, but not good enough for a leader of others. If no just and righteous God be anywhere, then I choose death. But I will not choose it for all of you. Each of you must make that choice for yourselves."

"My lord," said Zimran, "back at Arba we faced a lesser peril than this and you led us south. What has changed?"

Abram heaved a sigh. "If a man continues to flee from injustice, how will he learn if justice be anywhere? – or a God who loves it?" He looked around at their faces. None looked back. They all just stared blankly into the embers.

"Rest from your labors today. If you be here tomorrow, get to work." Abram rose and walked back to his tent. Others began doing likewise.

Eliezer turned to Zimran. "Why can he not be noble with but his own life, and let the rest of us stand in awe of him? Must he make us all great men?"

"Fret not," replied Zimran. "His name alone will be remembered for it."

In the next few weeks the tribe shrunk by half.

28 SALEM
the sacrifice

At Salem the fire on the temple altar was now burning day and night with bullocks and heifers lined up for slaughter. Drums beat on the north saddle-land as troops marched in and encamped, each unit proudly displaying emblems of its city to be sure they got credit for being there. When the final detachment arrived from far off Dimashki, the army totaled nearly six thousand – about one twelfth of the total man power.

On the morning appointed for the march, all of these were arrayed on the slope facing the city, their eyes glued to the parapet above the gate where the Son of El would appear. Priests began to file out onto the parapet and stand in two rows facing the army. Between them stepped a tall man in a purple mantle, a golden bull-horned miter on his head – Melchizedek, in full ceremonial regalia, his hair and beard powdered chalk-white. All cheered until he raised his staff to silence them.

"Soldiers of Canaan," he began, "you who gallantly dedicate yourselves to the service of El, and you who stand here in hope of advancement or money, as well as you who have no idea why you stand here. I have a word to say to all of you, and I wish you to hear me clearly. Glub begada boona fnod hargenflak tik rasamana geep nidyit. Shantakanova takabana homanahiya goppa tu. Kenshnedlio dunka tonama pook rendifigazur ad wadplop." Then, raising his staff, he declared, "Kamooch!"

He then thumped the floor with it, turned, and strode majestically past a dumbstruck Jebus and high clergy. He nodded confidently at them, and continued toward the palace.

The army remained frozen in silence for a full minute before men started turning their heads toward their officers, who then turned to superior officers, who turned to generals. The commander in chief then turned and hastened toward the city gate.

Meanwhile, Melchizedek entered his office and barred the doors and windows. He removed his bull-horned miter and flung it down. It bounced across the floor and stopped. He ignored the sounds of Jebus and the priests gathering at the door. Dropping his purple mantle, he grabbed a wall torch, went into the back library, and lit the lamps. There on the study table lay the Tablets of Noah neatly in a row, where he had placed them an hour previously. He had been planning the events of this day since shortly after the execution of Elizedek. But now, picking up the first tablet, he faltered for a moment, his heart racing. "Forgive me," he whispered. Then after a deep breath, "No. This is naught to forgive." He turned it face down on the second tablet, and rubbed in an orbital motion. The so called Word of El dissolved into clay dust and seeped out from between them.

The respectful calls of Jebus and the priests outside now turned to shouts. Doors were pounded and window shutters rattled, but as they were built stoutly enough to withstand military assault, Melchizedek took little note of it. The thump of a battering ram, however, caused him to hasten. Feeling pressed for time, he began slamming tablets face down onto other tablets. When the front doors finally gave way, the judge continued breaking pieces into smaller pieces.

Jebus was first to enter the library, followed by priests and generals, each in turn standing speechless at the sight of their judge at a table strewn with clumps of dirt. Jebus looked to the empty shelf where the Sacred Tablets had been.

"No!" he cried.

Melchizedek calmly rubbed a pair of clay fragments together between his hands, dust falling from them to the floor. Jebus snatched a sword from the belt of the commander and approached his former mentor. Melchizedek smiled, pulled his beard aside, and lifted his chin. Jebus slashed, and the judge was dead.

"Slay them," said Jebus trembling. He turned to a stunned audience. *"Slay them all!"*

The priests and generals stood there gaping.

"The Abramites have bewitched the judge himself!" Jebus shouted.

Those at the back recovered their wits enough to ease out the doorway. Jebus approached the commander to return his sword. "You must destroy them!" The commander instinctively stepped backward, and the whole group turned and fled.

Loyal only to their respective kings, the generals and their armies, wasted no time getting back home to report the bizarre news.

The official story was that Melchizedek had overdosed on mandrakes and gone mad. The idea that the Son of El had been bewitched by an upstart cult leader was theologically unthinkable, and dismissed out of hand. Having no legitimate heirs, his kingdom was up for grabs. Jebus, now the most powerful man in Salem, was made temporary dictator and gradually mustered enough support to secure the throne. But lacking the necessary charisma, his efforts to assume the judgeship were in vain. Canaan would never again be so united by judge or religion until it was conquered by the religion it spawned.

29 WILDERNESS
the beginning

Eliezer's first child turned out to be a girl, but by then he had become a fully committed Abramite, and had no intention of leaving. His daughter would grow up among plenty of friends in a peaceful community on the southern fringes of Canaan. And every laundry day, she would join her mother at the well and hear the stories of Canaan and of the tribe. Most interesting were the stories of Sarai, for she spoke not the words of others, but of her own experience. And though frail from age, her stories brought the undivided attention of all the women.

> "Then one day three men rode in from the north. They were dressed in black clothing not of Canaan. Abram knew at once that they were men of high standing, for he bade me serve them with great respect. These were they who foretold that I would bear a son, though my time for bearing was near its end.

> I laughed, for I thought them foolish. But Abram was wiser than I. He saw that they were men of El Most High. And when they foretold the destruction of Sodom and Gomorrah, he begged them show mercy."

Though the story varied slightly each time, she tried to keep variations to a minimum, knowing that consistency would be easier to remember by those she would leave behind.

A thirteen year old dared risk a question she knew better than to ask. "Tell us of when you went down to Egypt and got stolen by the king."

Sarai's jaw went slightly askew. "Not among my favored stories. You must ask Abram or Eliezer of that one."

As mistress of story, Sarai continued to tell the ancient Canaanite myth of creation on Shabbat, but some parts, which might conflict with Abramite theology, were now omitted, and new parts added to smooth over the surgery. This was not capricious, but the result of many laundry day conversations.

Shabbat now took on greater significance to the Abramites. No longer just a tribal dinner, it had become a social event opened up to visitors who might be curious about the new cult. The presence of strangers was to be expected and welcomed.

In this atmosphere, a certain hooded man went unnoticed in the crowd. Silently drifting from the periphery of one conversation to another, he chanced upon Korah, surrounded by many young folks.

> "It was dark when we arrived at Lot's dwelling. He of course bade us spend the night, and we declined. 'You are most gracious,' said we, 'but we will but sleep in the street.' He of course insisted, so we accepted and went inside. Then this crowd of… unspeakable creatures gathered around… Truly we could feel the demons in the air."

Korah had become quite popular among the Abramite youth, but his story was of no interest to the hooded lone wolf in his mid-twenties. Much more interesting was the story told by Isaac, who was also a center of attention.

"But remember, we left the sheep back at the cart. So I look around, and I see naught to sacrifice anywhere. So I look to Abram. 'Father,' says I, 'what offer we here?' And he is all calm like, 'Offer? Fret not. Our God will take care of all that.'"

After waiting until Isaac finished, the hooded man approached him and whispered, "I saw a viper at one of the tents."

"Which tent?" asked Isaac.

The man pointed to Abram's tent. Isaac immediately started toward it. "Where?" he asked.

Abram was at the center of a somewhat smaller circle consisting of men only. As usual on a Shabbat afternoon, he was engaged in theological discussion, this time with an elderly long-beard from Salem. "You say, Abram, that you serve no new el – that it is the same El Most High whom Canaan has known since the days of Noah."

"Yes. I say that."

"Why then did He take so long to change His heart on the matter of first-born sons?"

"I know not that He changed at all," replied Abram.

"The hearts of men change. I think He tells us what we should believe at the time we should believe it."

"I fail to understand."

"Men are all foolish, and frightened, and evil. When we needed a fearsome El to hold us back, He showed Himself fearsome."

"So you think men are less evil now?" asked the long-beard.

"Not less evil, but wiser as to how to punish evil."

"Then be us now so wise that we need not the Tablets of Noah?"

"Ach! The more I deny that, the more I am accused of it. I am not Elizedek. Nor would I destroy the Tablets like Melchizedek. I rejoice that we still have copies. For they show us that the laws of the Most High change to suit the times. Remember the law of blood vengeance. The Tablets of Noah say if a man slays my kinsman, I must slay his kinsman, perhaps many of his kinsmen. Now the greatest priests of that very cult say if a man slays my kinsman, I must slay only that man."

"The matter is still disputed."

"I think no man will dispute this. When the laws of the Most High make men more evil than they would have been otherwise, He will give them a way to change those laws without opposing Him."

The long-beard smiled. "And who is to judge what is good and what is evil?"

"Every one of us."

"Then surely we have chaos."

"Not if the El who made us gave us knowledge of good and evil."

"But the Tablets say Adam came to that knowledge by disobedience."

"So?" Abram shrugged. "How was Adam to know that disobedience was evil?"

The man had no reply.

"The end of it is this," said Abram. "I am stuck with knowledge of good and evil. I can act on it, or I can act against it. I choose to act on it, and without fear."

"Have you no fear of the Most High?"

"If He is good, then I fear Him. If He is evil, then I fear Him not."

"But surely an evil El is more fearsome than a good one."

Abram smiled. "That is where we disagree, my friend. I say an evil El is not worthy of fear."

"Hmm. Think you that He is good or evil?"

"Father," came the voice of Isaac at a distance.

Abram looked up and saw his son at the entrance to his tent. Isaac was motioning for him to approach.

"What?" Abram shouted. But Isaac just continued to beckon.

"Forgive me," said Abram to his audience, and went to see what was the matter.

"What?" he asked again, and Isaac was jerked back out of his sight. Abram entered the tent.

"Hello, father," said Ishmael. "Remember me?" His left arm was firmly around Isaac's neck.

"He has a dagger at my back," said Isaac calmly.

"It is not flint," said Ishmael. "Think you that El will forgive me this looseness of form?"

"What seek you?" asked Abram.

"Perhaps a bit of religious wisdom. Tell me of your just and righteous el. I have heard so much of him."

"Again I ask, What seek you?"

"You took things from me, and I wish them back."

"What?" asked Abram.

"You know what!" growled Ishmael as loud as he dare.

"I fear him not," said Isaac.

"Hold your tongue," responded Abram. "Money? Land?"

"That and so terribly much more," said Ishmael. "I want all that is now given to this sheep's turd."

"And if you slay him," said Abram, "what will that get you? Think you that I would pass my mantle to a brother-killer?"

"What choice have you?" asked Ishmael. "I would be your only son."

"And think you that I am so old I cannot make others? … Or will you then slay me too?"

Ishmael fumed silently.

"You can have what I have any time you wish, my son. But you must get it the same way I got it. And it will cost you."

Ishmael jerked his left arm tighter. "And what has it cost him?"

"Naught yet," said Abram. "But he has it not yet. What I have can be had by any man who will pay the price. Be you such a man?"

Ishmael paused, then flung Isaac hard to the ground. Pointing the dagger at him, he declared, "You will not rest until I am recompensed." Pushing Abram aside, he ran out.

Isaac jumped to his feet and bolted toward the entrance. Abram restrained him. "Follow not. He too is my son."

Isaac calmed down. "What meant you that I have it not?" he asked. "What have I not?"

"It was but a thing to say," replied Abram.

"You have never said anything but that you meant it… in some way."

Abram looked away from him. Isaac pressed it.

"I am your heir; am I not?"

"Yes."

"Not of your property alone, but of your people and your God."

"People and gods are not bequeathed."

"If not me, then who?… Eliezer?"

"You alone are my heir," said Abram. "Be content with it."

"'The son of Sarai shall inherit the covenant of the Most High.' So said Elizedek."

"Elizedek had hornets in his heart. Lean not on his words."

"And your dream said the sons of Sarai would conquer Canaan."

"Dreams cannot be trusted. Moreover, it was *my* dream, not yours. And if you hold not your tongue on it, you will surely bring down all Canaan on your head."

Isaac sulked. "Elizedek was the greatest man I have ever known."

"Perhaps," said Abram, "but he also made great errors."

"I know of none."

"Elizedek allowed no space for men less than himself to live. That is why Salem killed him."

"Salem killed him because its God is evil. An evil God is a God of fools."

"Fools need a God of fools."

"All men need the one true God. There can be but one true religion."

Abram flung his arm in a wide arc. "Look around

you!" he shouted. "If you were the One True God of this earth, how many religions would you allow?"

"One!" shouted Isaac back. "The true one!"

"And to whom would you address that religion? To wise men or to fools?"

They didn't speak to each other for the rest of the day.

Isaac had always felt an ambivalence toward his father ever since the ride home from Mount Moriah. When Abram had believed that El Most High wanted him to kill Isaac, he would have done it. When he believed the opposite, he did the opposite. Isaac could only conclude that his life depended on Abram's belief that his God had not changed his mind – again. Few if any men would contemplate the value of their own existence more than Isaac.

Zimran died! It came as a surprise to everyone. Of course, he was in his sixties, but in good health. Then one spring morning he just woke up dead. Even more strangely, Eliezer seemed to take it the hardest.

Korah, who had always hoped for invitation to Abram's inner circle, was once again politely rebuffed. *Why?* he thought. People liked him. Had he not experienced miracles of God, even greater miracles than Abram? – or at least testified to having experienced them? Had he not kissed up to Abram and the other three in the most humble of manners? How could a supposedly righteous God be so unjust? Korah just didn't get it. Now it was only Abram, Isaac, and Eliezer at the center, with Korah not even knowing if he was fourth.

On the night following Zimran's burial, the three remained awake after the others had gone to bed. Sitting on the dirt around the last embers of a fire, they quietly drank themselves numb.

Isaac broke silence. “One thing I see not.”

“One alone?” replied Abram.

“Last Shabbat when you told the story of Shechem, you left out the best part.”

“What part?”

“The part where you deceived the priests. The ambassador part.”

“Children and strangers were listening,” said Abram. “I wished not that they should learn that I deceived people.”

Isaac mulled it over. “So it is good for *us* to know it, but not them.”

“Yes. You know me. They know me not.”

“So it is not good for one to know that you deceive until they know you deceive.”

“If they know I lied to the priests, they may think I lie to them about my God.”

Again Isaac mulled it over. “So you lied to them so they would not think you a liar.”

“I lied not. I told the truth, but not *all* of it. They are different.”

“The end is the same.”

“For those who hear it, yes. But if I lie not, then I am not a liar.”

“Have you also not told us other things?”

“Many. Have *you* not told *me* things? Eliezer, Have you not told me things?”

“Surely,” replied the drowsy man.

Isaac pressed. “But have you not told me things of our God?”

Abram paused before responding. “Yes.”

“What?”

“Things you must learn for yourself.”

"If I take your place when you die, should I not learn all that you know?"

"It would be best. But you cannot ride on my back. You must learn to walk."

Isaac went silent. Abram felt that further explanation was needed. "You have no children, so you know this not, but it is not good to tell all things."

"But if you know things of your God, and tell them not even to me… it makes me suspicious."

"Good," said Abram. "I hope it makes you suspicious enough to go to Him and see if I tell the truth. You cannot *tell* the things of a righteous God; you must *show* them. And you cannot show them if you do them not."

"One thing I fear," said Isaac softly. "What if our God Himself keeps secrets from us?"

"He most surely does," replied Abram. "And He reveals naught to unprepared hearts."

Isaac stood. "I need to piss." He walked toward the latrine.

Abram took a gulp of wine. "All of them want a piece of the Most High God, but none want to earn it. I have one son who thinks he can steal it, and the other thinks he can inherit it… What think you, Eliezer?"

Eliezer focused. "Oh… I think it is a free gift."

"Hah!"

"Why not? That is what my younger daughter would make of it. Our God is a kindly old grandfather who wishes naught more than to shower blessings upon us. Mark you my word. Someone will claim that very thing. Wager?"

"Think you that either of us will live to collect"

"Not in these bodies. New ones perhaps? What think you?"

"Perhaps," said Abram. "Surely if the God who rules this world is just, then there must be a day of rewards and punishments."

"Then you believe we will live again?"

"I said *if.*"

Eliezer downed the last of his cup and released a belch. "Uhh… you make me to wonder, Abi. You have not held back anything from *me* of our God, have you?"

Abram remained silent. Then glancing toward Eliezer, he raised his eyebrows.

Eliezer was compelled to laugh. "How is this?" he said. "Truth is like a case of stairs. Religions are the steps. Every man thinks his own step the highest until he is persuaded otherwise. It is good to ascend. But if you take too big a step, you may well fall on your face."

Abram chuckled. "Beautiful. But food for gainsayers. Hide it in your heart."

As Isaac walked back from the latrine, Abram thought, *Yes Eliezer, I have kept back things of our God from you – things I will never tell anyone. If you wish to know them, go find them.*

His mind drifted back to that momentous day on Mount Moriah. The altar. The wood. Standing behind his son with a raised stick. The bleat of the sheep behind him. Somehow it appeared to be calling to him. He lowered the stick and followed the sound. A ram was caught in a thicket. The most sure footed of all mountain climbers had somehow made this fatal blunder. Abram went closer. Upon examination, he discovered that the ram was not only caught. It was also tied securely with a cord of purple flax.

EPILOG

To a twenty-first century reader a question arises in many minds which could not be addressed from within the context of the story. Having seen four millennia of horrific conflicts inherent within monotheism, why do we still bother with it? Why don't we just put it all on a shelf with the rest of Semitic mythology and go be pantheists? Well, actually pantheist history is no more peaceful. Nevertheless, if you can live with the irrationality, you're welcome to it.

Moreover, why bother with theism at all? Why not be atheists? Well, it's because as crazy as all religions ultimately show themselves to be when followed to their logical conclusions, atheism is even crazier. Clearly it's nihilistic, and offers no justification for ethics. But more basically, it simply can't explain the existence of anything, much less minds, much less intelligent minds, much less intelligent minds that would cut a leg off to survive, not because they enjoy living, but because they hope to *eventually* enjoy it.

Consider the Argument from Insufficient Stupidity:

> Unaided matter is not of itself stupid enough to bind together into self replicating units that end up being more irritable and frustrated than their component parts.

That bit of magic requires at least a devil. Therefore at least a devil must necessarily exist. But why would a devil create creatures that hate devils? Once again, could that degree of stupidity possibly exist without exploding?

The only alternative is that, despite all appearances, somehow there must be an ultimate infinite Sense Maker. And to this, those who need sense are inescapably drawn like Quixote to a windmill.

Abram never told anyone the whole truth about his God. Not that he didn't want to; no one wanted to hear it. They all talked like they did, but they didn't. They would rather have faith in certainty, than the certainty of the most reasonable gamble.

Neither did they truly want a just God hassling them about their ethics. Far easier to deal with an anthropic Lord who winks at all that, as long as He gets a fair cut of the profits. They wanted a shining miraculous Tyrant to whom they could bow down and worship on Shabbat, and then go on with business as usual. No one wants to invite a second mind into their brain – heart, whatever – even if that mind is the Head Honcho of all minds. And who can blame them? What if you invite in the wrong Guy? Or even if you get the *right* Guy, what's in it for you?

Abram could never be sure of any of that. But one thing of which he was absolutely certain is that he had placed the best possible bet. Without one shred of faith in an unlikely premise, he had bet his soul on the only possibility that had a chance of paying off – a just and righteous God. If that God exists, he wins big – assuming he dies with positive numbers on the books. If that God doesn't exist, what does he lose? If there's no afterlife, then he has wasted his life being more miserable than he would have been otherwise – probably. Or worst case scenario: God is evil, throws him into hell forever. So what? Better to jump into the hell of an evil God with your integrity intact, than to reign in his heaven as an eternal sell-out.

Isaac never met Abram's God. He saw no reason to. He would inherit the leadership of the tribe and the cult without any effort but to learn the pitch. Abram's God of Justice became Isaac's God of Inheritance, to be passed down to Esau – make that Jacob, as the God of those who love inheritance enough to rip it off. But rather than admit he served the God of inheritance rippers, Jacob spun Him into God the Person Chooser, and passed Him on to his twelve Chosen People.

Meanwhile, we may assume that the children of Ishmael met up with the children of Esau. Oh, the stories they could share! Can they be blamed for smoldering indignantly in the wings, ever waiting for a counter-prophet to take back what they understandably saw as their birthright?

And what of the God of Abram? Would He learn to quit sticking His finger in the pie? Would He learn the merits of apathy from His nauseating creation? Would He possibly become retarded from smacking His forehead?

All that is known is that Abram was puffed up by pious progeny into Abraham, and his God likewise puffed up into the modern monotheists' choice of omni-perfect contradiction bundles.

But the human race would continue to learn and evolve. And Abram's just and righteous God, if He/She /It exists at all, would continue to reveal bits and pieces of information, but only at appropriate times, only as much as can be tolerated at the time, and only to those who ask for it.

ABOUT THE AUTHOR

No credentials are necessary to write fiction. No credentials are adequate to claim the right to say what this fiction says. Either way, they're irrelevant. If you want credentials, see those of my endorsers on the back cover. If you want to know about me personally, visit my website: www.sanityquestpublishing.com.

Oh. And if *you've* got credentials, I can always use more endorsements. It's not easy telling the world something it doesn't yet know it needs to hear.

Or if you want to argue theology, that's fine too – long as you're rational. I don't actually *enjoy* arguing; I just like being right.

Cary Cook